A Holiday gift for readers
of Harlequin American Romance

Novellas from three of your favorite authors

Noelle and the Wise Man
ROZ DENNY FOX

One Magic Christmas
ANN DEFEE

Tanner and Baum
TANYA MICHAELS

ABOUT THE AUTHORS

Roz Denny Fox has been a prolific Harlequin writer for nearly twenty years, and has contributed to the American Romance, Superromance and Everlasting Love lines. Roz has been a RITA® Award finalist and has placed in a number of other contests. Her books have also appeared on the Waldenbooks bestseller list. Roz currently resides in Tucson, Arizona, with her husband, Denny.

Ann DeFee's debut novel, *A Texas State of Mind* (Harlequin American Romance) was a double finalist in the Romance Writers' of America's prestigious RITA® Awards in 2006. Ann, who writes for both the Harlequin American Romance and Harlequin Everlasting Love lines, lives in the state of Washington but grew up in Texas.

Tanya Michaels sold her first book, a romantic comedy, to Harlequin in 2003. Since then, Tanya's sold nearly twenty books and is a two-time recipient of Booksellers' Best Awards, as well as a finalist for a Holt Medallion, a National Readers' Choice Award and a Romance Writers of America RITA® Award. Tanya lives in Georgia with her husband, their two preschoolers and an unpredictable cat.

The Perfect Tree

ROZ DENNY FOX, ANN DEFEE, TANYA MICHAELS

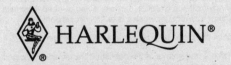

HARLEQUIN®

TORONTO • NEW YORK • LONDON
AMSTERDAM • PARIS • SYDNEY • HAMBURG
STOCKHOLM • ATHENS • TOKYO • MILAN • MADRID
PRAGUE • WARSAW • BUDAPEST • AUCKLAND

ISBN-13: 978-0-373-75189-1
ISBN-10: 0-373-75189-3

THE PERFECT TREE

Copyright © 2007 by Harlequin Books S.A.

The publisher acknowledges the copyright holders of the individual works as follows:

NOELLE AND THE WISE MAN
Copyright © 2007 by Rosaline Fox.

ONE MAGIC CHRISTMAS
Copyright © 2007 by Ann DeFee.

TANNER AND BAUM
Copyright © 2007 by Tanya Michna.

www.eHarlequin.com

Printed in U.S.A.

CONTENTS

NOELLE AND THE WISE MAN
Roz Denny Fox

Dear Reader,

I love Christmas and all its hustle and bustle. I know the season's getting more commercial, but there are traditions that can keep the magic alive. One is the real tree, which brings with it the look and feel and smell of an old-fashioned Christmas, and surely contributes to the spirit of this special time. Selecting the perfect tree for you and your family—or just you and that significant other you'll be spending the holiday with—is something that brings anticipation and joy.

What Tanya, Ann and I decided after our editors invited us each to write a Christmas story for this anthology is that there are perfect Christmas trees in every part of the country. And the qualities that make a tree perfect reside in the minds and hearts of the people who choose them (and those who grow them!).

It's our privilege to bring you three stories with different sets of characters, all in search of a perfect tree and—even more important—lasting love. My thanks to the editors for letting us tell our stories, and happy holidays to them, my fellow anthology authors and our readers. I hope you all find your perfect tree this year!

Sincerely,

Roz Denny Fox
P.O. Box 17480-101
Tucson, AZ 85731
rdfox@worldnet.att.net

This story is for everyone who loves the scent of a real Christmas tree.

Chapter One

Camden Latimer bumped his Viper off the gravel road he'd been driving for ten miles and ended up on a muddy path. Pulling under a big evergreen tree, he unfolded a map to which he'd taped a sticky note of additional directions. Overhanging branches blocked the steady downpour that had been giving his wiper blades a workout. Cam shut them off while he confirmed that he was still heading toward the Christmas tree farm he'd inherited from his grandfather. Cyrus Latimer had died a few months earlier of a heart problem he'd hidden from Cam.

The rain had turned the dirt road ahead to mud. Cam was no stranger to rain. For the past dozen years he'd been a Miami street cop and had worked in all kinds of weather. But when it rained in Florida the sun came out fifteen minutes later to dry everything. This was his second day in Oregon, and there was no sign of a letup.

Cam knew Christmas trees didn't grow low in the coastal valley. However, all the things Granddad Cy had imparted by phone and e-mail hadn't included the weather or condition of the roads. Cam's Viper, his pride and joy, was low-slung and jet-black. He eyed the muddy road with misgivings while massaging his aching right shoulder. Two weeks after what he hoped was his last surgery on a shattered upper arm, Cam wondered why he'd thought sitting on a porch watching trees grow was a good idea. But he'd sold his beach condo and said goodbye to his cop pals, so it was too late for second thoughts. His inheritance lay at the end of this road, and a new life awaited. A safer life, he hoped.

Putting the Viper back in gear, he stepped on the gas. The powerful engine growled, then roared. Cam felt his back wheels spin, but the car didn't move.

"Dammit!" He grabbed his black leather jacket, popped up the gull-wing doors, a modification he'd paid a mint for, and stepped out into the rain. His Italian loafers sank into the same muck that had the Viper's back tires mired up to their hubcaps. He needed either a miracle or a tow truck. Cam shrugged into his jacket and contemplated the empty road behind him—eight miles to the nearest town.

Flipping up his collar, he decided it would be smarter to walk the four miles to his property, mud or no mud. There was a neighbor, he knew, at Snowflake Farm—a big operation run by a woman Cy often referred to as the tree queen or witch, depending on his mood. Clearly there was no love lost between the two tree growers, but Cam only had Cy's impressions.

Cam squinted through towering firs at an angry gray sky and felt the plop, plop, plop of rain as he set off down the road. He figured he'd have to make nice with the queen snowflake so she'd give him a phone number for the nearest towing service. He'd gone barely ten yards when he heard the welcome sound of a vehicle approaching.

A well-used red pickup rounded the corner ahead of him. Cam moved to the center of the muddy ruts and waved both hands.

The pickup stopped a few yards away, and its driver rolled down a window and called, "Hey, what are you doing on this private back road? Didn't you read the sign back where you left the highway? You're trespassing on Snowflake Christmas Tree Farm property."

Hearing the feminine voice, Cam kept his distance from the truck. "I didn't see a sign. This road—and that's a joke, right?—is on a hand-drawn map I have. I'm looking for the Latimer tree farm."

The driver opened her door a crack. "No one's been there in at least two months. Not since Mr. Latimer died. If you're one of his commercial accounts, you'll want to ask in town whether he left anyone in charge."

"That would be me. I've just driven up from Florida. I'm Cy's grandson, Cam, uh, Camden Latimer. Do you happen to know the number of a towing company?" Cam gestured to his disabled car. Granted, he hadn't known his grandfather well, but from what he'd gleaned through their sporadic correspondence, it was typical of the old man to direct Cam down a shortcut belonging to a hostile neighbor. It would be his way of getting the last laugh.

"I'm Noelle Hale," the woman said. "I'm sorry for your loss. I manage Snowflake's enterprises next door. As it happens, my truck has a winch. I'll hook it onto your bumper and tow you to more solid ground. Then you can turn around. Drive back to a four-way stop, take a right and follow the main gravel road to where it splits. The right fork leads to Latimer's house. My home, lodge and gift shop are on the left." Shutting herself in the cab again, she aimed the truck straight for Cam, forcing him to jump aside. Even then her tires threw sloppy mud on his pant legs.

No longer wondering why Cy had had a running battle with Ms. Hale, Cam slipped and slid back to his car. Ms. Hale had exited her pickup and was apparently trying to find a place on his nonexistent back bumper to attach the steel cable she'd reeled out.

"You'll have to connect that to the back axle," he said. "Vipers have molded bodies. Hook anywhere else and you'll destroy the skin. Repairs would cost me a fortune."

"I'd say the dealer saw you coming a mile away. This quasi car won't last a month on our roads." She laughed and passed him the hook and cable. "I hope you plan to shimmy under the car and hook on to an axle. Me, I'm going to dinner in town. I don't plan to look like a mud pie."

Getting a better look at her as she stood there in jeans and a fall jacket, Cam realized she was attractive, if you discounted her smart mouth. Russet hair curled in the rain from under the backward ball cap she wore. She had rosy cheeks and warm hazel eyes. Actually, her sassy mouth was pretty appealing, too.

It wasn't until he'd finished his inspection that it dawned on Cam—Ms. Hale was less than impressed by him after her own equally thorough examination. Her attitude ticked him royally. So much so, he mentally relegated his pricey clothes to the trash can. Tossing his leather jacket to his startled neighbor, Cam grabbed the cable out of her hand, then flopped onto his back hard enough to splash her with mud as he slid under the chassis. He made a hitch-and-a-half over the axle and slid out. "Crank her up," he ordered. "We'll see what you've got under the hood of that gutless Sierra."

Noelle smirked and hesitated only long enough to open the Viper's door and toss his fancy jacket on his front seat before she climbed into her pickup and gave it plenty of gas.

Cam waited until she was concentrating on her task before he rotated his bad shoulder, the one he'd hit too hard on the ground just now trying to prove to feisty Ms. Snowflake what a macho jerk he was. *Noelle.* An appropriate name for a woman peddling Christmas trees. Was it her real name or an alias she'd chosen to be cutesy?

The Viper slid out of the mud with a sucking sound. Cam trailed behind on foot, trying to think what he had in his luggage that he could use to cover his leather upholstery.

He eased himself down to the ground again, this time on sharp gravel, and wiggled under the Viper to detach her cable. "Thanks for the tow," he called as he tossed out the hook. He lay there a moment, hoping she'd wind the damned thing up and be on her way before he had to scoot out. But she didn't budge, so Cam crawled out using his uninjured arm. His view was blocked by a dangling towel.

"To save your upholstery," Noelle said sweetly as he struggled to sit and then stand up.

"Thanks again." Cam accepted the towel and felt bad for misjudging her.

"Your grandfather wasn't exactly what you'd call neighborly. I didn't realize he'd ever been married or that he had a grandson. Have you come to sell his tree farm?"

"Do you know anyone in the market for one?" Cam wiped his hands before raising the custom-installed gull-wing doors. Then he spread the towel over the plush seat of his RT/10 Roadster.

"I might be interested," she said. "Or I should say, my family might be. Snowflake is owned jointly by me, my mom and dad and my two brothers. I'd need to consult with them, of course. The folks live in your neck of the woods. Key West. My brothers, Kent and Sloan, around here. They have private practices in town and they take care of any legal or accounting issues for the farm." Noelle rummaged in the cab of her pickup. She backed out, holding a business card, which she handed to Cam.

The card was pale blue with embossed snowflakes overlaid by Noelle Hale's name in white script, followed by her title: General Manager, Snowflake Christmas Trees. In smaller print was a phone number and a list of services, including wreaths, decorations and lodge rental for weddings, anniversaries and special events.

Cam pocketed the card before it got too soggy, since they were now in the rain. "Don't talk to them about it just yet. First, I'll want to evaluate Cy's holdings. How about if I let you know what I decide when I return the towel?" He slid into the car, pausing to clarify her earlier directions.

"That's right," she reiterated. "This back road is normally chained shut. Teens from town sometimes come up here to park. They probably forgot to close it when they left."

After saying goodbye, Cam turned his car around and wondered whether the tree queen had any personal knowledge of the make-out spot. Cam guessed she was probably close to thirty. No wedding ring. Cops, even ex-cops, noticed stuff like that. He'd also noticed she had nice hands. Unpainted nails, neither too long nor too short. He supposed some physical labor went with managing a tree farm. He'd probably discover how much—if he stayed on.

Last night he'd checked in to a hotel on the highway. In the lounge after dinner, he'd struck up a conversation with two men who'd given him their business cards once they heard he'd inherited a tree farm. Lewis Norman and Murphy Fletcher said they scouted land for local grape growers.

Cam remembered Cy mentioning that many once-prosperous Christmas tree farmers in the area had sold out to vintners. Owning a vineyard appealed to Cam somewhat more than raising, harvesting and selling Christmas trees, so he'd told the two men the same thing he told Noelle Hale—that he wanted to look things over, and that he'd be in touch if he decided to sell or convert to grapes.

Other than being wet, the drive along the county highway to his farm was much more pleasant than the back road had been. Here, on either side of the two lanes, stood sheared trees—the kind families decorated for Christmas.

Cam reached the fork in the road Noelle had told him to watch for. He turned right, hoping as Cy's lawyer had promised that the old man's house would have electricity and water ready and waiting. After his adventure in the mud and this rain, he was looking forward to a long, hot shower.

NOELLE SPENT SOME TIME ON THE five-mile drive into Beaver Falls thinking about the stranger who claimed to be Cy Latimer's grandson. In spite of his citified clothes, the guy didn't look soft. He was quite attractive with his short black hair that curled in the rain, and light blue eyes that didn't miss a trick. And those long eyelashes. Why did guys get to-die-for, thick black lashes?

Wait until her best friend, Zoe Blake, and Gwen Fortner, Zoe's part-time helper in the Snowflake shop, got a load of Camden Latimer. Noelle smiled to herself and fluffed hair that had gotten drenched while she'd helped her new neighbor. A neighbor for how long? He owned eight hundred acres to her family's twenty-five hundred. But if he was as crusty as his grandfather had been, a buyout wouldn't be easy. Cy had bickered about parking, seasonal workers and myriad other things. If Cam Latimer was aware of the checkered history between their families—beginning when her parents, Barb and Dan, took over Snowflake Farm from her grandpa—Noelle figured he'd make a heck of a poker player. Cy would've sold his farm to Lucifer rather than a Hale.

Well, if young Latimer sold, he sold. Noelle didn't have time to concern herself with Cy's grandson. She was approaching her busiest season. One she'd been born to love. Her mom said the fact that Noelle had arrived on Christmas day meant the all-important holiday was embedded in her soul. Everyone in the area knew Noelle would one day run Snowflake Farm. Adding hand-made wreaths and a gift-and-decoration shop had been her contribution to the success of an already thriving enterprise.

Still, for the past few years her parents had made noises suggesting that they'd rather she found a life partner like her brothers, Kent and Sloan, had done, and forget about expanding the business. As if she had time to hunt for Mr. Right. None of the men she'd met and managed to date had expressed any interest in tree farming. That automatically meant Noelle crossed them off her list of prospects. In reality, she told herself, she felt satisfied with her life as it was. Only one thing eluded her. *Producing the perfect Christmas tree.*

NOELLE PARKED OUTSIDE HER brother Kent's, accounting firm. She gathered up the sales receipts from the gift shop so he could match them with the computer version.

When she walked in, Kent and his wife, Lisa, who worked in his office, both rose and hugged Noelle. Kent took the folder and sat down to thumb through paper-clipped receipts. He unfolded a set of photocopies and glanced at his sister. "This year you entered three trees in the National Christmas Tree Association contest for a grand champion White House tree? I thought Sloan said you entered two."

Noelle tore up one form. "Two is right. A grand fir I planted eight years ago with the contest in mind, and a nine-year-old Fraser. I scratched the Douglas. It had flaws. I'll bet money the Fraser will earn a second look from the committee. It's gorgeous."

"Noelle, why do you keep entering that silly contest?" Lisa asked, frowning at her sister-in-law. "You were heartbroken when you thought you had a winner, but then they chose a white fir from Maine instead."

"Save your breath, Lisa," Kent said. "Noelle's wanted to produce a tree for the First Family since she was ten and saw all the hoopla on TV."

Noelle defended herself. "You can't *buy* the kind of lasting PR that comes with a winning tree. But we've been over this before. Come on, let's go eat. And not another word about this. It's Snow-flake Farm's turn to win. I can feel it in my bones."

They walked the short distance to the café, and the subject turned from the contest to news of Camden Latimer, Noelle's new neighbor.

Chapter Two

Cam had no doubt he was on the right road once he reached the fork his neighbor had mentioned. Noelle Hale's sign was a huge snowflake with arrows directing visitors to a gift shop, lodge and tree barn. His grandfather's lane was marked by a small wooden sign that read Latimer Trees. Cam knew Cy hadn't dealt with the touchy-feely end of selling Christmas trees; instead, he'd shipped truckloads of cut trees to commercial customers who sold them at urban tree lots.

The Viper's undercarriage scraped gravel even though Cam geared down to climb the knoll. Another point for the snow queen. If he didn't unload the tree farm he'd either have to grade the lane or sell the Viper.

The house came into view, and Cam whistled through his teeth. The log cabin was bigger than he'd expected. He thought again about the grandfather he hadn't really known. Overall, the Latimers were a dysfunctional, disconnected family. Cam had been shocked when Cy had first contacted him five years ago. Now he figured that must've been when the old boy had learned he had a bad ticker. If there'd been any hint that his granddad was living on borrowed time, Cam would've made a point of visiting—even though he'd never been invited.

He regretted not attending the funeral. The timing had been terrible. A formal letter from a law firm notifying him of his grandfather's death had arrived mere days after Cam had been shot in a Miami back alley. The letter had left him brooding for weeks about living and dying alone. The letter had also informed Cam that his grandfather had had a will and that he'd prearranged a funeral and cremation.

That was a damned sad commentary on a life. Cam didn't want

that said of him. He knew he needed to change direction, but now, he wasn't sure he'd made the right choice. In this remote locale, there wasn't much hope of finding anyone to connect with. In Miami, he'd at least had dates. There'd even been two women he'd stuck with for as long as a year each. Both had wanted him to quit being a street cop. Now that he had, they were married to safe, boring men. Perhaps that had helped him decide to move on.

Doubts surfaced again as Cam exited from his car and let himself into the house. Maybe he should sell out to Ms. Snowflake. What if he couldn't handle living here in the wild?

The interior barely felt lived in. The living room had a stone fireplace and navy blue, overstuffed furniture. The house was so eerily quiet Cam wished he owned a dog. The lawyer had told him there'd be instructions for him in Cy's office. Sure enough, a box of folders sat on a big mahogany desk with a note addressed to Cam. The folders contained information about the business, including typed notes for each phase of the operation. It was plain that Cy had expected Cam to carry on.

Cam had kidded with his cop buddies about coming here to sit on his back porch and do nothing but watch trees grow. All bullshit. Cam had always needed to keep busy. He carried the folders upstairs to the main bedroom, which he decided to use as his own.

After a blessedly hot shower, he went to bed to read up on what needed to be done first. *Final shearing. Cutting trees. Baling them before shipping.* Stifling a yawn, Cam set the box aside and promised himself that in the morning he'd go out and see firsthand what was what at Latimer Trees.

THE NEXT DAY AFTER breakfasting on stale Cheetos and coffee brewed from grounds he'd found in Cy's freezer, Cam set out to look over what he'd inherited. Trees, trees and more trees. There wasn't much else he could see from here; maybe he could get a better perspective from above. Back inside, he thumbed through the phone book until he found an ad for a nearby air park. Their hourly pilots did mostly crop dusting, but Cam talked to one who owned a helicopter and who agreed to take him up for a tour.

Once the helicopter was over his land, Cam became concerned that there didn't seem to be any fencing separating his trees from those owned by Noelle Hale. The pilot told him Ms. Hale owned approximately twenty-five hundred acres, and Cam had gotten the clear impression that she wasn't impressed with Cy's paltry eight hundred. The old cliché about good fences was relevant here, he thought. As a veteran cop, Cam had been called out to intervene in some pretty nasty arguments between neighbors. He'd seen property disputes end up in court, or even with one angry neighbor shooting another.

"Thanks for flying me around, Joe. I think I've seen enough. Do you know of any good local surveyors? Once I get my plat plan from the counry recorder's office I want my property surveyed and staked."

"Ron Halsey's your man if he's available. A lot of folks relied on Ron when other tree farmers sold out to grape growers."

"Really? Interesting. That's another option I'm considering. I'll talk to Ron Halsey."

Cam actually saw Halsey's sign on his way back to town, so he stopped in to see when Ron might be available. He couldn't believe his luck—Ron offered to go with him to the recorder's office and then out to the tree farm to start surveying ASAP.

"Might as well take advantage of the break in the rain," Ron said.

SOMETIME AFTER TWO O'CLOCK, one of Snowflake Farm's seasonal workers burst into the gift shop. "Zoe, where's Noelle? That new guy next door hired Ron Halsey to stake out his property. Ron and two other surveyors are driving stakes a good distance into rows of trees the boys and I have been shearing for Noelle. Not only that, but Noelle's special tree is there, too—the one she's been measuring and shearing herself."

Zoe grabbed a walkie-talkie. "Noelle, it's me. Can you come to the gift shop? George Tappan just told me something you need to hear. Okay, ten-four." The lanky blonde clicked off her unit. "She's at the lodge. Just finished with a customer, so she'll be right over."

Zoe and George met Noelle in front of the gift shop as she pulled up in the golf cart she used to zip between buildings. "What's the big flap, guys? I hope you haven't found bark beetles again after all the spraying we did in June."

Her seasonal staff manager repeated what he'd told Zoe.

"That's ridiculous," Noelle exploded. "Those trees are nine and ten years old. If I'd planted seedlings on Cy's land back then, he'd have been out mowing them down with a chain saw. Give me a minute to grab a utility vehicle, George. I'll follow you to where they're setting stakes. The surveyors will just have to move them."

Arriving at the site, Noelle was surprised to see Ron Halsey was the surveyor handling the job. She knew he had a flawless reputation. "Hey, Ron." Noelle slid out of her vehicle and stripped off her gloves as she stepped up to shake his hand. "You'll want to stop your crew. You're about a dozen rows onto my land."

Ron told his men to take a break. He went to his pack and pulled out a rolled plat plan. "I set my first stake at this northwest meridian from Cyrus Latimer's original deed, Noelle. If you've planted a dozen rows of trees beyond where I've set my stakes, then you planted on your neighbor's property."

"No way!"

Ron shook his head. "Now, Noelle. We're not disputing a few rows, are we? I mean, considering, how many acres you've got. Even if there's a thousand trees, you can probably work out a deal with Latimer. He seems reasonable."

"If he's so reasonable, why did he order a survey not twenty-four hours after he got here?"

Ron carefully refolded the plat plan along its creases. "He said he's an ex-cop, and he's doing this because he wants to avoid any possible property dispute."

Noelle marched back to her utility vehicle. She backed it down a row and turned around to address Ron one last time. "He's going to get a dispute like nothing he's ever seen. These are Snowflake trees. *My* trees," she added, gesturing at the rows east of Ron's stakes. "I'm going to go talk to my brother Sloan and if Mr. Latimer cuts down even one tree in these rows, we won't be discussing monetary restitution. There'll be hell to pay."

George Tappan waited until Noelle had started back to the lodge before he turned his ATV around. "I'd hold up driving stakes if I were you, Ron. Noelle's not one to give up easily." He shook his head. "When she took over this operation after Dan and Barb retired and moved south, Snowflake Farms went from a mom-and-pop business to turning a million dollars' profit a year."

CAM WAS OPENING THE living room windows to air out the house when Ron Halsey arrived. "Finished staking already?" Cam asked as he unlatched the screen door.

"Nope. I figure that'll take about a week. I came by to let you know we ran into a bit of a snag with Noelle Hale. Until the two of you iron out your differences, I'll have my men move to the back edge of your property line." Ron briefly covered what Noelle had said. "We'll stake the other three sides. When you kids settle all this, I'll finish staking between your farms."

At the sound of an engine, both men turned to see mud spewing from under the tires of Noelle's red pickup as she turned sharply out of her lane. Cam frowned. "Her brother's the lawyer for her business, right? I guess I'd better get myself into town and hire somebody to protect *my* interests."

"Sure you wouldn't rather try to solve this man to man or, in this case, man to woman?" When Cam didn't respond, Ron said, "Your best bet is probably James Vaughn. His office is on Vine Street."

Cam ran a thumb over his lower lip as he reflected on his encounter with Noelle Hale. He had a shirt and pants that were so crusted with mud they'd never be the same. "I've met Ms. Hale, Ron. I didn't get a whole lot of warm fuzzies, know what I mean? I believe I'll go talk to James Vaughn."

Chapter Three

"Slow down, Noelle. You're babbling." Sloan Hale rounded his desk and sat his sister in one of the nearby chairs. "I saw Cyrus's obituary a few months ago. It didn't mention any next of kin."

"His name is Cam, Camden Latimer. A grandson. So the old grouch must've had a family at some point. I met him yesterday—the grandson. He was trying to drive to his place on our back road, and he got his sports car stuck in the mud. I should've left him there." She bounded to her feet. "Instead of sitting here discussing Cy's family tree, call a judge. Get an injunction so Cam can't harvest those trees. *My* trees." She took a deep breath to calm herself. "Look, Sloan, I'm off to San Francisco for the holiday decoration show next week. When I get back I have events at the lodge. And there's mowing and trimming and cutting trees to ship. Next weekend, the ad for the gift shop will run in newspapers from here to the coast."

"Sit for a minute." Sloan waved her back to her chair with a freckled hand. Sloan and Noelle shared the same fair complexion, though his hair was more rust-coloured than red. He perched on the edge of his desk and toyed with his letter opener. "It's probably an honest mistake at the county recorder's office. I'll just go down and request a copy of our grandfather's original deed."

"Plus the six hundred acres Dad bought from Paul Redmond. These rows are probably in that parcel."

"Right. I was in college when they worked out that deal. Wasn't it a bone of contention between Dad and Cy Latimer?"

"A big bone. Mom says that's what turned Mr. Latimer into such a jerk." Noelle shrugged. "But at least she didn't fight a running battle with him like I did after I opened the gift shop and he put nasty notes on our customers' cars if they so much as parked an inch onto his parking strip."

"Hmm. Maybe it'd be better if you didn't start off antagonizing the grandson. Why not be generous for the sake of goodwill? Snowflake posted record profits last year. You can afford to write off a few hundred trees, Noelle."

She jumped out of the chair again and prowled his office, finally stopping in front of a bookcase to pick up a snow globe. All three Hale kids had one like it. The globe held a fully decorated Christmas tree and happy children. When shaken, flakes of snow dusted the tree. "Sloan, here's the thing. A tree I entered in this year's National Christmas Tree Association contest, the one I honest to God think can win, is smack in the middle of the rows in question."

"Jeez." Rising, Sloan took his snow globe out of Noelle's trembling hands and returned it to the shelf with his law books. "Before I request a copy of our plat documents, how about I send a letter to this Camden Latimer?" At Noelle's glum nod, Sloan added, "Okay, and I'll throw in some legal jargon saying that no tree in that particular area can be cut until this property mess is resolved. That should buy us a few weeks. Isn't the final decision on the White House tree made around the first of November?"

"Closer to the end of October. The committee has to arrange to have the tree cut and delivered to the First Lady by Thanksgiving weekend."

"So we have time yet." Sloan slipped an arm around his sister and ushered her to his office door. "You go about your business, Noelle. Leave this Latimer character to me." Sloan smiled warmly, and as Noelle left, he called for his secretary to take a letter to Cy Latimer's heir.

"Mr. Vaughn, I appreciate your seeing me without an appointment," Cam said, following the short, bald lawyer into an opulent office. The room smelled of expensive pipe tobacco. Cam glanced at the original oil paintings of the Oregon coast and could practically see the dollar signs adding up. As Vaughn motioned for him to take a seat across from a huge teak desk, Cam considered saying he'd had second thoughts about retaining a counsel. Maybe he should've tried to meet with Sloan Hale,

Snowflake Farm's attorney. They might have been able to reach an agreement on their own.

James Vaughn was dwarfed by a burgundy wingback chair. He picked up a pipe and tamped tobacco in the bowl before he addressed his visitor. "Let me make a few notes." Chewing the curved stem of his pipe, the lawyer opened a leather-bound binder, then picked up a gold pen. "I'll contact Ron Halsey and request a copy of your property documents. He's a good man to have on your side. Tomorrow I'll send someone out to estimate how many trees Noelle Hale has planted on your land. We'll calculate your lost revenue…well, in this instance, your grandfather's losses over the time period Ms. Hale usurped that space. There's also depleted soil minerals." When Cam frowned, the lawyer explained, "You'll have to buy artificial fertilizer to replace the natural minerals her trees used up. We can easily bypass small claims court and get onto the main docket. Hit them hard enough to make big guys like the Hales think twice before running over a smaller tree farmer like yourself."

Cam shifted in his seat. "Uh, I'm not after money, Mr. Vaughn. I don't even want the damned trees. I asked for a survey in order to put fencing around my farm. I'm looking into whether or not to continue with trees, or maybe grow grapes instead."

"I know you're a newcomer, so you have no idea how Dan Hale trained his brood to take over Beaver Falls. You just leave this to me. I wouldn't, however, rush out and install any fencing, or cut and ship those particular trees. Believe me, if they did encroach on your land, we'll prove that possession is *not* nine-tenths of the law. We can win this properly. I'll draft a letter to Ms. Hale with copies to her parents and brothers. They're all partners in the farm." Vaughn set aside his pipe, rose and puffed out his chest, until Cam feared the brass buttons on his snug vest might pop right off as he hustled Cam out of the office.

Cam stood outside a minute, feeling uneasy about having launched that salvo at his neighbor. But from what he'd heard Ron Halsey was reliable and honest, and Ron had recommended James Vaughn. Anyway, it wasn't as if he was the first to seek counsel. Ron said Noelle planned to have her lawyer brother get in on the act. And, when he'd driven past Sloan Hale's law office earlier, he'd seen her pickup parked outside.

It was after five o'clock, and since Cam wasn't in a rush to go home to his big empty house, he drove to the Falls Tavern. A burger with fries and a cold beer would hit the spot, to say nothing of some jukebox music and maybe conversation with a few locals. If Beaver Falls was going to be his new home, Cam figured he ought to chat with people and get the lowdown on the town.

Visiting the tavern proved helpful to Cam. He sat at the bar next to a man who knew a broker on the coast who'd had success turning several Christmas tree farms into vineyards. The man also said what Cam had already concluded. "Son, if I were you I'd cut and ship every tree your contractors will take this year. You can have your leftover trees mulched and plowed under to nurture fledgling grapevines. It takes a few years for them to produce."

After they finished talking, his new friend directed Cam to the main grocery store in town where he bought milk and cereal. He couldn't face another breakfast of stale Cheetos and black coffee.

THE NEXT DAY HE GOT UP FEELING rested and filled with new purpose. Over breakfast, he reread notes on the steps he needed to take to honor his grandfather's tree contracts.

His first stop was the equipment shed. He found a small tractor with a boom sprayer, a MURPHYMATIC shearing machine and several backpack shearers, plus a box marked Shearing Knives. The knives' edges were so sharp he could have shaved with them. In the corner sat a mower that Cy's notes said was to cut the grass and weeds that sprouted up between the rows.

Approximately a third of his trees needed a final shearing. All needed baling. Cam recognized the baler from Cy's description. Dragging the machine out of the shed, he plugged it into an outside socket. Casting about for a tree, he cut a small one to tinker with and to see how baling worked.

Carrying the tree back to the baler, he noticed a midsize school bus pull in and stop next door at Snowflake Farm. A group of noisy kids emerged. Boys and girls around ten or eleven, followed by a woman to whom Cam gave a shrewd once-over. Their teacher, he presumed. It had to be a field trip. Fussing over his baler, Cam saw Noelle Hale coming out of her gift shop to greet her visitors. She was dressed in snug, worn blue jeans, knee-high boots and a short denim jacket today. Even though the morning sun was weak, it was enough to set fire to the red strands in her hair.

Following a brief discussion, the women and children started walking and soon all disappeared into a grove of six-foot-high fir trees. Cam turned back to his work at hand.

Baling seemed simple enough. He flipped the switch, then tucked his sacrificial tree into the metal barrel. Voilà, out came the small tree, tightly bound in plastic mesh.

Cam tried a few more to get the hang of baling. Satisfied, he shut down the machine and hiked uphill to where well-shaped trees all seemed to be tagged for cutting.

He hadn't gone far when suddenly he heard the boisterous shouts of kids horsing around. Boys. Street cops could certainly identify *that* sound. But it was the hum of his baler motor that sent Cam racing out from the rows of trees.

Skidding and sliding downhill, he arrived back at his shed with his heart pounding. He heard hoots and raucous laughter, and saw that two boys had a third, smaller boy trussed up like a goose for cooking. Or rather baled like a tree for shipping.

"What the hell are you doing?" Cam yelled as he ran toward the baled child. The two perpetrators stopped laughing and started to run but Cam had longer legs. He quickly caught both by their jacket collars and hauled them back to the baler, where their victim was rolling around on the ground. "What on earth possessed you… If he's hurt…" Cam sputtered, letting them go so he could crouch over the boy on the ground.

"He's not hurt," the taller of the two boys declared indignantly.

"Yeah," his coconspirator agreed. "It feels kinda weird, but it doesn't hurt. My brother did it to me one year."

"We'll see. No one move until I get back with clippers to cut him loose." Cam saw that they looked appropriately contrite.

He found a pair of clippers but before he made it back to the baler, Noelle, the teacher and the rest of the students bolted out of her trees, ran across the road and onto his property. The kids danced around their unfortunate classmate, laughing up a storm at his expense.

Noelle stood back, clearly evaluating the situation. Cam swore she almost smiled as he cautioned the baled-up child to lie perfectly still so he could snip the plastic-coated wire.

Instead of joining in the mirth or even lending Cam a hand, Noelle frowned at him and went on the attack. "Mr. Latimer, anyone in the tree business knows it's extremely negligent to leave a baler unattended and plugged in. From now until Christmas Eve, I'll have loads of families with children parking near here to go to my Cut and Carry section." She gestured to her driveway and the trees beyond. "You may have assumed that because baling is designed to be a gentle process it won't hurt a child. But things can go wrong. Children aren't trees, Mr. Latimer. What if Jason hadn't stayed still? What if he hadn't kept his hands against his sides?"

Cam sensed the young teacher's growing concern. She couldn't be long out of college herself and she was probably dreading having to deal with Jason's irate parents.

Noelle Hale's stern features and crossed arms didn't help matters. Hoping she wouldn't mention the word *lawsuit*, Cam clipped through the last of the mesh binding Jason's ankles and set him on his feet. Once the boy was free, Cam folded the mesh and tossed it into his shed.

"I'm Camden Latimer," he said, aiming his smile at the teacher. "You strike me as a reasonable person who's well aware that boys will be boys. As you can see, Jason is fine." Cam lowered his voice so the kids couldn't hear. "A scrawny kid like Jason probably gets picked on a lot. He survived this prank without crying, so he's already gained points with his classmates. Now, Miss… I'm sorry, I didn't catch your name." He tucked the clippers in his back pocket as he bent nearer the teacher.

"Amber Swanson," she said, sounding short of breath. "You're so right about Jason being teased, Mr., ah, Latimer, is it?"

"Call me Cam. I'm new at this. New to Beaver Falls, too. I've only been here two days. I clearly have a lot to learn. Do you live in town, Amber?"

She nodded. "All my life. I did my practice teaching at Beaver Falls Elementary last year. This is my second year bringing students out to Snowflake Farm to see the trees in the Forevergreen Program. When I was a kid, I participated in the adopt-a-tree program here," she said, glancing at Noelle. "Every year kindergartners plant seedlings, and the class follows their growth through the years. In sixth grade the trees are cut and donated to the school. Our PTA sells them as a fundraiser," Amber said. "Maybe you'd like to get involved, too. I could tell you more about the program." She started to lead her students back to the bus and didn't object when Cam took her arm and went along. "Maybe we could get together some evening after school," she murmured.

Left alone by her neighbor's shed, Noelle marveled at how easily Camden Latimer had sweet-talked that poor gullible teacher.

And what a departure from crusty Cy Latimer he was. Cy would've scared the three mischievous boys into the middle of January. Noelle had gotten so used to battling him over every little detail, she wasn't at all sure what to think about this change in dynamics.

Unlike Amber, Noelle rarely had to fight off hopeful Don Juans—much to the disappointment of her mom, who wanted all three of her children happily married and giving her grandbabies. As if Noelle could do that and manage a busy tree farm.

Cam and Amber were still talking next to the bus. As Noelle watched them, she recalled how even her brothers' friends had never wanted to date her. They claimed she was too intimidating. Not that she'd intimidated Camden Latimer. And yet he'd quickly dismissed her and turned his attention to Amber Swanson. *Snake charmer,* Noelle thought, grimacing as the bus pulled out and he crossed the road toward her. She should've gone home while he smooth-talked Amber into the bus.

Here she was stuck. What was she going to say?

Chapter Four

Cam walked up to Noelle, preventing her escape. She'd been staring at the ground, but when she looked up, her wary expression told Cam that she'd rather have been anywhere but there, where she might be forced to speak to him.

"I'm sorry I left the baler plugged in," he said. "It never occurred to me that the kids might wander onto my property. It probably seems like common sense to you but you grew up in the tree business, Noelle. I walked into it yesterday so I have to learn as I go." He gave her a self-deprecating smile. "I'm on a read-and-practice crash course. Next up is shearing. I don't suppose you have paramedics on standby?" he said jokingly.

"Shearing is easy once you get the hang of it." Noelle tucked her hands in her jacket pockets. "If you'd like, I can show you." As soon as the offer was made, she immediately wanted to retract it.

"You'd do that? Well, sure, that would be great," Cam said. "What kind of tools should I bring?"

"Knives. I assume you're working on trees about to be shipped," she muttered, still not looking directly at him. "They've probably been through two shapings already." Noelle paused, unsure how to broach the subject she needed to discuss. "I imagine Ron Halsey's mentioned the mistake in Cy's plat map. I've spoken to my brother Sloan about it. I'm sure he'll have it straightened out soon."

They'd reached Cam's shed. He passed Noelle a shearing knife from the box and selected one for himself. "I've hired James Vaughn to look into it, too."

"Vaughn? That arrogant..." Noelle clamped her lips closed before she said anything nasty.

"Maybe I should hold on to that knife while we talk about this."

Noelle realized she'd been gesturing with the hand gripping the knife and quickly let it fall to her side. "Just so we're clear, I planted that section of trees. A dozen or more rows."

"You can prove that, I assume."

"Everyone who works at Snowflake Farm knows," she retorted. "They've all seen me care for those trees." Noelle didn't want to say anything about the Fraser fir she'd entered in the contest. She couldn't explain why, other than her history with Cam's grandfather. Cy had joined the National Christmas Tree Association in order to sell his trees, and he'd made it very clear that he thought the contest was silly. At the moment, Camden Latimer looked every inch the tough-guy street cop he'd once been, and Noelle could just hear him scoffing at her dream of producing the perfect tree.

She scowled at Cam. "My brother will prove everything. Meanwhile, keep your hands off those trees."

"Fine. I have plenty of others to keep me occupied. The ones with the white tags need a final shearing...I think."

"Let's go find them. If your quad is gassed up, it's the fastest way to get around."

The first quad Cam cranked over sputtered a bit, but did run. It didn't have side-by-side seating, which Noelle would've preferred, so she was forced to sit behind him. She hadn't planned on touching him, but he drove like a maniac and she had to grab hold of his waist or be tossed off after he hit the first rut. She wasn't prepared to have the scent of his aftershave drift back and drown out the earthy smell of the fir trees. Noelle tried to analyze the fragrance as the wind carried it back to her, but couldn't. It was manly, and probably more subtle to someone who wasn't this close. Noelle grudgingly admitted she liked it.

All at once Cam stopped the quad, climbed off and left her sniffing the scent of fir trees again. Embarrassed, Noelle dismounted, keeping the vehicle between them. She noticed they were surrounded by trees bearing white tags and reminded herself of what they were there to do.

"Circle around the tree before you shear any branch," she said, squeezing between Cam and the nearest fir. "You want it to look like an A from every angle." Her circle complete, Noelle made several clean cuts starting at the top of the tree. The result was perfection, if she did say so herself.

"Now you do one," she said, stepping back.

Cam might have managed had the tree she pointed to next been five feet tall, not seven. Reaching up, he stretched his injured shoulder muscles too far too fast. The pain nearly drove him to his knees. He grabbed his shoulder and swore as the knife slipped from his grasp.

"What's wrong?" Noelle asked, rushing to his side. Without thinking, she covered the hand massaging his sore arm with her own.

"It's nothing. Uh…I was shot a couple of months ago by a suspect who'd already killed a convenience-store clerk." As his immediate pain eased, Cam began to be aware of his surroundings again. He saw the shock emanating from Noelle's wide hazel eyes, and felt the warm breath escape her lips. And her small hand was remarkably strong as she helped him massage away the pain.

"I'm so sorry," she said softly. "I knew you'd been a cop, but I had no idea you'd been shot!"

He shrugged off her concern and reluctantly stepped back. They were isolated out here—just them and acres of silence among the trees—and Cam didn't like what her touch on his shoulder was doing to other parts of his body.

"It's not the first time I caught a bullet," he said gruffly. "But it was the worst. That's why I decided to make a career change. Well, that, and the fact that Cy left me this farm." Cam's gaze flitted from tree to tree. "I'm sure you thought I was a cold-hearted bastard for not coming to his funeral. I was laid up with this arm is why."

Noelle bit her lip guiltily. "I have to confess I didn't know about his death until the city clerk who posts births and deaths put Cy's out in our local paper. There'd been some rumors because he hadn't been active in the tree growers' organization for several months but no one realized he was that sick." She briefly touched his arm. "I'm really sorry for your loss, Cam. You were obviously close to your grandfather."

Cam shook his head. "My dad was Cy's only son, but they had a falling out years ago. I don't know who was at fault or what it was about," he said curtly. "Five years ago I got an e-mail from the old man. Dad had died a year earlier. An enraged husband killed him during a domestic violence stand-off. I had to run a background check to be sure Cy wasn't a lying scumbag Dad or I had put away." He shrugged. "As you can tell, we weren't exactly a close-knit family." Ending his personal disclosures, Cam gave his shoulder a final rotation then climbed back on the quad.

Noelle started to get on, as well, but hesitated. "If you swing past my house, I have phone numbers for seasonal workers I've used in the past but didn't need this year. Any of them can shear your trees in about a week. They're good people," she said. "Deserving of a fair wage, even though they're here on green cards. You know about those?"

"Oh, yeah. I'm from Miami, remember."

She threw a leg over the backseat of the quad and held on to his jacket. Noelle knew Zoe would tell her to let her troublesome, and possibly troubled, neighbor flounder on his own—maybe then he'd sell her his farm. But she couldn't do that. Something about his story touched her heart and she wouldn't be able to turn her back on him now. She refused to turn her back on a neighbor in need.

CAM PULLED UP IN FRONT OF Noelle's home. The house had a huge porch and cupolas on the second floor that reminded Cam of eyes. He stayed on the quad prepared to wait outside.

Noelle was already on the porch when she noticed. "Aren't you coming in? It'll take me a bit to find the phone numbers and confirm who needs the work. I'll throw on a pot of coffee. You should try to enjoy whatever breaks you can get before the season gets crazy." She unlocked the front door and stepped into the foyer.

Cam made sure his boots were clean before he joined her in a wide entry that faced a curved staircase. A three-tiered chandelier sent light dancing across a parquet floor as Noelle flipped a switch.

"Wow, I thought I rattled around in Cy's house. You live here alone?" he exclaimed as he peered into a room off the hall that proved to be a well-appointed living room.

Noelle laughed self-consciously. "I was born in this house. Thirty years ago on Christmas Day. Which explains my name. I guess I should be thankful they didn't call me Snowflake." She gave a self-deprecating laugh as she opened a door at the end of the hallway. Camden followed her into an oversize kitchen with gleaming stainless steel appliances and granite counters.

"I refurbished the kitchen two years ago, thinking I'd build a smaller home on the property and turn this into a bed-and-breakfast. We rent out the lodge for big events, but this would be cozier and more intimate. I just haven't found the time to see an architect about drawing up the plans." She set up the coffeemaker and got it brewing. As steam began to form inside the carafe, she shrugged. "Kent—that's my brother who's in charge of finances—claims I'm too sentimental to realistically look at the potential of turning this place into a B and B."

Cam shoved both hands in his back pockets and studied the room. The big window over the sink looked out on a serene pond not visible from the front. "My parents split when I was about three," he murmured. "They shared custody but both moved around so often I don't remember any one place feeling like home."

"How sad." Noelle felt her expression soften. "Oh, jeez, I shouldn't be so blunt. Your place in Miami probably became home."

"A cramped, aging condo in a rundown neighborhood? Not really. But I didn't spend enough time there to justify paying for a nicer place. I worked a lot of night stakeouts and double shifts. I just crashed there."

"Take anything in your coffee?" Noelle asked. She watched him discreetly as she filled a mug. His stance was confident, as though he was denying the inner turmoil his tone implied.

"Black's fine," he said. As he reached for the cup, he went on, "Look, women get more attached to surroundings than men do. I shouldn't be standing here, drinking your coffee and taking up your break time just to ramble on about houses."

She waved her hand dismissively, as if to erase Cam's comment. "Pull out a stool and make yourself at home. I'll dig out the number and call an experienced shearer I know is still in town." She booted up a computer that was tucked in a far corner of the room and tapped into a file of seasonal employees. After making a couple of phone calls, she smiled and handed Cam a name. Miguel Bonillas. "Miguel has two sons you may be able to hire later when you get ready to cut and load trees. There's an art to shearing and in cutting trees to keep enough sap flowing so they're still pliable for the holidays."

"I wondered about that. Some of Granddad's customers are pretty far away."

"I assumed so. Cy didn't think it was profitable to encourage cut-and-carry trade, and he wasn't shy about letting me know that. But I love seeing the faces of kids who tramp around for an hour with their parents until they finally find the right tree," Noelle said as she stirred cream into her own coffee.

"Don't take this the wrong way, but I wasn't expecting you to be nice or helpful at all from things Cy wrote in his e-mails. Now I feel guilty." Cam folded the paper with Miguel's name and stuffed it in his shirt pocket. "Mind telling me what happened between you two, so I don't repeat his mistakes?"

Noelle took a sip before responding. "The bad blood didn't start with me, Cam. It goes back to when I was a teenager and Cy and my parents both wanted the Redmond tree farm. It was a six-hundred-acre wedge sitting between our two properties, and Cy claimed he had a gentleman's agreement with Tom Redmond to buy it if he ever sold. But then Tom died and his son, Paul, wanted sealed bids. My dad bid highest. Cy insisted there was an under-the-table deal. Dad got the land, but Cy was so furious, he stole some of our commercial accounts. Times were tough. The market had been flooded by new growers planting trees just to turn fallow land into cash. It wouldn't have been so bad except that my parents were in the middle of building the lodge. They had to mortgage the house. It took years but we paid down the debt and we're finally solvent and well. But who knows for how long? The trend keeps moving toward pre-lit fake trees." She didn't add that it was the main reason she hoped her tree would be selected for the White House. The publicity from the TV coverage alone was guaranteed to bring new customers to Snowflake farm.

Cam blew out a sigh. "I feel I ought to apologize for my grandfather. It's nowhere near enough, but I'd like to cook you dinner as a first step toward clearing the air between us, Noelle. What do you say to this coming Saturday night?"

"You don't need to do that."

"Please, I want to."

Good sense told Noelle to stand firm, but she was tempted to see what he'd cook. Given her brief glimpse into his life, Noelle bet he was a fast-food takeout kinda guy. "Okay, if we make it early. I'm driving to Portland the next morning to catch a noon flight. I'm going to California for a holiday decoration showcase. What can I bring?" she asked as she moved to the door.

"Just yourself. Shall we say five for wine, with dinner to follow?" At her nod, Cam set down his cup and went out to the driveway.

He was on his quad and gone before Noelle could even begin to withdraw her ill-thought-out acceptance.

Chapter Five

Early the next morning, Cam answered a knock at his door, coffee cup in hand. His early visitor was obviously the tree shearer Noelle had contacted for him yesterday. Miguel Bonillas stood on the porch, a small, wiry man who'd brought his own razor-sharp shearing knives. Two wicked-looking blades hung from his belt. Cam noticed that Miguel's hands were scarred and nicked.

"My sons and I cut trees sometimes for Mister Cy. Shearing, though, he did for himself. My wife saw his death notice in the paper. She said a novena for him because we thought he had no family."

"Not much of one. Thank your wife for me. Come in, I'll get you a cup of coffee and then we can go over what I need done."

"Ms. Hale said you need trees with white tags sheared. It'll be better if I skip coffee and get to work. There aren't as many tree farms as there used to be. I haven't worked in weeks. My sons are learning to prune grapes." His grimace and tart "Bah!" made his feelings clear.

"You don't like vineyards?"

"Vines are touchy. Fickle. Need extra care, like a woman." Miguel smiled crookedly and left Cam to ponder that logic as he descended the steps.

"Hey," Cam called. "Rather than risk scratching the paint on your Toyota, take the quad to scope out the white tags." He dug the key out of his pocket and tossed it to Miguel.

"What time will you knock off?" Cam asked. "Noelle said you get paid at the end of each shift but I have a meeting with a man down the coast. I want to be sure and make it back in time to get you your money."

"Don't worry, Ms. Hale vouched for you. I'll work until dark and finish by Friday. She said eight hundred trees and that you pay the same as she does."

"Uh, okay. Eight hundred was my grandfather's estimate, but it should be about that," Cam added, hoping his grandfather hadn't been mistaken.

Miguel fired up the quad and motored out through the trees. Cam racked his brain, trying to remember if Noelle had mentioned what she paid her shearers. He rummaged through a basket on the kitchen counter where he'd put the business card she'd given him—in case he wanted to sell his farm. He punched in the first number on the card and an unfamiliar voice answered. "This is Camden Latimer. I need a word with Noelle. Is she around?"

"You've reached the gift shop. This is Zoe Blake. Noelle is out on the property. May I take a message?"

"No, thanks, I see her cell number now." Cam hung up and tried the next number. This time Noelle answered. He recognized her slightly smoky voice and couldn't stop the quick flush it always prompted. "It's Cam Latimer," he mumbled. "Did you tell me yesterday how much to pay the shearer? He's here and I can't remember."

"I did," she said, but told him again anyway. "All my wages are spelled out on a flyer you can pick up at the gift shop. We distribute them around town so day laborers know exactly what to expect."

"I'll go grab one, since I'll be needing to hire tree cutters soon."

"I'd run one over to you, but I'm setting up the lodge for a Kiwanis luncheon. They're having their annual charity awards this afternoon. I'm warning you now, expect cars parked everywhere."

"That's all right. I'll be gone most of the day. By the way, thanks again for calling Miguel for me, and for helping me figure out what to pay him."

"No problem. Zoe should be at the shop if you want one of those flyers. She was coming in at eight."

"She's there now. I called that number first. Well, thanks and see you later," Cam said as he hung up. He poured his coffee down the drain and as he walked out to his car, he decided to stop by the gift shop on his way out. He didn't know how long his meeting with Murphy Fletcher, the man he'd met in the hotel bar his first night in Oregon—the vineyard broker—might take.

Cam had deliberately not told Noelle where he was spending the day because an idiot could tell how much she loved the tree business. He doubted she'd be pleased to learn he was considering dumping his trees for grapes. Besides, he hadn't made up his mind.

Once parked in Noelle's driveway, Cam shoved open the gift-shop door, triggering an instrumental chorus of "O Christmas Tree" that made him smile. He wasn't sure what he'd expected of the gift shop, but it certainly wasn't to be instantly and totally immersed in Christmas so early in the season. The room smelled of fresh-cut fir. And no wonder. Wreaths hung everywhere, many tied with white or silver snowflakes. In fact, there were snowflake cutouts of every description hanging from the ceiling. And all over the shop were trees decorated to fit any imaginable theme.

"May I help you?"

Cam finally spotted the speaker, a bean-pole blonde just getting to her feet from where she'd been sitting on the floor, surrounded by boxes of shimmery ornaments.

"You must be Zoe. I spoke with you on the phone earlier. I'm Cam Latimer from next door. Noelle said I could pick up a flyer of day-labor rates here."

Zoe dropped back into a cross-legged position. "On the counter. The green sheet," she said curtly.

"You think I'm trying to steal Noelle's pay rates?" Cam asked after picking up the list.

"I think you're trying to steal Noelle's trees," Zoe snapped.

"I beg your pardon?" Cam rested a hand on a door that had been decorated to look like a chimney, with gaily wrapped presents spilling out onto the hearth.

"Beg away. We all think it's crappy of you to steal trees everyone knows she planted in good faith."

Cam could almost see the daggers flying from Zoe's pale blue eyes. "That issue is being handled by our attorneys." He paused by the door and added, "Noelle seems content to let them sort it out. She hasn't mentioned it, and we talked twice yesterday and once this morning." This time his tone matched Zoe's for curtness.

"Noelle has a soft heart and she tends to let people stomp all over it. The rest of us aren't so nice. Or didn't your grandfather tell you that? I figure the old SOB is laughing in his grave for putting you up to claiming those trees."

"Something special about those particular trees?" Cam's antennae shot up, curious as to what this woman was accusing him of. Zoe turned her back and picked up an ornament and a clipboard, then pulled a pen from her hair. Obviously, she wasn't going to tell him any more.

He grumbled over the exchange long after he'd reached the coastal highway. Plainly, Zoe thought he should write off—or simply hand over—a plot of land Ron Halsey said he owned. Cam doubted Noelle would be so generous if the situation were reversed. Was her friend concerned about more than the survey? He would think they'd want the boundaries clearly defined.

Cam hadn't set out to stomp on Noelle's heart. Maybe her staff was reading more into his dinner invitation than he'd intended. Probably so. After he'd left her house yesterday he'd asked himself if it was wise to spend a whole evening with a woman who could be so prickly at times. He wasn't going to lead her on. But he wanted to prove he could be a better neighbor than his grandfather had been.

MURPHY FLETCHER, ONE OF THE two wine guys Cam had met at the hotel where he'd spent a night on his way to claim his inheritance, turned out also to be the broker recommended by the guy at the tavern in Beaver Falls. They shook hands by way of reintroduction. "Can I buy you lunch?" Fletcher asked. "I was just heading down the street to get a bowl of clam chowder."

"Sounds good." A rumbling in his belly reminded Cam that he'd skipped breakfast.

Murphy locked up his office and pocketed his key. "So, you've decided that being a Christmas tree farmer isn't your gig." The broker rambled on, not realizing that Cam wasn't keeping up. His eye had been caught by something in a shop window, and he'd stopped for a closer look.

Fletcher started back, but Cam met him half way, deciding he'd check out the shop later. "I'm still weighing my options. I just came for some information. Judging by what I've heard from another tree farmer, I'll soon be so swamped cutting, baling and shipping trees I won't have time for anything but sleep. If grapes have to be planted in the spring, which is also when new tree seedlings go in, I'd like to see profit and loss projections for each operation."

"Well, if it's a fast buck you're after, converting to grapes doesn't make sense. You'd be starting from scratch. But it's also true that a single tree planted next spring will take longer to become profitable than a grape vine planted at the same time." Murphy held a café door open and flashed two fingers at a waitress, who smiled and called to the cook for two bowls of chowder. The broker led Cam to a table. "Trees are a revolving crop. The night we met, you said you'd inherited eight or nine hundred acres of mature Christmas trees. This year you'll probably harvest a hundred acres. Next year a different hundred, and so on. Each spring you plant, fertilize and turn one new batch."

The waitress brought over two steaming bowls of creamy chowder. Cam picked up his soup spoon and prepared to dig in. "My granddad left detailed notes about raising Christmas trees. I need you to tell me how grapes differ."

Fletcher talked for twenty minutes between sips of soup and said more over pie and coffee. He didn't idealize the wine grape industry. Both crops, any crop, Cam concluded, took faith, hard work and a whole lot of luck.

"I'll pay for my own," he declared when the bill arrived. "When it comes time to make a decision about this, I'd rather not be beholden."

"Tell you what. One day next week, I'll run out to Beaver Falls and evaluate your soil. That's the best place to start when it comes to grapes."

They shook hands and Cam left, returning to the shop where he'd seen a trinket he thought was tailor-made for Noelle. He hesitated only briefly, then bought the bauble. On the drive home, however, he recalled his parting words to Murphy Fletcher and worried whether Noelle would see the gift as an attempt to make her feel obligated. *Obligated how?* He argued with his conscience.

Rolling his head from side to side, Cam rubbed the back of his neck. His internal debate raged for so long he almost forgot to stop at the bank and get cash for Miguel. After leaving the bank, he made a quick stop at the grocery store to get supplies for his dinner with Noelle.

Cam skidded into the farm, late. Miguel reclined against the porch steps. He rose when Cam climbed from the Viper, and whistled admiringly at the car.

"I'm gonna sell it," Cam said. "Twice already the undercarriage has scraped rock, causing sparks. Big fire hazard. Next free day I get, I'm going to see about trading it in for a pickup."

"How much you want for it?"

Cam named a figure below the seventy grand he'd paid. He hated to see the Viper go, but he needed to unload it fast and get something more practical.

"I know a fellow who recently bought a fully decked-out pickup but it's not the babe magnet he was after. He may be interested in trading."

"Send him over. I'd be happy to talk to him." Cam counted out Miguel's pay. They said goodbye and Cam went inside to store his groceries.

THAT EVENING, NOELLE STARED AT her neighbor's door and paused with her hand ready to knock. She hadn't dressed up for the occasion. Well, other than switching her jeans and sweatshirt for black pants and a gold sweater Zoe and Gwen insisted looked fabulous on her. Taking a deep breath, she knocked. Curiosity had gotten the best of her. She'd never been inside her neighbor's log house.

"I like a guest who's on time." Cam greeted her with a chilled glass of white wine, which surprised Noelle, as did seeing an apron tied loosely around his narrow hips. "I'm in the kitchen finishing up. I thought we'd eat in there, if it's okay?"

"Fine by me." She sipped from her glass and glanced around the living room. She was struck by the masculine feel of the dark blue overstuffed furniture and wood-paneled walls flanking both sides of a log-size fireplace. Hardwood floor gleamed under her feet. "This wine is very good."

"It's a local Riesling. I picked it up at the coast. I generally drink beer."

"You probably noticed all the foothills covered in grapes on your drive to the coast," Noelle said, wrinkling her nose. "Those used to be Christmas tree farms, but the farmers sold out."

"Ouch, you make that sound like an offense punishable by death."

Noelle raised an eyebrow and let his comment slide.

Cam finished tossing a fresh Caesar salad, then served it at a cozy table for two. Noelle watched, both astonished and impressed. "You put my cooking to shame. I tend toward junk food on the fly."

"This isn't how I eat when it's just me. I discovered Cy's garden. I hope you like steamed zucchini. There's not much left out there but I did find that. I stole his recipes, too. From what I could see in his freezer, I think he ate well."

Noelle took another bite of salad, and they concentrated on eating. When she got to the bottom of her salad, she blotted her lips with a napkin, then said, "Cy was a cold and distant man. But maybe he was lonely. I should've made an effort to settle our differences," she said earnestly.

Cam didn't respond immediately. Collecting their salad bowls, he topped up their wine. He put two halibut steaks on to grill and slid Parmesan-crusted potato wedges into a preheated oven. "I almost forgot," he said, reaching for a small sack on the counter. Smiling, he dug out a four-inch square white box and dropped it on the table beside Noelle's wineglass. "I saw this in a shop window at the coast and it made me think of you." Returning to the stove, he flipped the fish.

Noelle stared at the box as if it might bite her.

"Open it. It's nothing huge. Call it a bury-the-hatchet gift," he said off-handedly.

She lifted the lid and took out a silver snowflake on a sterling silver chain. "Cam, it's beautiful. And you bought this for me, for no reason?"

He watched her expression go from surprise to delight as she put the necklace on and kept touching and adjusting the pendant.

Slightly flustered, Cam dished up the fish, the potato wedges and zucchini he took from the microwave. "You could've left me stuck in the mud," he said finally, after he passed her a plate. "Or made trouble over the baler incident. Instead, you showed me how to shear trees, and when I couldn't manage, you sent me Miguel Bonillas. Anyway," he said, winding down, "I saw all the snowflake doodads in your shop right before I went to the coast. For all I know, you sell these trinkets, too." Cam cut into his halibut.

"We don't," she said, adjusting the snowflake on her sweater. "Thank you, Cam," she said, lifting her eyes to his.

"Your shop is chock-full. And aren't you off to buy more tomorrow?"

"For next season. Everything we do is in preparation for next season. You should be ordering fertilizer now so that as soon as the trees are cut, you can plow and fertilize before the snow falls. Over the winter, you'll order seedlings to plant next spring."

"So, it's not good soil without adding commercial fertilizer?"

Noelle relaxed visibly as she explained the nutrients trees needed, and went on to talk about how to ward off bark disease and insects. She talked about her trees the way some of Cam's former friends spoke about their kids, he noticed. Her voice and passion were hypnotic. He briefly wondered if he should come clean about considering a move from Christmas trees to grapes. But he lost the opportunity when Noelle skipped on to a story about the time she sprayed, then it rained for a week and washed off all her expensive spray, and that prompted another story.

Discussing her work softened Noelle's eyes and took the starch out of her backbone. Cam liked the way she talked with her hands when she got excited, too.

All at once, Noelle glanced at her watch and gasped. "It's eleven o'clock. I don't know where the time's gone. Let me help with the dishes, and then I have to go. That early flight out of Portland, remember?" She got up and began busily stacking their plates.

Cam reached out and stilled her hand. "Leave those," he said. "I'll walk you home." Sliding back his chair, he led her to the door.

She freed her hand from his and nervously fluffed her hair over her shoulders. "There's no need. I've roamed this land since I was a baby."

"All the same. It's late, and it's dark." Recapturing her hand, Cam shut his front door and set off down the steps.

Noelle matched his stride. Between walking her home and giving her the pendant because it reminded him of her, she found Cam Latimer unexpectedly chivalrous. They spoke little, except when he noted he could see their breath under the light of her porch lamp.

"Fall. I love it." She stopped and turned to face him squarely. "Cam, thanks for the loveliest evening I've had in a long, long while."

LATER, AS HE WALKED HOME ALONE, Cam would blame the wine for the way he'd kissed Noelle goodnight and then requested a real date when she returned from her trip. He'd surprised them both. When the kiss ended, Noelle blurted out another stuttering rush of thanks for the snowflake necklace.

Cam hadn't wanted her thanks, so he'd toyed with the charm as it hung from her neck. That had led to a second kiss, which really steamed up the night air.

Arriving back at his house, he tramped up to the door thinking it was a good thing she was going out of town the next day. By the time she got back, she'd probably have second thoughts about going out with him.

He fully expected to get a call the next morning from Noelle, making an excuse to cancel. But no such phone call came.

Chapter Six

Sunday morning, Noelle rushed around throwing last-minute toiletries into her luggage. She was angry with herself. She'd let Cam Latimer's good-night kiss rattle her enough to interrupt her sleep. Well, their second kiss had been pretty spectacular. But, for Pete's sake, she'd been kissed plenty of times.

She slipped the necklace over her head and saw in the mirror how it gleamed against the black silk blouse she had on. That placed Cam in a category by himself. And he'd asked her to go out on a real date when she got back from San Francisco.

A giddy ripple of excitement ran through her, reminding her of her adolescence. Frowning, she turned from the mirror and grabbed her bags and a checklist she needed to drop off with Zoe before she left town.

Noelle refused to glance toward Cam's house as she drove out of her lane. Three blocks from town, she pulled up at Zoe's. Her best friend came to the door, yawning and tying her robe. "Look at you," she exclaimed. "Aren't you California chic? Ooh, and check out the bling. Cool necklace. I've never seen it before."

Noelle's fingers flew to the snowflake. Flustered, she shoved the checklist into Zoe's hand. "I'll touch base Tuesday, after I see what the vendors are selling this year. Oh, remember our ad comes out today. You and Gwen will be up to your ears while I'm gone. Sorry for the timing. Just do the best you can." Noelle consulted her watch. "Shoot! I'm running late. If any questions come up, call me on my cell."

Zoe quickly skimmed over the list. "Hang on, Noelle. You want George Tappan to mow around both trees you entered in the contest?"

"That's right," Noelle called back. "The committee begins

evaluations soon. No one knows the exact date. The way a tree presents counts in their decision."

"So, Sloan cleared up the problem with Latimer? I forgot to tell you that jerk came by the shop yesterday. I nearly bit his head off, but he said you were okay with letting the lawyers decide. Wait, didn't you have a meeting or something with him last night? I guess you set him straight. Way to go, Noelle." Zoe gave her a thumbs-up.

The truth of it, Noelle realized belatedly, was that neither she nor Cam had mentioned their land dispute the night before. Now, remembering their parting kisses brought a rush of heat. She held back a smile. "I think it's safe to say he and I took a big step toward repairing the relationship. If he drops in again, Zoe, be nice."

"I'll try. And I'll pass that on to Gwen. Although, she thinks he's hot. Even I have to agree with that," Zoe admitted, fanning herself with Noelle's checklist.

Leaving well enough alone, Noelle said goodbye and climbed into her pickup. Unofficially, Zoe was engaged to a soldier on tour in Korea. Gwen, a red-haired firebrand who worked part-time in the gift shop, was unattached. Cam might well be swept off his feet by her.

Out of habit, Noelle's inner voice asked, *So who cares?* And the realization came that *she* did.

With several hours of driving to the airport ahead of her, Noelle examined the shift in her thinking. She wanted a husband and kids as much as any woman. Her dates never worked out. She hadn't told anyone, but she'd fallen pretty hard for the carpenter she'd hired to remodel the lodge. Owen Rasmussen had dumped her right when Noelle had thought things were getting serious. He'd claimed she was too wedded to the farm. That hurt. Was she supposed to set her work aside when he snapped his fingers? She couldn't. She loved the Christmas tree business. Surely there was a man some-where who would understand and share that philosophy.

Cam Latimer? Noelle shoved his name to the back of her mind.

TUESDAY AFTER HIS DINNER with Noelle Hale, Cam spent the morning phoning Cy's customers who'd preordered truckloads of trees. He introduced himself, explained his grandfather's sudden death, and assured them he'd fill their orders this year. He carefully made no promises for the future.

Right after lunch, Miguel Bonillas showed up with a man he said might be interested in swapping his pickup for the Viper. The cop in Cam smelled Mexican mob all over the smooth-talking young dude who drooled on the car. Nick Sanchez walked with a swagger and drove a customized pickup with a power plant capable of outrunning any police car on the road. Even then, Cam's asking price of sixty grand meant his buyer needed to kick in about thirty g's in cash. The souped-up maroon truck had fire decals running from front to rear, and a plush interior boasting every electronic gadget known to man. Cam sniffed for the slightest hint of weed. Smelling nothing but leather, he turned to Nick and said, "Let's talk terms."

Nick pulled a wad of crisp hundred-dollar bills out of his pocket. There was no quibble when Cam named his asking price. And it was plain both car and pickup were in prime condition. The men shook hands, exchanged keys and signed certificates of registration. Miguel smiled so broadly as he slid into the Viper, Cam figured he'd earned a healthy finder's fee. That would please Noelle. She'd expressed concern that the Bonillas family might have to move out of the area to find work.

Cam spent a moment admiring the pickup. He anticipated Noelle's reaction when she found out he'd taken her suggestion to get rid of the impractical sports car.

Just as Nick stepped into the Viper, Cam heard the crunch of tires on gravel. A black Lincoln and a dark blue Mercedes with smoked windows slowed at the fork in the road. Nick saw them and became visibly agitated. Cam wondered if the cars might belong to Feds looking for Nick. They were both relieved when the two cars turned left into Snowflake Farms.

Nick flashed Cam a smile, then revved up the Viper and sped out of the driveway. Cam had intended to speak to Miguel to arrange for him and one of his sons to cut trees in a week or so. Now he'd have to take care of that by phone.

Still in no hurry to test-drive his new pickup because he prided himself on knowing a smooth engine when he heard one, Cam hung around, inspecting it. He was curious about the well-dressed men and women getting out of the two luxury cars over at Snowflake Farm, and lingered long enough to see Zoe and another woman, a voluptuous redhead, emerge from the gift shop. The women greeted the new arrivals enthusiastically. Zoe gestured with both hands, and quite abruptly they all piled into two utility carriers and drove off into the section of trees separating Noelle's farm from Cam's.

Cam might have grabbed one of his quads to follow at a discreet distance, had Murphy Fletcher not arrived just then.

"Glad I caught you at home," Murphy said as he stepped from his SUV. "I was visiting a friend in Beaver Falls today, so I thought I'd drop by to have a look at your soil. Nice land," he added, scanning the property. "Once the trees are gone, I'm sure you'll get enough sun to raise juicy grapes."

"Can I get that in writing?" Cam joked.

"Can't do that, but I did bring brochures from some local vineyards so you can see the success other farmers-turned-vintners have had."

"Thanks. I'll look them over before I get too swamped with cutting and baling. And I'll try to visit one of the operations."

"I wouldn't expect you to go into this blind. How about we start with samples of your soil?"

Fletcher took half a dozen test tubes from the backseat of his SUV before following Cam to the quad. "I'll take samples from six different sites. Lou Norman, the man with me the night we met you in Medford, will analyze the mineral content in your soil. If it all checks out, we can meet again in town at Lou's office and go over details. Just as an aside, how well do you know your neighbor?"

"We've met," Cam said, starting the engine and aiming the quad uphill. "Why?"

"Sloan Hale fought to keep us from buying Christmas tree farms for grape growers. I'm sure you've heard of him. He considers himself an expert on environmental law. He claims that trees give off more oxygen than grape vines. He also claims that dumping trees and planting grapes hastens soil erosion. Sloan blocked us for months on acquiring a farm east of here. I can imagine how much legal crap he'll throw at us for trying to move a vineyard next door to the family enterprise."

"You mean I can't do what I want with my farm?" Cam asked, just as he passed Noelle's utility vehicles traveling downhill a couple of tree-rows over. Zoe, who drove the larger cargo vehicle, let up on the gas. Cam would have sworn she glowered at him, but he supposed it could have been a shadow.

When Cam stopped the quad, Murphy got off and dug his samples. He was scooping up the last one when Cam noticed a new tag flying from the tallest tree in one of the disputed rows. The shiny ribbon was blue and gold. Cam was further surprised to see that all the rows in this section had recently been mowed. He wondered why Noelle's crew would waste the time.

Cam and his guest returned to the equipment shed, where he parked the quad. Walking back to Murphy's car, Cam noticed Noelle's crew and visitors emerging from a stand of trees beyond her lodge.

Zoe and the redhead walked the somber-looking group back to the two ritzy cars. There were handshakes all around, then the guests climbed into their cars and took off.

Cam and Murphy heard Zoe and her friend whoop. The women did a quick victory dance before disappearing into the gift shop.

"What was that all about?" Murphy asked, handing Cam a stack of brochures.

"I have no idea. Their boss is out of town for a few days. Maybe they made a big sale to a church group or something."

"I'll be in touch," Murphy promised, clapping Cam on the shoulder. And Cam couldn't even catch his breath to say it was on his bad arm.

INSIDE THE GIFT SHOP, ZOE snatched up the phone. "Come on, Noelle, pick up, pick up," she muttered.

They'd hung a Closed sign in the window when the National Christmas Tree Association Contest Committee had paid them a surprise visit, and now Gwen flipped it to Open again.

"Noelle, call me as soon as you get this message. You are not going to believe it. Your tree's been tagged by the contest committee as one of five in the running for the White House again this year.

It's the Fraser fir. George had finished mowing that area not even an hour before the committee showed up. Your tree looked positively regal. Oh, I wish you'd been here to do the happy Snoopy dance with Gwen and me. Call ASAP, okay? Because…I have a bit of disturbing news. Your friend squired that vineyard land broker all around his property today. I'm sure they saw the blue ribbon hanging from your tree."

NOELLE DIDN'T GET BACK TO HER hotel until midnight. A group of vendors had invited her out for a seafood dinner on Fisherman's Wharf. They'd finalized several ornament and decoration orders over the course of the evening. Enough that she was satisfied and able to go home a day earlier than planned.

It surprised her to see the message light blinking on the phone as she let herself into her room. Kicking off the high heels she wasn't used to wearing, Noelle wondered if someone had called her room by mistake but then she noticed she'd accidentally shut off her cell.

Zoe's message caused happy butterflies in Noelle's stomach. She danced around the room, but was sorry she hadn't been home to hear the committee pronounce her tree a viable entry. She threw herself onto the bed and bounced. This was the second time she'd nurtured and grown one of five near-perfect trees. The single most perfect of those five would be selected by staff for the First Family in a matter of weeks.

It was too late to phone her parents and brothers. Too late to call Zoe. Noelle thought about Cam and her fingers brushed the phone buttons. But…what had Zoe said at the end of her message?

Noelle replayed the message. *Cam met with a vineyard broker?* Those leeches had already sucked up some prime tree farms. The creeps had undoubtedly seen Cy's death notice. Noelle had no difficulty believing they'd pay Cam a visit and even pressure him to sell. Surely he wouldn't be so easily conned. But what if he was? Sobered, she got up and took off her work clothes.

It wasn't until she stood under the shower that Noelle remembered Cam pouring the wine the other evening and saying it was a local. Why make that point?

She shrugged it off and crawled into bed, too excited by Zoe's other news to fret anymore. Besides, she faced a potentially bigger problem with Cam. Her perfect tree sat in the middle of the land Ron Halsey said belonged to Latimer's Farm. Her first order of business once she got home tomorrow had to be visiting Sloan— even before she drove out to take pictures of the blue ribbon that proclaimed to the world that she had a perfect tree.

Chapter Seven

Noelle phoned Zoe from the airport. "I wish I'd been there when the committee came. How did they sound? Did you get a feel for where my tree ranks in the top five?"

"You know they'd never say! They always *claim* they have no input whatsoever when it comes to selecting the final winner." Zoe laughed at her friend's excitement.

"I know, I know. The White House Superintendent of Grounds and Chief Usher have the final say. The suspense is killing me, Zoe. I really thought I had a chance last year, but then I lost to that spruce farm from Maine. I don't think I can handle the disappointment twice."

"That tree was exceptional, Noelle. You said so yourself. But so is your Fraser fir. And look on the bright side. You have far better odds of winning this than I have of winning the lottery. The staff had mimosas this morning to celebrate. We toasted the fact that you settled everything with Cam Latimer *before* you went to California. I mean, no one can say that it's not your tree now!"

"Uh…I'm not sure anything *is* settled, Zoe. We'll just have to hope Sloan worked his magic. I'm planning to see him on my way home from the airport tonight."

"What do you mean you're not sure? I thought—"

"I've gotta run, Zoe," Noelle interrupted as she heard her flight announced. "I should have some answers tomorrow. Cross your fingers, okay? Bye." Noelle closed her phone and quickly joined the lineup of passengers. Once on the plane, she found her seat, buckled in and pulled out a book. She wouldn't borrow trouble worrying about a problem that Sloan had no doubt already solved. Her brother knew property law better than any other local lawyer.

Fog in Portland delayed her plane's landing.

Noelle loved the thick white mist and the smell of wood smoke hanging over the valley as she drove back into Beaver Falls. Those things meant autumn, and they were a clear sign that the winter season she lived for wasn't far off.

Noelle caught Sloan locking his office door. "This is a surprise, little sister. I thought you were whooping it up in San Francisco until tomorrow."

"I spent all our ornament and decoration budget fast, so I caught an earlier flight home. There was some really gorgeous stuff!"

"Save the money details for Kent. As a matter of fact, I'm meeting our esteemed brother at Lon's Tavern for pizza and beer. Cheryl and Lisa are at a scrapbooking party tonight. Would you like to come along?"

Noelle experienced fleeting envy for her sisters-in-law, who were free enough to spend an evening on a hobby. Although Noelle designed Christmas wreaths to sell in the shop as her creative outlet, it wasn't quite the same. "No. Thanks. I just I stopped by to see if you've settled the property-line discrepancy I asked about."

"Oh, that." Sloan buttoned his coat as they stepped from the doorway out into the fog. "The original deed for Grandpa Hale's land is okay. It's like you suspected—the overlap is in the pie-shaped wedge Mom and Dad purchased from Paul Redmond. Paul thought he owned those hundred and fifty yards, but they really belonged to Cy Latimer. Dad should've had a survey done before he paid for them."

"But those are *my* trees. I mean, I planted them and cared for them."

"Kiss them goodbye, Noelle. Listen, if you're that worried over the cost involved, come to dinner. Surely Kent can find a way to write it all off as a business loss."

"But I entered one of those trees in the White House Christmas Tree contest! And while I was gone, the committee paid us a visit. That tree is among the five finalists. Now you tell me it's growing on land we don't own. Did you send that letter to Cam Latimer, warning him not to cut those trees?"

"No, not after I learned the truth. It didn't seem worth it for so few rows. And I decided it was better to let it go after I heard that Latimer had hired James Vaughn. Vaughn's had it in for me since

I set up practice in Beaver Falls and some of his clients switched over to me."

"Are you saying it was an honest mistake, Sloan? There's really nothing I can do?"

They'd reached Noelle's pickup and Sloan paused beside the driver's door. "I can petition James for all of us to sit down and discuss an equitable solution. Just remember, we aren't sure your tree will win, kiddo. If it does, and Camden Latimer is anything like Cyrus, negotiations could get trickier."

"He's not like Cyrus. Cam is far nicer."

"Cam, is it? You're positive he's nicer…how?" Sloan brushed her hair back from her face.

Noelle slapped his hand away. "I gave him a lesson in shearing trees—and he was far friendlier than Cy was in all the years we lived next to each other. I ended up referring him to Miguel Bonillas to do his shearing. He and Miguel get on well."

"There's a rumor going around that Latimer may be considering selling out to a grape grower, or that he'll bulldoze his trees and plant grapes himself."

"What? Why would he? His tree farm is well established and I know Cy made a good living. It's just a rumor, Sloan. Those grape brokers always pester people who own prime land." Noelle jerked open the door to her pickup. "All the same, send Vaughn a letter. I probably shouldn't muddy the waters by talking to Cam about this myself. It's better to keep it legal."

"Good, because my advice would be not to let him know he has something important to you. Believe me, a lot of nice guys aren't so nice when it comes to the bottom line. Anyway, your tree might not win, and then you'll have caused trouble with a new neighbor for nothing."

"Right. Anyway, enjoy your boys' night out. Tell Kent I'll be sending him our quarterly reports so he can do taxes."

Noelle arrived home just before dark. The cottony fog cast a fine mist over the trees. As a rule, these were the kind of evenings Noelle loved. She'd build a fire in the big fireplace, then sit at the trestle table and decorate Christmas wreaths. Tonight, though, she was restless and the house felt deserted as she unpacked and stored her suitcases in the closet.

Throwing on a jacket and boots, she hiked out to view *her* tree—and the gold-edged ribbon identifying it as one of the top five in the country.

All Fraser firs were classy by nature, she thought, walking around the tree. They were sturdy and had dense, dark green needles with silver undersides. What made this one exceptional was its shape. Carefully sheared not to look sheared at all.

Where was the thrill she'd expected to feel?

Taking out her phone, Noelle called her folks. Her mom answered. "Hold on a minute, honey, I can't hear you. We're having a pool party. There, that's better. What was that you said? You have another blue-ribbon tree? That's wonderful! I'm happy for you."

Noelle heard her mother turn away from the phone and say, "Dan, there's more artichoke dip in the fridge. What? I'm talking to Noelle. No, she hasn't phoned to say it's snowing *or* to tell us about a new boyfriend. She received another Tree Association award."

Barb Hale came back on the line. "Your father adds his congratulations. But, dear, there's more to life than winning a contest with a tree. You also need to get out a bit, date, maybe think about a family."

Her mom's comments left Noelle feeling hollow as she stood in the fog admiring her perfect tree. "I…ah…want to win for Snowflake Farms, Mom. For the publicity. Winning could make our farm a household name in the industry."

"Honey, I have to go. We have guests. Just let me say that Dad and I worry about the farm dominating your life. Is more growth necessary? The business is successful. *You* are successful. I think you should know Dad and I are seriously thinking of selling Snowflake Farm. We were going to discuss it with you and the boys when we come for Thanksgiving."

"Sell the farm?" Noelle almost couldn't say the words aloud, she was so stunned. She'd worked hard to make her family proud. Didn't they care?

"Maybe not sell it, but possibly hire a manager so you can cut back and have a social life. Oh, I shouldn't have gotten into this right now. Noelle, we really can go into all the pros and cons on our visit. Your dad needs me to bring out the cake. It's our neighbor's fortieth anniversary. Next year will be ours. I don't feel sixty-five, but the years do fly by. In January, Sloan and Cheryl will have been married ten years. Eight for Kent and Lisa in June. Now I should go before your father drops the cake."

The line went dead and so did something inside Noelle. But her mom was right. Noelle had planted the Fraser fir and others in this fifty-acre section the year Sloan got married. Maybe if she'd given her personal life the same kind of attention, she could have been married by now.

On the hike home, she thought about her brothers' weddings. And about her parents' fortieth anniversary in another year. She, Sloan and Kent should start planning a bash for them at the lodge. Except that most of their circle had moved on. And their new friends were in Florida.

Noelle loved this old house and lodge. She loved the tree farm and the town. Although, the town had changed and grown with the influx of vineyards. There'd been a time when the lodge had been *the* place when anyone in town chose to celebrate birthdays and anniversaries. However, one of the big grape growers had recently built an attractive alternative to Snowflake Lodge. Noelle had a wedding booked for this weekend, but the reservations weren't as numerous as they'd once been.

It pained her to think she was the only Hale left who was a hundred percent devoted to Snowflake Farm. Her brothers had other pursuits, but even they wouldn't want the farm to go to a vintner.

Noelle knew this kind of thinking wouldn't help. Nevertheless, she wallowed in self-pity as she worked on her wreaths until finally going to bed after midnight.

The next morning she was plunged back into helping out during the first week of their opening sale at the gift shop.

Noelle, Zoe and Gwen were busy with customers from the time they arrived until the shop closed at six. "Phew, what a day," Zoe exclaimed, locking the door and turning over the Closed sign. "Thank goodness you made those extra wreaths when you got home last night, Noelle. We haven't even had a minute to ask what new items you bought for next year. And what did Sloan say about the tree? Since you didn't come in ranting or in tears, I assume the news is good."

Actually, Noelle had done her best to not think about the tree, or the property dispute. She and Cam Latimer had exchanged a brief wave earlier. He and Miguel Bonillas were in Cam's equipment shed sharpening knives when Noelle came to the shop. "It's not good, Zoe. The fault lies in the parcel land my parents acquired from Paul Redmond. He listed the wrong boundaries on his bill of sale."

"You don't own the perfect tree?" Gwen gasped.

"Don't jinx it by calling it the perfect tree, Gwen," Zoe cautioned. "Gosh, what can you do now, Noelle? Throw yourself on Latimer's mercy and beg him to let you have the tree?"

"I can't do that. Sloan's going to try and resolve the situation with Cam's attorney. If that doesn't work out, then I guess it really is his tree." Noelle's shoulders sagged. Given the conversation she'd had last evening with her mother, losing one tree paled in comparison to losing the farm.

Gwen shook a finger. "Are you nuts? Give Cyrus Latimer's grandson a tree guaranteed to put his farm on the map?"

Zoe rallied. "Gwen's right. Noelle, promise you'll chop down the Fraser fir before you hand our tree over to a Latimer."

Noelle rubbed her forehead trying to ease the headache beginning to develop. "I'd never destroy such a beautiful tree for purely selfish reasons. And…you're assuming my tree will be chosen before Sloan can get us a meeting with Cam's lawyer. Maybe Cam will be a gentleman and not say anything to the committee. Even if he does, we'll still know we planted and raised this year's most perfect tree."

Zoe snorted. "A mess like that would be the end of the Association ever letting you enter the contest again. I'm sure Sloan knows his law, and there's no offense meant, but he hasn't been here the last few years getting grief from Cy Latimer like we have. Noelle, we're your best friends, and we want the best for you. You need to go on the offensive. Aren't I right, Gwen?" Zoe nudged the suddenly silent clerk, who finally came to her aid.

"Right. You have to march next door and tell Latimer that's your tree and to keep his grubby paws off it."

Noelle just didn't have the spirit left for confronting Cam. But she owed allegiance to her coworkers who gave their all to her business. "Maybe not quite like that, but I'll find a nonconfrontational way of approaching Cam. I will, I will," she promised, raising her right hand.

TWO DAYS PASSED BEFORE SHE SAW Cam alone, cutting limbs off trees near the public road. Noelle parked her utility vehicle and lined up what she wanted to say. The noise of his saw and the sight of his muscles straining as he worked sent all coherent thought straight out of her head.

"Hey, I'm glad to see you back home," Cam shouted over the buzz of the saw before Noelle could say a word. Raising his left arm, he blotted the sweat from his forehead. "I'm too ripe for company, Noelle, but I'm really looking forward to Saturday." At her blank look, he said, "You haven't forgotten about our date, have you?"

She had. But right now she needed to get this problem off her chest and explain her situation without making a mess of it. She gestured up the hill. "Cam, remember the rows of trees Ron Halsey said were yours, but that I told you I'd planted years ago? There's one tree in the middle of the bunch that is…well, it's special. And I want it," she said firmly, moving to where she thought he could read her lips, even if he couldn't hear her.

Cam's saw hit a knot in a limb. The knot flew up and cut his cheek. "Damn, Noelle, I can't talk to you while I'm doing this. Sorry, I don't get why one tree is such a big deal. It's not like you don't own thousands. That's pretty possessive even for the Snowflake Queen," he said curtly, setting his blade to another tree.

That was probably too harsh, Cam thought, wincing as Noelle's face fell and she hurried away. There was something about the way she stood there making demands that reminded Cam of his grandfather's warning him about his neighbors' wanting to corner the entire tree market. Noelle Hale, Cy had said, presided over her fiefdom, three times his acreage. And now she claimed she had one pet tree? He swore as another knot struck him hard.

Cam had bigger worries, such as meeting his harvest commitment. Rumors about his meeting with Murphy Fletcher had spread through Beaver Falls, and Miguel claimed they were turning seasonal tree workers off working for Cam because the shearers' loyalties lay with the tree growers like Noelle. Thanksgiving week, he should be cutting and baling his trees for shipment but he and Miguel couldn't handle the job alone. Even the limbing Cam was doing with the small saw caused him a great deal of pain. "Okay!" Cam grunted to himself as he gazed after Noelle.

Cam knew he'd have to phone her later, once he'd cleaned up, and attempt to smooth her ruffled feathers. He'd leave a message if he had to. Considering how things had stood between them, she'd probably cancel their date and he wouldn't blame her.

HER TESTY ENCOUNTER WITH CAM had left a sinking sensation in Noelle's stomach. She'd afforded him ample opportunity to give back her tree. His snarl—when he'd called her the Snowflake Queen in that nasty tone—was something she might have expected of his grandfather, not of Cam. Noelle thought they'd developed a rapport. Better than merely a rapport. She was relieved she hadn't mentioned their kisses to Zoe or Gwen. She was a fool to have let a few kisses mean anything to her.

All afternoon a melancholy gripped Noelle because she'd allowed herself to believe Cam genuinely liked her.

Her disappointment in him, coupled with the sting of his sharp words, left her more confused than ever when she arrived home late that night to find a message from him on her recorder. His voice sounded unexpectedly cheerful. "Noelle, I know we're both stressed, but I forgot to ask what time to pick you up for our date on Saturday. I thought dinner and a movie, if you can get away. Give me a call, or leave a time on my voice mail. Oh— one other thing. You didn't say a word today about my latest acquisition. You're the reason I traded my car for a pickup. But you'll die laughing when you see it. I swear it's grown more garish since I bought it, so be prepared."

She hadn't seen any pickup around except Miguel's battered Toyota. Cam's good-natured message was a greater puzzle. *Darn*. Noelle didn't need him being hostile one minute and the next pretending they were bosom buddies. Pretending everything was fine between them. It wasn't. That tree. It was the tree of her dreams. She had every right to be angry at Cam Latimer.

Chapter Eight

By Friday afternoon, when Cam hadn't heard from Noelle, he worried that she was waiting until the eleventh hour to cancel their date. It was pathetic, he acknowledged, how he kept dashing home throughout the day to check his messages.

In fairness to Noelle, though, Snowflake Farm had been in high gear from dawn to dusk since she got back from San Francisco. As near as Cam could figure, families came out from town to choose and tag a Christmas tree they would cut and take home closer to the holiday. The echo of children's happy laughter drifting through the trees made Cam feel all the lonelier. As he watched cars come and go from Noelle's gift shop and lodge, he wondered why his grandfather had chosen his method of cut-and-ship over dealing directly with consumers. Christmas was all about kids and family. To Cam's way of thinking, Cy's approach missed out on an important part of the holiday spirit.

Who was he to talk? He hadn't gone out of his way to celebrate the season in years. As a cop, he'd volunteered to work Christmas so that the married officers could spend the day with their families. Cops on duty often saw the less festive side of the holiday. Boozers not only drank the money needed to buy food and presents for their children, but alcohol caused some guys to get physical. Domestic violence calls tripled over Santa season, and Cam kept busy with calls from neighborhood bars. Traffic accidents also rose. So, no, he'd never been a Christmas person.

Even before he'd followed in his dad's footsteps and joined the force, Christmas had held no special meaning. When he was a kid, he'd alternated holidays between his mom and dad until his mother married an old jerk with money and moved somewhere in California. Cam didn't know where she ended up. He'd been ten when she took him aside and told him her new husband didn't want the burden of a part-time kid. And Cam didn't miss traipsing off to visit her. She never saw the need to keep in touch, so they left it there. But once he lived full-time with his dad, Cam had found out his dad was a more dedicated cop than father. So, like father, like son.

While he had little personal experience with good parenting, Cam did want kids of his own someday. He'd had two work partners at different times who were great dads. John Traynor and Phil Smith both posted pictures of their wives and kids on the squad car visor. They each bragged about their offspring. Cam remembered soaking in all of John's and Phil's stories, or tuning them out when he felt too rootless.

Miguel rang in on the walkie-talkie. "Cam," he said, "I've probably cut a full truckload of limbs. You want to gather them to take for mulching? Or I could bring my pickup back and fill it. But I'd planned to knock off early today. It's my oldest grandson's birthday."

"I remember. Leave the limbs. You go have fun with your relatives."

"Ten-four." Miguel signed off using the cop-speak Cam had taught him.

Cam was glad to have the physical distraction of loading limbs to take his mind off feeling sorry for himself. He'd accepted long ago that he couldn't change his family. Likewise, he had no power over whether Noelle Hale would cancel their date tomorrow night.

After Miguel left, Cam had just enough time to load the limbs and make a quick trip to the plant at the edge of town that turned them into mulch. Mulch he'd plow back into the earth next spring before setting out seedlings. But only if he stuck with growing Christmas trees.

Cam waffled on that issue. One day yes, the next, no. He'd asked Murphy Fletcher to give him until after he cut and shipped this year's crop to make a decision on switching to grapes or not. The vineyard broker expressed disappointment although he had no choice but to agree.

AFTER ANOTHER LONG DAY OF work, Cam toweled off after his
shower a few minutes to six on Saturday, still with no message from
Noelle. It didn't matter, Cam decided. He wasn't going to mope
around the house tonight. There were places he could go in town
to be with people. Not Noelle, though. And darn it, he'd looked
forward to spending the evening with her.

He was pulling on a clean pair of jeans from his closet when his
phone rang.

Noelle was on the other end, sounding harried. "Cam, I don't
know what I was thinking when I agreed to our date. I'm afraid I
can't go anywhere tonight."

He'd been expecting her to cancel, but was let down nevertheless.

"Cam? Are you there? I forgot I'd booked a wedding reception in the lodge tonight. I've spent all day decorating. I'm sorry
I didn't give you more notice, but Lacy, my caterer, just phoned
to say two servers are down with the flu. She's frantic. I have to
fill in and help her out."

"Need an extra hand?" Cam asked, mostly to teach Noelle not
to concoct such an elaborate lie.

"Do I ever, if you're serious. It's the mayor's daughter's reception. Not an event I want to screw up."

"If *you're* serious I can be there in ten minutes. Do I need a tie?"

"Lacy's crew wear dark pants, white tops and black bow ties.
I'd already planned to wear a navy dress, and I'm not switching.
Lacy can take what she gets. Oh, shoot, there's a limo pulling in
already. I haven't finished putting out the fresh flowers. Cam, I'll
thank you now, because there may not be time later."

Cam felt guilty for having doubted her. He quickly pulled on
the dressiest pants and shirt he owned. He didn't have a bow tie, so
he substituted a regular dark one. Hurrying out without a jacket, he
noticed a frosty nip in the air on his walk to the lodge. He probably
shouldn't be surprised. In a few weeks, he'd be cutting and shipping
the bulk of his contracted trees. Maybe he *would* continue with the
tree farm. Although, Cy had said once that a lot could happen to
derail profits. An early snowstorm. A major power outage shutting
down the baler. A lack of seasonal workers. Last-minute cancela-
tions if neighboring tree farmers underbid old customers. Cam

knew now that Cy must have meant Noelle, but he had a difficult time believing that of her.

Closer to the lodge, the smell of fresh-cut fir mixed with the more pungent scent of wood smoke. Indeed, smoke curled from a big brick chimney protruding above the roof of the lodge. Cam had never been inside but when he entered, he found it exactly as he'd pictured it. The big room, decked out in corn shocks and baskets of fall leaves, looked like he imagined an old hunting lodge would with high, beamed ceilings, knotty pine walls and gleaming plank floors. Cam spotted Noelle talking to an elegantly dressed older couple, and he hung back, waiting for her to be free.

She finished her conversation and began to rush off, but changed direction when she saw him. "That's the mayor and his wife," she said. "They're here to check things for their daughter, Traci. Just let me set out baskets of chrysanthemums and fall foliage, then I'll give you a tour of the kitchen. It's a buffet dinner, but we'll pass hors d'oeuvres among the guests."

Cam inclined his head and followed as Noelle entered a smaller room, where she'd obviously been assembling flower baskets. When she struggled to pick up two baskets at once, Cam relieved her of the larger arrangement. "Thanks," she said. "That one goes on the bandstand. This is for the center of the buffet table. I have smaller ones to hang on those wooden wall pegs around the room."

They split up and came back together near the kitchen when the chore was done. "It looks nice," he observed, eyeing the finished product.

"Traci's wedding colors are burgundy and amber. If it were me, I'd have gone for a winter wonderland theme. You should see the lodge decked out in fir boughs, white poinsettias and miles of white twinkle lights. It's so beautiful then."

Her sigh told Cam that Noelle dreamed of having a winter wedding. He studied her obliquely, fantasizing how she'd look as a bride. Tonight she wore a softly sexy blue dress, black boots with narrow heels and sparkling blue earrings. He realized he'd never seen her in anything but work clothes. She cleaned up nice. *Very nice.*

"Oh, one second, Cam. I forgot to turn on the sconce lights."

"Take your time. I'm yours for the duration." He ran a hand gently down her arm.

She smiled. The private smile prompted Cam to wonder why Noelle Hale was still single. It was no mystery why *he* hadn't married. Police marriages suffered from a high divorce rate. His folks were only one example. But until he'd moved here, Cam hadn't understood how alone a man could feel rattling around a big house. How had Cy done it for so long?

Noelle sped off, flipped on the lights, then rushed back. "I saw Lacy's catering truck pulling around to the kitchen door. Let's go help her unload food for the warming ovens."

The band arrived soon after Lacy. And then guests began to straggle in. All at once, the room exploded with gyrating figures and loud music. Cam pulled more champagne corks than he could count. He and Noelle spoke a few words in passing. But mostly, he watched her float among the guests. She handled everything from a too-long bridesmaid's dress to a harried guest's crying baby with calm efficiency. Noelle flew around picking up the pieces. Cam imagined having her there to pick up the pieces of his own often chaotic life. His pulse tripped wildly when, in the midst of tickling the baby, she met his eyes and smiled, apparently just because she was happy to see him. His breath stalled in his chest and was followed by a tightening in his belly that he recognized as attraction. It had hit him fast. He recognized how fast as he gave in to the feeling and contemplated what he might do to keep her smiling.

Various ideas flashed through Cam's mind. One lingered. He could hand over that blasted tree she'd ranted about the other day. Why that one tree mattered so much he didn't know.

But he did know that he didn't want whatever was developing between them to depend on the fate of one silly tree. He wanted a lot more from Noelle.

As rapidly as the lodge had filled to overflowing, it emptied at the end of the evening.

Cam shook out a large garbage bag. "I'll pick up in the main lodge," he told Noelle, who stood at the back door signing a check for Lacy, the caterer.

"Cam, you've already saved my life by pitching in with the serving tonight. There's no need to help me clean up."

"I heard you tell someone you began decorating at four-thirty this morning. Uh…yesterday," he said, glancing at his watch. "Two sets of hands can put everything in order twice as fast."

"All right," she said, after waving to Lacy and locking the back door. "Thanks."

They each worked on different areas, but moved quickly and finally met up again to scrub the kitchen. When they finished, Noelle threw her dirty sponge in the last open garbage bag. She let Cam cinch it shut, then straightened and eased the tension out of her back.

"Do you believe it? The mayor and his wife absconded with every last morsel of food. Usually there are leftovers for the workers. I'm starved. And I'm sure neither of us slowed down long enough to eat anything tonight."

"I put an almost full bottle of champagne in the fridge," Cam said as he stuffed the last bag into the overflowing can.

"I'm no gourmet cook," Noelle said, "but I may have fixings at home for scrambled eggs and toast. Will that go with champagne?"

"Everything goes with champagne." He rescued the bottle, declared it hadn't yet lost its fizz, and trailed her into the frosty night.

"Brr." Hearing Noelle's comment, Cam draped an arm around her. He'd been dying to get his hands on her all evening. Once inside her kitchen, he steered her to a chair. "Let me pour the bubbly, and then I'll cobble together a midnight breakfast." He yanked open her fridge door, but stopped to tease her about its meager contents.

Noelle stifled a yawn. "It takes every hour of every day to run Snowflake Farm. My mother would tell you it's not how a woman ought to live." As Noelle tested the champagne, she still felt a sting from her mom's latest comments.

She watched Cam combine the ingredients for a cheese and herb omelet. While it cooked, he made toast. He was deft in the way he later slid the omelet onto plates and topped off their glasses as he sat down across from her.

"This looks delicious," Noelle said as she tucked into the food. "If you hadn't come home with me, I'd have probably skipped eating." She briefly raised her eyes to his.

"I know what you mean. Cooking for one hardly seems worth dirtying dishes." Cam touched his wineglass to hers. "It's a heck of a lot nicer having someone across the table. Especially a someone of the opposite sex."

Noelle scoffed, sparking a lively discussion about the pluses and minuses of living alone. They both had regrets, they learned. And they both endured bouts of loneliness.

A bit self-consciously, Noelle replenished their glasses this time. "My brothers and I were born in this house. It's way too big for me, but I love it. I should stop procrastinating and turn it into a bed-and-breakfast. Lacy would run it. But I can't seem to take the steps." She gazed soulfully around the big, family-size kitchen.

Cam heard the uncertainty in her voice. He had a similarly ambivalent response to possibly replacing his grandfather's Christmas trees with grape vines. "I rattle around in Cy's house, too," he admitted. "These places were built for families with kids."

They finished their food in silence.

Holding the champagne bottle to the light, Cam said, "There's about a half glass apiece. Shall we polish it off?"

Noelle held out her flute. "Care for the fifty-cent tour of my home before you leave?" Cam heard the request for the delaying tactic it was. Clearly, Noelle didn't want him to go yet.

"Sure," he agreed. "If you're not anxious to get to bed."

"It takes me a while to unwind." She rose and headed into the next room, taking her glass with her.

Cam set their dishes in the sink, then followed. He could see this place as a B and B. The living room was huge, and farther down the hall was an office/library. They turned the corner and Noelle flipped a switch to light the stairwell.

She stumbled on the first step. "Careful," Cam murmured, sliding an arm around her. He could have let her go, but frankly he liked holding her.

"Sorry. I probably shouldn't drink any more of this." She smiled into his eyes and raised her glass, but Cam only tightened his grip on her waist.

"You deserve champagne for all the work you did today. Are all brides so picky? I heard Traci complain about the color of the candles, and she said one napkin on her table didn't match the rest of them."

"Well, it's a day most women have planned in their heads for a long time." Noelle sounded pensive. Until she briskly shoved open a door and explained this was one of two bedrooms separated by a common bath. "My brothers' space when they lived at home." She gestured to the door at the end of the hall. "My parents' suite. They'll use it when they come for Thanksgiving. It's our one yearly family gathering since my brothers got married. Cam, if you're going to be alone on Thanksgiving, why don't you share the day with us?" she asked as she led him into the last room on the tour.

A host of feelings overwhelmed Cam. Noelle's offer touched him in ways he couldn't explain. Rather than try, he caught her chin in one hand and kissed her. It wasn't a fast kiss, and Cam prolonged it as much as possible. When it finally ended, Noelle drew back, plainly shaken, and stammered, "W-what was that f-for?"

"Calling it a thank-you doesn't go nearly far enough," he said, gazing down on her flushed face. Cam tugged the glass from her hand and set it with his on the dresser beside them. Cam knew it was her room without asking. The hodgepodge of Christmas dolls and Santas in the bay window, the snowflake valance and matching bedspread all put Noelle's stamp on the room.

Cam brushed his thumbs across her cheeks. "This may be rushing things, but…" There was more he wanted to say, but he couldn't seem to manage anything except to kiss her again.

Suddenly breathless, Noelle took a step back. "I could blame kissing you back on too much champagne. But that would be a lie." She wanted to be honest because she'd sensed in Cam a bone-deep loneliness that echoed her own. She supposed she was still upset by what her mom had said, and the fact that tonight's bride was seven years her junior didn't help. But it was the sense that time was slipping away that led her to seek comfort from Cam. Noelle had never felt as attracted to any man this quickly.

Although it had been a long time since her last relationship, Noelle had some condoms stashed in her dresser. However, before things progressed too far, Cam wedged a space between them on the bed and tilted up her chin, looking for reassurance. "I need you to tell me this feels right, Noelle. Promise me you won't regret it in the morning."

She tugged his head back down to the pillow and let her body answer for her. It was the first of many discoveries they made about each other in the hours that followed.

Chapter Nine

Noelle's alarm blared. She shut it off but felt so warm and content she wanted to snuggle back under the covers. Then she recalled the reason for her contentment and sat up. The imprint on the pillow next to hers was proof that Cam Latimer hadn't been a dream. Vaguely, Noelle remembered him kissing her awake to say he was leaving. She'd smiled against his lips and murmured, "Stay." But Cam had reminded her that their farms were in full seven-day-a-week mode, and her workers and his would be arriving within the hour. And he didn't want to give anyone a reason to gossip. *That was nice*.

In the shower, Noelle realized she was humming. Out of happiness, she supposed. Who would ever have guessed that she and Cam had as much personally in common as a night of pillow talk had revealed? And, the man deserved an award for his *other* skills.

Thinking *award* dealt Noelle her first dose of reality. In all their whispers and confessions, neither of them had said a word about her prize fir. Should she have done as Zoe and Gwen had urged—come straight out and asked Cam for the tree?

She dried off and dressed for work, wondering why he hadn't said anything about either the tree or their litigation. Thinking back, Noelle admitted that it wasn't any surprise business hadn't come up in conversation. Cam was good at keeping her mind on other things. Delicious things.

CAM WANDERED THROUGH HIS HOUSE with a cup of strong coffee. His thoughts were focused on the woman he'd left in bed. Noelle Hale's passions ran deep. It was pure luck that he'd lived this long and traveled this far to find a woman who shared his values and aspirations for the future—and that he'd found her living next door.

Roots meant a lot to Noelle. She wanted a home filled with love, family and laughter. Her kids would have the childhood Cam used to dream about.

Still high from their lovemaking, Cam began picturing how he and Noelle could someday merge their farms. She'd mentioned turning her family home into a bed-and-breakfast, so he imagined them living in his house—a husband, wife, two or three kids and maybe a dog and cat. His backyard had enough room for a swing set, a fort or two and a playhouse.

Those were big plans when he hadn't even met Noelle's parents yet. She'd invited him to do that at Thanksgiving, and Cam was prepared to like them if for no other reason than the way they'd raised their daughter.

What if the Hales thought he was only after Snowflake Farm? He needed to prove his intentions were honorable. Dumping his rapidly cooling coffee, Cam sat at his desk to type a letter to James Vaughn. The letter stated his decision to cancel any inquiries regarding the property issue. He enclosed a check for the lawyer's services to date as they'd agreed when he'd retained the man. Then he rousted Miguel on the walkie-talkie. "Hey, it's Cam. How was your grandson's birthday bash?"

"Good. I ate too much. You sound cheerful this morning. Did your date with Miss Noelle turn out okay?"

"We didn't actually go out. I helped her with a wedding reception at the lodge for the mayor's daughter. The caterer had two of her staff phone in sick."

"That doesn't seem too exciting to me. Did you win the lottery?"

"No." Cam laughed. "I came to some conclusions about my life. That's why I'm taking a run to the coast this morning. I'm leaving you in charge. You'll be glad to hear I'm going to sit down man to man and tell Murphy Fletcher there's no deal. I'm sticking with Christmas trees."

"That *is* welcome news. Too many vineyards threaten to destroy this beautiful countryside. Now may not be a good time to tell you but I found about a hundred trees in next year's crop with their bark eaten by mice or voles. They'll have to go."

"Do what you have to do. I want healthy trees. If you see Noelle, let her know what you found. I'd hate to see the mice go to her farm once they leave here."

Cam signed off, and whistled on his way to the pickup.

WHEN NOELLE WALKED INTO THE gift shop. Zoe immediately cornered her. "I talked to Lacy this morning. She said Cam Latimer helped you at the wedding reception last night. She said you and he were the only two in the place when she left, and that you guys were smiling at each other all evening. What gives?"

Noelle picked up the previous day's mail and riffled through it. "Cam's a great guy. We had him pegged all wrong, Zoe." Pulling an envelope from the stack, Noelle slit it open.

"I hope that means he's relinquished all rights to those trees."

"What?" Noelle glanced up from the paper she'd been reading, her brow puckered. "This is a letter from Cam's attorney. He says that since Sloan refused to discuss a monetary resolution to the matter of the trees I planted on Cy's land and instead demanded that the involved parties meet to talk, we can do our talking in court. This is a notice of a hearing in Judge Winslow's courtroom mid-January." The paper fluttered in Noelle's unsteady hand.

"Well, isn't that fabulous timing?" Clearly disgusted, Zoe stalked around, setting ornaments to right. "On my way in today, I saw Miguel getting stuff out of Latimer's shed. He said Cam went to the coast this morning. You know why he made the last visit to the coast—to meet with the grape broker. Oh, yeah, Latimer's a real friend, Noelle."

Noelle refolded the letter. She felt more betrayed by Cam than she could ever admit to Zoe. After their night together in her bed, this was a huge blow. "If he thinks for a minute that I'll hand over those trees without a whimper, he's misjudged me. Will you watch the shop for an hour? I'm going to Sloan and have him try to get that court date bumped up. Oh, and if Cam Latimer darkens this door, kick him out on his rear!" Noelle said, wrenching open the door to storm out.

IT WAS LATE BY THE TIME CAM returned home. He'd been firm with Murphy Fletcher about not switching to grapes. Fletcher hadn't taken the news well, but Cam felt he'd effectively closed the door on any future vineyard prospects.

It wasn't too late to call Noelle. He thought he might talk her into coming down for a drink—and who knew what after that. Her phone rang a dozen times, but she didn't pick up. Cam considered hiking up to her house. She'd shown him where she spent a lot of evenings making wreaths. Maybe she hadn't taken her cell with her.

But before he could head over, he got sidetracked. His answering machine produced some new orders. He needed to fax the customers first to set delivery dates. And when all was said and done, it really had gotten too late for a surprise visit to Noelle.

The next day, he tried several times to reach her to ask her out on another date. A replacement for the one they'd missed. She deserved a night out focused on her, not on business. He'd suggest an evening between now and Thanksgiving. After that, they'd both be too busy to slip away.

All that week and into the next they played phone tag. Or at least Cam assumed the hang-up calls on his machine must be from Noelle. Except that he'd left his cell number on her call-back feature a bunch of times.

His first clue that all wasn't well between them was on a busy Friday morning when he dashed into her gift shop to buy a ball of twine.

Zoe Blake lifted the twine right out of his hand and plopped the roll back on the shelf. "We don't sell to traitors," she said bluntly. "Drive to Beaver Falls and see if your fancy-schmancy lawyer can get Lon Mackey at the hardware store to serve you. But don't be surprised if no one in our community wants your money. Now get out!" She hustled Cam to the door and slammed it behind him before he got a word in edgewise. He heard the lock click into place.

What did she mean by calling him a traitor? Or even that reference to his lawyer?

Cam jogged home. He recalled seeing a letter from James Vaughn in a stack of mail he'd set aside to handle later. He'd assumed it was a receipt acknowledging his payment in full, blah, blah, blah.

Digging through the stack, he found it and tore open the envelope, then quickly scanned its contents. "Dammit," he said, reaching for his cell phone when he saw Vaughan had cc'd Snow-flake Farm. He punched in half of Vaughn's number when he noticed the date on the letter. The lawyer had dictated this note two days before Cam had canceled further representation.

Letter in hand, Cam raced out of his house in search of Noelle. A workman reluctantly pointed him in the right direction. He started down the path on foot, and met her driving toward him in the big utility vehicle. She would've passed by without acknowledging him, but Cam planted himself in the middle of the narrow road and waved the letter at her. "Just give me a minute to explain." He bent over the hood of the vehicle and implored her to hear him out. "This letter Vaughn sent me, of which you have a copy, he wrote before our night together." Cam could only pray she'd understand. "I sent him a check the very next morning with a note saying I no longer needed his services. I care about you, Noelle. A lot. You think I give a damn about the few hundred trees he wants us to go to court over? I don't," he said, wadding up the letter. "They're yours. All of them."

"It's too late, Cam."

"Too late for what?"

"I thought you knew. There's one tree in that batch that means the world to me. It's on the National Christmas Tree Association Contest Committee short list for the White House tree. You've caught me driving back to the house right now because the committee chairman and two representatives from the White House are due to arrive here within the hour. My tree is the last one of five they'll be vetting for the top honor."

"So then it's not too late! We can clear everything up before they get here."

Distress showed clearly in Noelle's eyes. "I got a letter from the court this morning. If you didn't receive one, you'll probably get a copy tomorrow. The upshot is that neither you nor I can cut a single tree in that stand until after Judge Winslow hears our case in January. And that's *way* too late."

Cam exploded. "This is the stupidest thing I've ever heard. We're the two parties involved. It's my land and your trees, and I opted out of pressing charges. Let me ride home with you. While you change clothes to meet those bigwigs, I'll phone James Vaughn's office and tell him to straighten this out with the judge."

Noelle motioned for him to climb in and passed him her cell phone so he could call the lawyer. Some of her crew and Zoe and Gwen were waiting as they drove in. They scowled when they saw Cam but perked up as Noelle explained that he was waiting for the receptionist to ring Vaughn's office.

Cam waved his hand in the air, calling for silence. "Mrs. Mickelson, this is Cam Latimer. I need to speak to Mr. Vaughn. It's urgent."

He hauled in such a deep breath that everyone standing around pressed in closer to where he still sat in Noelle's utility vehicle. "He's out of the office until after Thanksgiving," Cam whispered. "Mrs. Mickelson, you must be able to get hold of him in an emergency. This is one. Give me the number where he can be reached, and I'll take full responsibility for interrupting your boss's vacation."

Noelle gripped the upright strut on the ATV. She felt her stomach drop when he shut his eyes and muttered, "He's on a deep-sea fishing vessel in the Bahamas? No, no, I understand he's unreachable. Thanks, anyway." Cam snapped his phone shut and ran his left hand through his hair in a gesture of frustration.

A fir cone fell from a tree. The sound echoed like a rifle shot since the entire group had gone silent. Cam felt daggers shooting from all eyes but Noelle's. Her eyes were filmy with tears that cut to his heart.

Chapter Ten

Frustrated, Cam wrapped a hand around Noelle's arm to hold her fast while he attempted to clear up a few things once and for all. He didn't care who else was listening. "Maybe I'm wrong, but after the other night I went away believing everything had changed. Since then I've been operating under the assumption that you and I had turned a corner." Feeling Noelle tug away, Cam released her arm. "*Together*," he stressed. "I said that night that it was fast, but I fell hard, Noelle. We're not kids. I guess it sometimes happens this way—a man knows when he's met the one and only woman for him. And if you meant half of what *you* said, it seems to me we're heading down a path where in the not-too-distant future, all my trees will be yours and vice versa. With any luck, it seems to me we'll have plenty of years to grow the perfect tree. A lot of years, I hope."

"Cam…" Noelle's knees threatened to give out. "That night when we talked about us…it almost doesn't seem real. I was so moved. You've got no idea how much. I…want you to meet my family. Their blessing is important to me. But about this tree… You don't understand. Growing the winning tree is a lifelong dream. A once-in-a-lifetime deal. Nothing can compare—" Unable to complete her sentence, Noelle tore her eyes away from Cam's to stare weepily at her crew, then at her trees.

Zoe insinuated herself between the pair, forcing Cam to take another step away from Noelle. "You can't trust a Latimer, Noelle. Cy stole customers from your folks. And this guy's full of pretty, meaningless words. Look, I see some cars turning off the highway. Those have to be the committee members. If they choose your tree, Snowflake Farm gains prestige. Why can't you see he'd do anything to make you lose this opportunity?"

Gwen cut off Noelle's view of the approaching vehicles.

"Zoe's right. Cy probably saw you babying this tree. It would be so like him to leave instructions for his grandson to exact the ultimate revenge."

Uttering an oath, Cam broke out of the circle. "How would I have any idea why the damn tree was tagged with that ribbon? If my granddad even knew the White House put up a tree, or that it could come from a farm all the way across the country, he never breathed a word of it to me. He's dead, let him rest in peace. Surveying the property was my idea and mine alone." Cam stalked a few paces down the path, then he spun around again, making sure he had Noelle's full attention. "You told me that sometimes you feel so alone and lonely you cry yourself to sleep. Maybe I didn't explain myself very well a minute ago. I was offering you a lifetime of love, a shoulder to lean on and a partner to share…well, everything with. Granted, I'm a shot-up ex-cop who doesn't know zip about any of this, but I'd say it's shallow and superficial to place more importance on a little bit of fame than a lifetime of love. And you know what? I'm sorry I *didn't* sell out to Murphy Fletcher to turn this into a vineyard. So, here's the thing. I'm giving you that tree, Noelle. Without strings. I don't care what you do with it. You'll do it without me."

Cam brushed past a well-dressed woman and several men in three-piece suits, walking toward Noelle and her staff.

Dismissing Cam's outburst, Zoe sent George Tappan and a second member of his crew, Dave, to the equipment barn for two more utility vehicles to carry the committee and the judges out to the tree. A ripple of excitement traveled through the crew. "This is Noelle Hale," Zoe said, yanking Noelle over to meet the committee chairman, the first person to have tagged the tree. "Noelle is manager and part owner of Snowflake Farm. She was out of town the last time you were here."

Noelle offered a feeble handshake. Dazed, she felt herself being swept along in the euphoria of her crew after George and Dave returned and everyone piled into the three conveyances. She turned around to watch Cam until he disappeared from view.

The Fraser fir was already in sight when Noelle tapped George on the shoulder. "Stop!" she said. He steered to the side of the row and braked.

Noelle hopped out. "I'm sorry, everyone. But I'm withdrawing my tree from this year's competition." She started hiking back the way they'd come. Toward where she'd last seen Cam.

Zoe, traveling in the vehicle directly ahead, jumped out and ran back to intercept her boss. She gestured to the dignitaries who'd gotten out of the first utility transporter and were already inspecting the Fraser fir. "Noelle, you can't throw ten years away! What about your family, who'll benefit if your tree wins? And what about your crew?" Zoe wailed. "We've worked hard for this, too."

"I know that," Noelle said, her fingers going to the snowflake necklace which she'd worn every day since Cam had given it to her. "I didn't plan to fall for Cam Latimer. All I can say is that it's suddenly clear to me that winning this contest is nothing compared to that."

"Don't you at least want to stay and hear if your tree actually does win?" Zoe attempted to urge Noelle on up the row.

"We all know that, in spite of Cam's offer, it's not legally my tree. And if I stick around to hear them announce if we've won, I *would* be as shallow as Cam said. Zoe, please explain to the committee. Tell them we'll read about the winner in the newsletter." Noelle turned and ran down the row, picking up speed as she cut over to Cam's property.

She was out of breath by the time she reached his house. Cam was just climbing into his flashy pickup, the one he'd bought because she'd said he was foolish to drive a sports car in this country.

"Cam, wait. Please stop."

He hesitated, half in, half out of the cab.

Noelle could tell he wanted to slam the door and leave, to be done with her and the whole mess. She trusted he was too much of a gentleman not to stay and hear her out, and she was right. He dropped back to the ground as she ran over to him, and flung her arms around his neck.

"I choose you, Cam Latimer. I choose *us* over my foolish, childish wish to grow a White House tree. I told Zoe to withdraw the Fraser fir from the contest."

"Sweetheart, that makes me feel like the biggest jerk who ever lived. I should be drop-kicked from here to Beaver Falls.

Hurry, go back and tell them you've changed your mind. We'll confess to cutting a tree when we go to court. What can the judge do after the fact?"

"But the thing is, Cam, I haven't changed my mind. I thought I wanted my tree in the Blue Room more than anything in the world. You've made me see that there's something I want more. I want someone to love me for myself. I want a family of my own so I can pass on the love of raising Christmas trees. I don't need to grow the perfect tree. I want to try to have the perfect life. I'm missing that now."

They heard car doors slamming, and it was plain to both of them that the committee members and the emissaries from Washington, D.C., were leaving. The glum faces of Noelle's crew told Cam that they weren't feeling magnanimous.

Zoe, always outspoken, approached the couple while the other workers trailed in her wake. "Cam Latimer, I'll hate you forever for making Noelle choose."

"I'm sorry, too, Zoe. But I want you to know, in my whole life, she's the only person who's ever put me first. I'll never forget that," he said with feeling.

In front of everyone, Noelle rose on her tiptoes and kissed Cam. A lengthy kiss that was obviously grounded in love. When it ended, she kept both hands against Cam's chest, and said stoutly, "My parents recognized that I've been putting so much into the business that I left no time for me. For me and the real reason anyone gets into growing Christmas trees. So children can wake up Christmas morning and find presents under a tree they think is the most perfect Christmas tree ever. Thanks to everyone at Snowflake Farm, loads of families get their version of the Blue Room tree every single year."

Cam pulled her close so that together they faced her disheartened staff. "We'll grow perfect trees together for many Christmases to come," he promised.

Zoe glanced around the circle of long faces, then stepped forward to hug Noelle and Cam. "I'm sorry for what I said, Cam. I can see now how good you are for our boss. Hey, I'm always willing to be the first to say it's time to make lemonade out of lemons. I happen to know the lodge has no event booked the weekend before Christmas. If we all put our heads together we could throw a bang-up wedding and reception then!"

Noelle blushed to the tips of her ears. Even though they declared they hadn't nearly reached the point of booking the lodge, Zoe, Gwen, George and the others went off merrily making plans anyway.

"Cam, will you walk with me to look at the Fraser fir one more time, please?" Noelle interlaced her fingers with his.

"Because you regret being so hasty in sending the committee away?" He angled his head to look into her eyes as they started walking.

"No. To see if it's too tall to fit in the lodge, since it's going to preside over our wedding."

Cam kissed her so passionately it took them quite a long time to reach the tree.

Besides which, Noelle stopped in at the gift shop to grab a disposable camera.

"I want a picture of it as it stands. One day we'll open an album and show our grandchildren the tree that was almost in the White House, but ended up bringing us even greater happiness."

The sun was sinking and the afternoon was turning frosty, so when they reached the tree, the tips of the fir were gilded white. Viewing the magnificent tree as they stood hand in hand, Cam said, "It's such a beauty it would be a shame to chop it down, Noelle. What if we began a brand-new tradition? We can call it the Hale-Latimer anniversary tree and make it a family affair to decorate this tree every year in celebration of what it means to us."

Noelle paused, her finger on the shutter button. "Cam, that's brilliant." As their frosty breath mingled, Cam lifted Noelle and swung her around and around. When her feet touched earth again, his lips warmed hers for a long moment before she murmured, "Cam, what do you think Cy would say if he knew sending you down Snowflake Farm's private back road would result in our merging the two of our lives and our farms?"

"Truthfully? I think he was a lonely old man who'd probably tell me to grab love with both hands and hang on to it for all I'm worth. And maybe it's exactly what he had in mind when he left a banged-up cop the house next door to the most beautiful woman in the world."

Noelle smiled at that, and snapped a picture of Cam standing in front of what truly was her perfect tree.

Epilogue

Thanksgiving came and went in a whirlwind of Hale family business meetings and feasting, combined with vetting Cam and accepting him as one of their own. Really, acceptance came down to one fact—Noelle's parents and brothers saw the love shimmering between the pair. That held more weight with the close-knit group than did any comments they heard from staff about Noelle's sacrifice of her long-held dream. And before the Hale clan shook hands, hugged and went their separate ways, Latimer Trees was legally merged with Snowflake Enterprises.

Weeks later, as Christmas Eve loomed and Noelle and Cam's operations were winding down, the discussions that had taken place at Thanksgiving were little more than a blip on the busy couple's radar.

Noelle speed-dialed Cam's cell phone as she sent Zoe and Gwen off to load his pickup with the last of the boxed holiday dinners the three women had assembled in the lodge kitchen. Cam, George and Miguel were cutting trees to be delivered, along with the dinners, to the town's less fortunate families. "Hey," Noelle said as Cam picked up, "are you guys done yet?"

"We're bringing them down now. Have you looked outside? It's snowing."

She heard the chug of the utility vehicle's engine, so she grabbed the envelope with bonus checks and a sturdy box of ornaments and ran out to meet Cam. "We're going to have a white Christmas," she exclaimed happily as she handed out the envelopes and told everyone, except Cam, "Merry Christmas. Thanks, guys. We'll see you all in the new year."

Zoe glanced up the hill toward the anniversary tree. Its blinking white lights made fuzzy halos through the gently falling snow. "Next year at this time, you and Cam will be leaving on your honeymoon. Zany as both farms got after the paper ran your story and a picture of the tree, I'm glad we didn't have to cobble together a wedding."

Noelle nodded. "Take care driving home, everyone. Cam, we'd better get these deliveries made before the roads are too bad. I'd hate it if the kids we're visiting had to forego Christmas dinner and a decorated tree this year."

Cam double-knotted the rope he'd used to tie the load into the back of his pickup. "Can we spare a few minutes to hike out to our tree? It is Christmas Eve."

It was on the tip of Noelle's tongue to say there wasn't time. But something in Cam's expression reached her heart, already filled with the spirit of the season. She put out one hand, and he pulled her close and folded an arm around her as they walked. "Zoe said she saw you crying during the televised presentation of the White House tree. And a minute ago, when she mentioned the wedding, you didn't say you wished we'd made time to get married, which was my reaction." Cam paused. "I wonder if…well, do you regret your hasty decision?"

Noelle stopped a foot short of the regal and sparkling tree. "I cry every year at the presentation. Wait…you really wish we'd had a quickie wedding? I thought…" She grimaced.

"What?"

"When my mom wanted to plunge ahead with wedding plans, you kept changing the subject. Sloan heard. He said you had cold feet."

"That's absurd." Cam kissed away the snow melting on her lips. "Your mother talked about an April wedding in Florida—held during the break after planting and fertilizing trees. I was pretty sure you wanted a winter wedding at the lodge."

"How did you know…? Ah. Because you're a very wise man. Cam, I'm totally behind our decision to wait until next Christmas. Now, if that's settled, don't you think we should go play Santa to a dozen or so Beaver Falls families?"

As the snow fell faster, Noelle extracted two red-and-white Santa hats from her parka pocket. She laughed and tugged one over Cam's damp head. The other she settled on her own snowy curls. "Ho, ho, ho. I have plans for you after our deliveries are done, Mr. Latimer. Like cuddling in front of a blazing fire in your living room."

Cam's lips quirked oddly. "Then I should probably wait on this, Noelle. Except it seems more fitting to do it here by our tree." Dropping to one knee, he drew a small velvet jewelry box out of his pocket. He opened the lid and light from the tree hit the square-cut diamond, striking fire from its depths. "I love you, Noelle. Say you'll be my wife and make this my happiest Christmas ever."

Noelle's yes got lost in strains of "I'm Dreaming of a White Christmas" because she threw her arms around Cam's neck and tumbled him flat into an electrical box situated at the base of their tree. When it was switched on, it piped music from her shop to patrons wandering the rows in search of their own perfect Christmas tree.

And, following a brief, understandable delay, all the trees and Christmas meals did get delivered on Christmas Eve.

* * * * *

ONE MAGIC CHRISTMAS
Ann DeFee

Dear Reader,

Years ago, back when dinosaurs were roaming the earth, we lived in New Hampshire. I'd grown up in south Texas, so the only white stuff I'd ever seen was in the ice-cream section of the grocery store. And as far as anything frozen falling from the sky—well, as far as I was concerned, it wasn't going to happen. So, needless to say, my first experience with a nor'easter came as a huge surprise. I had two little kids, a neurotic cat and a husband with his leg in a cast—courtesy of an intramural basketball game. Before that blizzard was over, almost the entire first floor of my town house was covered in wind-driven snow. I watched with fascination as it piled higher and higher against the patio door, until finally all I could see was a wall of white. That was my introduction to the wacky world of winter.

So when I had the opportunity to become part of this anthology, I knew exactly how my story would begin. In this tale of Christmas magic, heavenly forces conspire with Mother Nature to reunite Honey Campbell and Matt De Luca—a delightful pair of star-crossed lovers. And, of course, there's a happy ending. What else could possibly happen in a world reminiscent of a Norman Rockwell painting?

As we enter this holiday season, I hope you enjoy the magic of Christmas.

Ann

P.S. I love to hear from readers. You can reach me at www.ann-defee.com or write to me at P.O. Box 97313, Tacoma, WA 98497.

To everyone who believes in the magic of Christmas.

Chapter One

Bah humbug!

Fifty weeks out of the year Honoria "Honey" Westfield Campbell was a shoo-in for Miss Congeniality. However, when it came to Christmas she morphed into a Scrooge-arina who would've made Dickens proud.

Every year, Honey promised herself she'd jingle her bells and deck her halls, but alas, the season *always* made her nuts. When the calendar flipped to December a black cloud would appear out of nowhere and wrap her in a malaise that'd last well into January.

Honey didn't need a therapist to understand what was happening or why; she simply didn't know what to do about it. On a cold Christmas Day when she was seventeen she'd betrayed the only man she'd ever loved. They'd believed their passion was eternal. But when faced with the wrath of her parents, she'd left him to fend for himself. Honey sometimes wondered what her life would be like if things had turned out differently. It might all be in the past, but guilt, like love, didn't have a statute of limitations.

Damn, she hated the Christmas blues!

So when her friend and business partner invited her to spend the holidays skiing in New Hampshire, Honey jumped at the chance. Boston wasn't her favorite place during the holidays.

She'd been on the road for almost an hour when the "William Tell Overture" blared from the depths of her purse. *Memo to self: that ring tone has to go.*

"Hey, where are you?" The familiar voice belonged to Bitsy Cornforth, her soon-to-be hostess. Bitsy was the business manager of their advertising firm, while Honey was responsible for the graphic arts division. Poor Bitsy had also been Honey's roommate and confidante when her parents had exiled her to Le Rosey, a Swiss boarding school.

"I'm on my way. Mother called and I couldn't get off the phone. Darling, *Paris* is the *only* place to spend Christmas," Honey said, mimicking her mother's Back Bay accent.

"Color me surprised. What did her majesty want?"

Honey chuckled. "She said she called to wish me a Merry Christmas, but I suspect she was trying to make me jealous. When Lucinda Campbell wants to chat, you shut up and listen."

Bitsy broke into a belly laugh. "You are *so* right. That woman can monopolize a conversation." She paused as she spoke to someone in the background before continuing. "So, when should we expect you?"

"I don't know. I got a late start and the traffic was hideous. Everyone in the city seemed to be heading out for the holidays. I'm making good time now, though." Honey flipped her wipers to a higher setting. "The snow's coming down hard, but I hope to be at your house in about two hours. If I get delayed I'll call."

"They're predicting about six inches of new snow, but I'm sure you'll be fine," Bitsy assured her.

Honey could hear a party in progress. "See you soon. I can't wait to get on the slopes." It had been a long, hard year and she was ready to kick back and relax. A roaring fire and a hot toddy sounded wonderful.

In this case, however, the best-laid plans of mice and Boston yuppies had definitely gone awry. New England winters could be mercurial, but today the forecasters had been spectacularly wrong with their predictions.

When Honey had left Boston there were a few flakes in the air. By the time she hit the New Hampshire border the flurries had turned into a steady snowfall. And now, a little over three hours into the trip, the windshield wipers were beating themselves silly, and they still couldn't compete with the fury of winter. With all the white stuff pummeling her little BMW, Honey couldn't see past the end of her hood.

Her heart skipped a beat as she skidded on a patch of glaze ice. This was a freakin' blizzard. *Damn. Damn. Double damn!* Her chances of sipping hot buttered rum were slipping into the not-anytime-soon category.

Whap. Whap. Whap. The wipers made a valiant but fruitless effort to keep up. The overwhelming whiteness was as strangely hypnotic and beautiful as it was relentless and deadly. For miles Honey had had her eyes glued to the highway fog line. Now, even that had disappeared under the drifts, and it had been at least an hour since she'd last seen a snowplow. To make matters worse, Honey was afraid she was lost.

If she'd had half a brain, she would've stopped at the last village to wait out the storm. But no, when Honey Campbell was on a mission she didn't let anything get in her way—not even the blizzard of the century—and that was exactly what they were calling this abomination. If she could make it another thirty miles, she'd be snug and cozy in Bitsy's living room.

Thirty miles.

Thirty short miles.

Who did she think she was kidding?

At the speed she was going, thirty miles would take her two weeks. Then, before Honey could blink an eye, her car did a one-eighty and she ended up facing the opposite direction.

One by one, Honey loosened her white-knuckled fingers from the steering wheel. She couldn't decide whether she wanted to scream, moan or curse—so she resorted to beating on the dashboard.

"I could use a little help here." She didn't expect an answer. Hildegard, her guardian angel and imaginary childhood friend, never said a word, but she'd gotten Honey out of more than one scrape.

As usual, the response was silence. So what to do? There wasn't a house for miles, Honey's cell wasn't working and even the devil was too smart to be out in this blizzard.

Get a grip, girl! So a little bad weather wasn't going to get the best of a Campbell. Her family had come across the Atlantic on the *Mayflower* and signing up for *that* voyage took the guts of a river-boat gambler. She'd find a way out of this or die trying. And *die* was not the operative word.

Tap, tap, tap. "Aaaah!" Honey screeched. Someone, or something, was knocking on the window. Should she or shouldn't she open it? That was a no-brainer; she needed any help she could get.

Honey hit the electric-window button and found herself nose-to-nose with a grizzled old man wearing a red down jacket and black leather chaps. Had Santa joined a biker gang?

"Hey there, little lady." He rubbed his scraggly white beard. "Looks like you're in a spot of trouble."

No kidding! "Yes, sir, I am. If you could get me to the Ironstone Condominiums near North Conway, or to civilization of any kind, I'd be forever grateful."

He chuckled. "I'm sure you would be. Put on your woollies and follow me." He indicated a snowmobile decorated in twinkle lights with a ribbon-bedecked wreath on the front.

Where had that come from?

"Were you driving behind me?" Honey asked. He didn't answer so she continued. "I'm Honey Campbell." She extended her hand.

"Glad to meet you. You can call me Pete," her newest best friend said with a wink. "I know a fellow who lives a couple of miles down yonder. Grab your smallest bag and we'll strap it on the back of Jenny," he said, patting the side of the snowmobile. "Yep, he'll be glad to help a pretty little thing like you," he muttered as he helped Honey onto the back of the big machine. "Real glad."

What did he mean by that? Scenes from every B-grade horror movie Honey had ever seen flitted through her brain—shades of Freddy Krueger and *The Texas Chainsaw Massacre*.

Unfortunately, the drifts on the highway were at least two feet deep. So it was either freeze to death in her Beemer or meet her Maker on the back of a wannabe Harley without wheels. In that case the Arctic Cat won hands down.

"Are you sure you know where you're going?" she asked, seconds before they rocketed off. Her question was drowned out by the low growl of the engine.

Twenty *very* cold minutes later, Honey spotted a sprawling farmhouse. With its wraparound porch, glittery lights and huge evergreen wreath, it could easily have been the setting for a Norman Rockwell Christmas card.

"This place is beautiful. Almost too pretty to be real," she said, not sure whether Pete could hear her.

Obviously he had. "It's right lovely," he said, pulling close to the front porch.

"Run up and bang on the door. Bang loud. He might be in the back," he instructed, handing Honey her duffel bag before making shooing motions with his hands.

He didn't have to tell her twice. Her designer boots and coat were *not* made for this sub-zero weather. Not to mention the fact that her buns were freezing. Honey lifted the heavy brass knocker and beat a tattoo that would wake the dead. *Hurry up, guy!*

It took a second rat-a-tat before the door was flung open, revealing an absolutely gorgeous man.

Oh. My. God!

It was Matt De Luca—her first love. The one she'd pledged to be with forever. The person she'd abandoned at the first sign of trouble. The man she'd never been able to forget.

This was the ultimate good news/bad news scenario. The good news was that Matt was even better-looking than he'd been at seventeen. The really, really bad news was that he had every reason to hate her—with an undying passion. It didn't take ten seconds for his astonishment to turn into a ferocious scowl, and that didn't bode well for her current situation.

What was the probability of running into her *ex-husband* in the middle of a New England blizzard? Any Las Vegas bookmaker worth his salt could tell you those were astronomical odds.

Chapter Two

"What the…" Matt's first thought was he'd had one too many snickerdoodles. Obviously, it didn't take illicit drugs for him to conjure up a hallucination of epic proportions. Honey Campbell had haunted his dreams for more years than he wanted to count, and here she was—in the flesh. Matt closed his eyes and counted to ten, positive that when he opened them all he'd see was snow, snow and more snow.

No such luck. "I'll be damned if it isn't Honoria Campbell," he mumbled. Even half-frozen, she still had that "hands-off" aura of a Back Bay debutante. In high school, he'd been in awe of her delicate blond beauty.

Looking back, Matt knew he'd been a naive jerk. Everyone had warned him, but had he listened? No way. A typical teenager, he thought he knew everything.

Some lessons were meant to be learned the hard way, and Honey's old man had been a master educator. Guys who grew up over a grocery story in the North End didn't marry Daddy's little princess—at least not without major repercussions.

"Talk about an ill wind," he muttered, attempting to slam the door, but she was too quick. Before Matt knew what hit him, his unexpected guest executed an NFL-worthy tackle, landing them on the floor in a tangle of arms and legs.

Matt's gut reaction when he saw his ex-wife had been white-hot rage. Half a second later that anger was surpassed by lust. Whoa, boy! The last time he'd gone down that path he'd ended up in the county jail—no place for a teenage kid to spend Christmas.

To be totally honest, what he'd felt for Honey back then hadn't been lust, it had been love. And, much as it galled him to admit it, he'd probably feel like that right up to the day he died. But that didn't mean he'd ever be that vulnerable again. Another broken heart was *not* on his horizon.

HONEY COULDN'T BELIEVE SHE'D knocked him over. But it didn't take a rocket scientist to realize Matt had been about to slam the door. And no way in hell was she willing to sit on the porch and freeze-dry her patootie.

"Funny, I don't remember you wanting to be on top," he quipped.

That did it—his sexy smile wasn't all *that* great. Here she was, in trouble up to her eyebrows, and he was being smartass. The last time she'd seen Matt, her father had been blustering about having him arrested on a statutory rape charge. He'd followed through with his threat to have their marriage annulled.

Suddenly she became aware that Matt's hand was resting on her hip. "Stop that," she said, accomplishing the dual task of swatting him and getting to her knees. Not an easy feat when every bone in her body had turned to Jell-O. He moved his hand but gave her the look he'd used in high school—the one that had captivated her heart.

"And stop staring at me," she demanded. He had the nerve to laugh. Astonished though she was at seeing her ex, she appreciated the irony of the situation, if not his response to it. She used to think about him all the time, wondering where he was and what he was doing.

Then several years back her curiosity finally got the best of her. That's when she'd done a Google search and discovered that Matt De Luca owned an art gallery on Newbury Street. For a couple of months she had wandered by it so often she felt like a stalker. One time she'd even seen him through the window, but all things considered, she couldn't work up enough courage to go in. Looking back, Honey knew she'd missed an opportunity.

"Okay," Matt said, rising to his feet and offering her a hand up. "I guess I'm stuck with you. Let's close the door. Then you can fill me in on what's happening. I'm dying to find out how you managed to stumble across the Magic Tree Farm in the middle of a nor'easter. If you haven't noticed, we live south of nowhere."

Honey brushed the snow off her coat. Matt's bland expression made it impossible to tell what he was thinking.

"I'm sorry, I'll clean that up." She indicated the water puddle on the floor.

"Not to worry. Give me your jacket. I'll hang it up."

"Oh, okay." Honey took off her hat and shook out her hair. "When my car got stuck on the highway an old guy on a snowmobile rescued me." She glanced at the door. "I thought he was coming in."

"Someone brought you here?" Matt asked, peering out the side window. "I can't see anything out there. But in that whiteout I'm not surprised. What did he look like?"

"Um, sort of like Santa Claus with a little bit of Hell's Angel thrown in."

"That's quite a combination."

Honey laughed, somewhat embarrassed. "His snowmobile was all decked out with a wreath and twinkle lights. Add that to his red coat and white beard, and voilà—I made the leap to Santa. The Hell's Angel part was courtesy of his chaps and do-rag." Honey realized her story sounded a bit far-fetched but that was exactly the way it happened.

"I don't know who that could have been, but it doesn't matter." Matt took another look out the window. "I'm sure he's well on his way home. Come on in and get warm. We have a lot to talk about."

Matt led her through the house to an inviting great room. A huge Christmas tree dominated one corner while a wood-burning stove provided another focal point. It was rustic, colonial and charming, and it contained all the paraphernalia of a family—toys, dolls, an Xbox and a golden retriever. The dog jumped to her feet, her tail wagging so hard her entire body wiggled.

"Her name is Sweet Pea. She'll love you to death if you let her," Matt said, calling the pooch to his side. Sweet Pea gave Honey one last adoring gaze before slowly following her master's command.

"Why don't you have a seat while I make us some coffee?" he said, busying himself at the kitchen island.

Matt appeared to be as nervous as Honey felt—and why not? This situation was not only surreal, it was also incredibly uncomfortable. From the look of things, he had a wife, a passel of kids and a dog. Poor guy, how was he going to explain an old sweetheart showing up in the middle of a blizzard?

Sitting wasn't an option when she was feeling sorry for herself—fidgeting was more her style. So what was her problem? Was it longing for what should have been? Or was she jealous of what he had with someone else?

Sometimes you had to pull up your big-girl knickers and act like an adult, although stalling did hold a certain appeal. Honey wandered over to the woodstove to warm her backside.

"I think we should clear the air." She paused, waiting for Matt to agree. Instead, he simply handed her a cup of coffee and sat down. That should have put her off, but she knew they had to have this conversation. "We didn't part on good terms and I should've contacted you after all that—" she waved a hand in the air "—stuff with Father and the police, but I was young and scared. Before I could get my head on straight, I was in Europe and I didn't have access to a phone. The head mistress was a bit stodgy about students making calls to the U.S. Anyway, I thought about writing you, but I chickened out."

"Yeah, well, I was in jail," he said, folding his hands behind his head.

"Oh, no!"

Matt grinned at her outburst. "Don't worry. My family bailed me out, so I wasn't in the slammer very long. My dad hocked everything he had to get me a good lawyer. I ended up doing five hundred hours of community service. I also had to promise I'd never contact you again. I wonder if this little visit counts."

Father hadn't been making idle threats; he'd had Matt arrested. Everyone in the De Luca family must hate her, and she couldn't blame them. "I have no idea what to say, other than I am *so* sorry. I thought he was just venting. I never thought he'd actually do anything that vile."

"I guess he wasn't. Venting, that is."

"Yeah, well, uh, did anyone at school miss me?" Her segue lacked finesse, but it was a question she'd always wanted to ask. For some reason, embarrassment or whatever, she hadn't worked up the nerve to talk to any of her old friends.

Matt flashed a wry smile. "Believe me, news of your dramatic exit went through the Boston Arts Academy like wildfire. There were all kinds of rumors. If I'd known you were skiing in Switzerland while I was picking up trash on the freeway, I'd have been a pissed-off puppy."

The entrance of a dark-haired toddler with a red bow sitting askew on her curly locks saved Honey from having to respond. The child, a tiny female version of Matt, was blessed with his gorgeous chocolate-brown eyes. Honey's fingers itched to paint a portrait of this child. She was a Botticelli cherub in the flesh.

"Uncle Matt, I'm hungwy," the little girl proclaimed, climbing into Matt's lap and putting her arms around his neck.

Uncle Matt?

So if he wasn't her dad, what was he—her guardian or her babysitter? And why was it relevant? Silly girl—it mattered because she was dying to know if he was married. What if he was still single? Just the thought sent Honey's heart into an uncharacteristic barrel roll. Please God, he wouldn't notice the red tinge creeping up her neck.

"This is Mary Margaret. We call her M&M." He kissed the top of the child's head. "Sweetheart, say hi to Miss Campbell."

"Hi, Miss… Uh." She got Matt's attention. "Who's she?"

"Her name is Honey. She's an old friend of mine," he answered.

"Oh." The toddler quickly went on to a more interesting topic. "I saw Santa outside."

Matt blew a raspberry on her neck. "Santa doesn't come for two more days, remember?"

"Nope, he was here," M&M said emphatically.

"Okay." Matt's acquiescence obviously made her happy. She hopped off his lap and scooted over to Honey, holding her arms out in the universal signal for "pick me up."

Honey's heart almost broke. If things had been different, she and Matt could have a precious child like this one. Until that moment, she hadn't quite realized how much she wanted children.

Honey knew miracles in the twenty-first century were rare, and the chances of experiencing one would be…well, it would be a miracle. But if magic existed, what better place for it to happen than the Magic Tree Farm at Christmas?

Chapter Three

Children were unfamiliar territory, but holding M&M seemed as natural as breathing. "How does your wife like living this far out in the country?" she asked, cuddling the toddler.

Obviously, Honey's question wasn't as subtle as she'd thought—not if Matt's sexy grin was any indication. She surreptitiously checked his left hand. He wasn't wearing a ring, but that didn't mean anything.

"No wife, it's just me, the kids, the dog and a two-hundred-acre Christmas tree farm. Between work and the children, I don't have much time for a social life," he continued. "If we're not trimming trees, we're planting or cutting or something. We send our products all over the East Coast. In the fall we open our retail store and cut-your-own-tree operation. It keeps me busy and I love it. You can't tell with all the snow, but we have a spectacular view of the White Mountains."

"I thought you wanted to run an art gallery," she blurted out. Wondering where her research had gone wrong.

"I owned a studio for a couple of years, but when I inherited the farm I knew it was time to leave the city. This is a family operation and as a kid I spent my summers here. Way back when my uncle Pietro came over from the old country, he wanted to start a winery. But that didn't work, so he decided to grow Christmas trees instead. He was a smart old goat," Matt said with a grin.

"My brother took over when Uncle Pietro moved to assisted living. That's when I started spending more time out here helping him. Learning the business, so to speak," Matt said with a shrug. "I have a degree in business and I'm interested in agriculture, so the transition wasn't that hard."

"I didn't know your family owned a farm."

Matt looked at her in a way she couldn't quite interpret. "There were a lot of things we didn't discuss. I suspect our minds were elsewhere."

Wasn't that the truth!

"Come on, snookums, let me get you washed up. Then I'll fix you some dinner." Matt held out his hand and Mary Margaret obediently ran to him. "You can help me introduce Miss Campbell to the rest of the crew."

"Then she can watch pwincesses wif me."

Matt shrugged when Honey glanced at him for help.

"Okay," she agreed.

"Sit here," M&M said, pulling Honey toward an inviting couch.

How could Honey resist? She was destined to enjoy the dancing princesses. In the Disney film, the prince and princess found true love, but Honey knew from experience that happy endings rarely occurred in real life. The prince of her dreams—the one who probably wanted to toss her out into the blizzard—was about ten feet away flipping grilled cheese sandwiches. Although he was polite and superficially friendly, Honey was pretty darned sure she wouldn't make his Christmas card list.

Matt walked to the bottom of the stairs and yelled, "Kids, come down for supper." A lone screech indicated that the message had been received.

"We're pretty casual around here." He stacked a pile of plates on the kitchen island. "We normally have a housekeeper but she went to Florida for Christmas. So we're on our own.

"Kids," he called again and was rewarded by a noise that sounded like a herd of elephants stampeding toward their favorite watering hole.

"Out of the way, jerkwad."

That feminine command was answered by a young male voice. "You can't make me," he said in singsong fashion.

Matt grinned. "Another day in paradise.

"Hey, you two, cut it out," he ordered as the children tumbled down the last two steps. "I want you to meet someone. Try to act civilized for a minute, please."

Honey was an only child, so she wasn't an expert on sibling rivalry, but for some reason this seemed normal. There wasn't any blood and Matt didn't appear to be distressed—that was good. It took a second for the combatants to realize they had an audience. When they did, they lapsed into silence.

"How did you get here?" the dark-haired boy asked.

"Before you start grilling our guest, don't you think you should meet her?"

"Yes, Uncle Matt. I'm sorry." A twinkle in the kid's eye belied the sincerity of his apology.

During the introductions, Honey discovered that Colleen was thirteen, Patrick was nine and M&M was three. She also found out that when Matt's brother and his wife had died in a car crash, Matt was left not only the farm, but also a ready-made family.

The fact that he'd dropped everything to become the children's guardian told her that Matt was the same wonderful person she'd loved at seventeen. But their relationship had been a lifetime ago, and while she knew she still loved *him*, he seemed ambivalent about her. And who could blame him?

The meal was unlike anything Honey had ever experienced. M&M spilled milk all over her sister, precipitating a full-blown teenage meltdown. Patrick wanted peanut butter instead of grilled cheese. Sweet Pea took begging to new heights, and Matt seemed oblivious to all the antics.

But somehow it felt right. Honey had dedicated so much of her life to her career that she was afraid she'd missed out on the truly important things—family, home and someone to love.

Fortunately, before she could get really depressed, M&M spoke up, breaking the spell. "Santa Claus was here. He browt Miss Honey," she announced in a display of kiddie wisdom.

"No way! He doesn't come till Christmas Eve," Patrick declared.

Did the boy really believe in Saint Nick, or was he was protecting his little sister's innocence?

"He was. I saw him out the window." M&M was adamant. "Wasn't he?" She patted Honey's face, expecting an answer.

"Sweetie." Honey cupped the toddler's chin. "He was just a man with a snowmobile."

"No."

When she crossed her arms over her chest, it was all Honey could do not to laugh.

"It *was* Santa," the child said with conviction.

Oooh-kay. Matt could deal with this.

"I'm a little curious, too. Why don't you tell me more about how you ended up here?" Matt asked.

Honey hesitated a moment, considering what to say. "I was on my way to my friend's ski lodge in North Conway, and, oh my gosh, I've got to call Bitsy to tell her I'm okay."

He indicated the phone on the wall. "You'd better give her a buzz before the lines go down. Your cell won't work in this blizzard."

She made a quick call to Bitsy explaining her predicament, but she chose not mention the identity of her host. During their year as roommates, Bitsy had heard more than her share of Matt stories.

After Honey had finished, she came back to the table and continued her narrative. "I got stranded in the snow and the next thing I knew, there was a man tapping on my window."

"You didn't see him drive up?" Matt asked.

"No."

"Tell me again what he looked like."

The three children listened with rapt attention.

"He was wiry and had this gnarly beard." Honey chuckled, thinking about her rescuer. "He was wearing a red down jacket and had a do-rag under his helmet. Best of all, he was driving a snowmobile decorated like Santa's sleigh."

"Sounds like a Willie Nelson wannabe to me," Colleen said.

"No way. Santa doesn't look anything like Willie Nelson. The guy must have been one of Santa's elves." That pearl of wisdom came from Patrick.

"Like, duh. Do you think an elf would be caught dead in a do-rag?" Colleen commented with a smirk.

"Kids, let her finish."

Honey was impressed with the way Matt responded to his niece and nephew. "I hadn't thought of him resembling Willie Nelson, but, yeah, I suppose he did," Honey said with a smile. Leave it to a kid to nail it.

For a moment, Matt looked puzzled. "Actually, that description reminds me of my uncle Pietro, but he's been gone almost ten years. It must've been..." He was obviously about to say *Santa,* but Honey cut him off with a nod toward M&M.

"It must've been one of the men from the fire station. They do all types of rescue work," Matt said. "We're glad you're here, aren't we, kids?"

Honey was glad, too. In an incredible twist of fate she was stranded with a man she'd loved forever. Things could have been much, much worse.

Chapter Four

Honey couldn't help wondering how her rescuer *had* managed to find her. Even Rudolph—the super reindeer—couldn't make his way through a New Hampshire nor'easter.

But also curious about more mundane matters, Honey broached another subject. "Does your power usually stay on during a snowstorm?"

In unison, Matt said, "Sometimes," Colleen tossed in an "Are you kidding?" and Patrick expressed a decisive "Nope." M&M obviously didn't have an opinion concerning New Hampshire Power and Light.

As if their conversation had been an omen, everything suddenly went dark.

"Don't worry, we've got it under control. I'll start the generator. Kids, you know your assignments. Honey, would you watch M&M while we get everything headed in the right direction?"

"Sure, we'll be fine. Won't we, M&M?"

She giggled in reply.

Several minutes later, Matt returned with a load of firewood while Colleen arranged a display of candles. Not to be outdone, Patrick retrieved several camp lanterns from the pantry and placed them on the kitchen island. It was efficiency perfected by practice.

"We use the woodstove for heat. Although it's nice and warm down here, it gets mighty cold upstairs," Matt said.

"Frigid is more like it," Colleen threw in.

He laughed at his niece's observation. "Yeah, it is. I have a generator, but I primarily use it for the industrial freezer we have out in the store. My latest business venture is in its infancy, but so far, we're on a roll. Last summer I started a wholesale operation providing frozen fruit pies for some of the biggest supermarkets in Boston. It's become something of a cottage industry for the whole comunity. Several of my neighbors have orchards and their wives love to bake. It's a win-win situation," Matt said with a grin. "I have the house appliances wired into the generator, but that still leaves us without lights. I hope you're not afraid of the dark."

She actually thought it was rather romantic. That, however, wasn't something she was willing to share, so she decided to go with an innocuous comment. "It's kind of homey."

Her response drew a snort from Patrick.

"It's a pain in the rear and it happens all the time."

"Patrick," Matt admonished.

"Well, it is. I can't play with my Xbox."

"You are such a dork," his sister responded.

"And you're—"

"Okay, guys, that's enough. Polish up your company manners."

"Okay, Uncle Matt." Patrick appeared properly chastised.

Colleen's muttered "Whatever" indicated she might not be quite as compliant as her brother.

Honey could tell by M&M's heavy breathing that she'd drifted off.

"M&M's asleep."

"Why don't you give her to me. I'll put her to bed."

She reluctantly handed Matt the sleeping child. "What do you do for entertainment when the lights go out?" she asked the two older children, who were watching her suspiciously. As unfamiliar as she was with little ones, she was even more out of her element with pubescent and prepubescent creatures.

"We play poker," Colleen said with a straight face.

Patrick nudged his sister. "Uncle Matt taught us how to play Texas hold 'em. Do you know how?"

"Not really. Maybe you could teach me."

"Yeah, sure. I'll get the cards." Patrick hopped up, retrieving two decks and a huge jar of pennies.

Honey watched the process with trepidation. She was beginning to feel as if she'd jumped into a shark pool. But how hard could it be to gamble with a couple of kids? Two hours later, she'd not only lost her pile of pennies, she was also deep in debt. She owed Colleen a manicure and was scheduled for several hours of Nintendo with Patrick.

"You should've told me they were pros."

Matt shrugged. "When you live out in the country with an iffy power system, you get resourceful."

"Why didn't *you* play cards with them?"

"Are you kidding? I'm too smart. Okay, kids, it's time to close the casino. Then you need to get ready for bed."

Colleen and Patrick trudged up the stairs, grumbling all the way.

"I can't let Sweet Pea out in this blizzard by herself, so I have to take her to a little sheltered area we have in the backyard." Sweet Pea bounced in anticipation when Matt picked up the leash. "We'll only be gone a few minutes. I'll show you our guest accommodations when I get back."

Honey wandered aimlessly around the family room. It was an inviting place, perfect for a busy family. She could imagine cuddling up on the couch with a bowl of popcorn and a good movie. This house was light years away from her professionally decorated, and somewhat sterile, condo.

"Okay, that's done." Matt was brushing snow off his shoulders. They were such nice broad shoulders, Honey thought. Matt as a teenager had been enticing, but as an adult he was every woman's fantasy.

"Let me grab your bag and then I'll take you upstairs."

Honey presumed her duffel was still sitting in the hall. When she'd first seen Matt, she'd completely forgotten about her luggage. Good thing her rescuer had reminded her to bring it or she'd be stranded without a toothbrush or clean undies.

"Thanks, that's fine." They'd reverted to formality, which was ironic considering she'd give up her considerable 401(k) for the opportunity to snuggle under a fluffy duvet with Matt De Luca. So what did that say about her? That her life wasn't fulfilling, or that she'd never gotten over him? More than likely it was a little of each.

"Here we go." Matt handed her a lantern. "You'll need this."

Honey followed her host upstairs wondering how things had

gone so wrong all those years ago. Was it possible to rekindle the feelings they'd had for each other? That was a question she couldn't answer. She could only hope that this was her second chance at happiness.

Chapter Five

In a world of unlikely scenarios, having Honey Campbell show up on his doorstep definitely fell in the "are you kidding me" category. True, he'd kept track of her through the years, but long ago Matt had decided to work on the *once burned, twice shy* theory of self-protection. So, even though they lived in the same city, he'd kept his distance.

What should he do now? The woman of his dreams—and his nightmares—was sound asleep upstairs. Morning had dawned, and the blizzard didn't show any signs of abating—and that meant she'd have to stay here with him and the kids. *Mama mia!*

Matt was trying to think of something—anything—he could do to preserve his sanity while also tamping down his libido. Then reality in the form of a crash intruded.

"What are you guys up to?" he called to the kids, who were playing in the family room.

"Nothing." Colleen was the first to answer, but Patrick muttered something indecipherable. That wasn't a good sign.

They were bored, and they were also excited about Christmas, but give a guy a break. Family togetherness could get really old. "Keep it down so Miss Campbell can sleep," he yelled.

"Okay." Patrick's answer was accompanied by a giggle from Colleen.

This had all the earmarks of being a *long* couple of days!

HONEY WAS COZY AND COMFY snuggled down in the duvet. It couldn't possibly be time to wake up. But what was that noise? And where was she?

This wasn't her room at home, and it was too stark to be a ritzy bed-and-breakfast—there wasn't a Ralph Lauren pillow in sight.

Then it came back in a flash—the blizzard, the Santa rescue and, miracle of miracles, her Matt encounter. The racket she heard was children playing downstairs.

Honey rolled over and decided to sneak in a little nap. She was on vacation, so why not? Then she felt a cold nose and opened her eyes—Sweet Pea.

"Whatcha doin'?" Honey reached out to pet the pup and quickly discovered the room was as frigid as an igloo. There was actually frost on the inside of the window.

If she managed to dress without flash-freezing, it would be a wonder. And did she even own anything suitable for a power outage in a nor'easter? Highly unlikely—Honoria Campbell was not an L.L. Bean kind of girl.

Honey tiptoed across the icy floor in search of the oversize robe Matt had lent her. *Crap,* being marooned in the Arctic was bad enough, but the worst of it was that most of her clothes were in a suitcase back at the car. God only knew when she'd be able to retrieve them.

She'd stuffed a pair of jeans, a Rhode Island School of Design sweatshirt and a pair of wool socks in her duffel. She wasn't going to be dressed for success, or glamour or even seduction. But, hey, this was an extraordinary situation.

Last night she'd thought spending time with the De Luca family was wonderful. In the bright light of day, she wasn't quite so sure, especially considering she still loved Matt. Oh boy, this was a recipe for disaster. If the snow would only stop, she'd be on her way—and sooner rather than later would be preferable.

This odyssey into her ex-husband's life was so bizarre that even Hollywood wouldn't believe it. Truth *was* stranger than fiction.

Sweet Pea thought Honey was playing a game when she made a mad scramble for her clothes. The dog bounced, barked and acted like a goofy golden. Honey had always wanted a dog, but her mother wouldn't hear of it. And her condominium association had a no-pet policy. What else had she missed during her laserlike pursuit of a career?

Stop that! Second-guessing was not going to solve any of her problems. Honey peeked out the window, hoping to see that the blizzard had subsided. No such luck—the white stuff was coming down with a vengeance, obliterating the landscape.

Halfway down the stairs she was greeted by the cacophony of an active family. Colleen and Patrick were engaged in another bout of sibling rivalry. While it was hard to tell what they were arguing about, she couldn't miss the words *dummy* and *dipwad*. M&M was banging on a drum set, and Sweet Pea had joined in the fun.

Her condo was pristine and quiet, so this type of chaos was unfamiliar. However, it did bring back her childhood dream of being part of a big family. How had life gotten so far off the path she'd once envisioned?

"Hi, Honey." M&M abandoned her drum, raising her arms to be picked up.

Honey obliged, nuzzling her neck. The child smelled like a tantalizing combination of baby shampoo and talc. What was it about this place that turned her thoughts to home and hearth?

"Are you hungry?" Matt asked, holding up a spatula.

With his rumpled hair, dark stubble and black outfit he was enticingly male. Never mind that he was wearing a frilly apron. Some guys could pull off anything, and Matt De Luca was one of them.

"Yes. Can I help?"

"Nope. I have it handled. The coffee's on the stove." He gestured at an old-fashioned percolator. "I think I told you we have the appliances plugged into the generator. We can make do without everything else."

Honey sniffed. The aroma of fresh-brewed java was inviting. This whole experience was making her feel as if she were on a camping trip. Not that she was an expert on the subject of the great outdoors. Her parents' idea of roughing it was a three-star hotel without room service.

"French toast?"

"Sure." *Why not?* Calories didn't matter, not when you were in survival mode. And if she could make it through sharing a house with her first love—without jumping his bones—it would be astonishing.

Too bad Matt hadn't sent any vibes that he was interested in her. *Darn it!*

"The weather report said the storm might go on for at least

Play the Lucky Hearts Game

and get...

2 FREE BOOKS and
2 FREE MYSTERY GIFTS...
YOURS to KEEP!

yes! I have scratched off the silver card. Please send me my *2 FREE BOOKS* and *2 FREE mystery GIFTS*. I understand that I am under no obligation to purchase any books as explained on the back of this card.

Scratch Here!
then look below to see what your cards get you... 2 Free Books & 2 Free Mystery Gifts!

354 HDL ENQ9   **154 HDL ENX9**

FIRST NAME

LAST NAME

ADDRESS

APT.#

CITY

STATE/PROV.

ZIP/POSTAL CODE

(H-AR-11/07)

Twenty-one gets you
2 FREE BOOKS and
2 FREE MYSTERY GIFTS!

Twenty gets you
2 FREE BOOKS!

Nineteen gets you
1 FREE BOOK!

TRY AGAIN!

▼ DETACH AND MAIL CARD TODAY! ▼

The Harlequin Reader Service® — Here's how it works:

BUSINESS REPLY MAIL

FIRST-CLASS MAIL   PERMIT NO. 717   BUFFALO, NY

POSTAGE WILL BE PAID BY ADDRESSEE

HARLEQUIN READER SERVICE
3010 WALDEN AVE
PO BOX 1867
BUFFALO NY 14240-9952

NO POSTAGE
NECESSARY
IF MAILED
IN THE
UNITED STATES

another day." Matt indicated the portable radio on the counter. "Before this is over we'll probably have more than two feet of new powder." His expression said it all. They were well and truly stranded. There wasn't a snowplow invented that could get through that mess.

"Has this happened before?"

"We've had blizzards, but nothing this bad. Good thing you're here, and not out in that." He nodded at the swirl of white outside the window. "We have everything we need to make it. I just hope the natives don't get too restless." The kids were squabbling over who was going to get the Scottie dog in Monopoly.

Honey was glad she'd been able to contact Bitsy—otherwise her friend would've eventually had the cops looking for her. Not that *anyone* was out and about in that weather.

"Come on, guys. Breakfast is ready."

The family room was warm, the food was delicious and the company delightful, even if Colleen and Patrick were still arguing.

"Mind your manners," Matt admonished, grabbing the empty plates and placing them in the sink.

"You guys have dish duty." His command was greeted by a chorus of moans. "Our water heater isn't on the generator, so we have to heat dishwater on the stove," Matt explained.

"Does the oven work?" Honey asked.

"Yeah."

"Do you think the kids and I could make cookies?" Where had that come from? She was so far from being Susie Homemaker it wasn't even funny. Nevertheless, there were bound to be some recipe books, so it'd be a piece of cake—pun intended.

Their baking was successful thanks to a family effort. Colleen was a much better cook than Honey had expected, and of course, M&M ended up with dough in her hair. Matt and Patrick were marginally helpful, but everyone had a good time, and that was the point, after all. Sweet Pea even contributed to the effort by eating every scrap that fell on the floor.

"This was fun. I'm glad you suggested it," Matt said.

The cookies were cooling, M&M was finally down for a nap, and the other kids had wandered off. For the first time all day, Honey was alone with Matt.

"Let's sit down and talk," he said.

Honey wasn't sure she was ready for a serious discussion, so she stalled. "How about a cup of coffee?" She held up the percolator.

"Great," he agreed. He was wearing *that* grin again.

"Come on. Sit down with me." He tapped the seat next to him. "We have a lot to discuss."

Who'd ever heard of a guy who wanted to talk? That kind of thing upset the natural order of the universe—didn't it?

Honey acquiesced and sat beside him. But, if he wanted to talk, *he* could start the conversation.

MATT TWINED HIS FINGERS through hers. He didn't know what had prompted him to suggest a discussion, other than that he was dying to find out if she was involved with anyone. But why would that matter? He was *not* interested in Honey Campbell. Her father was responsible for sending him to jail. Jail!

Still, he couldn't resist rubbing sensual little circles on her palm. "Why don't you start by telling me what you've been doing since high school?"

Damn, he was nervous—but even so, he should've been able to come up with something a bit more intelligent. Asking her to synopsize the past fifteen years—talk about lame.

Honey shrugged. "I've spent my entire adult life concentrating on my career. I work a lot, but I don't do much else."

"Is there someone special waiting for you?"

"No." She paused before continuing. "I've dated, but I haven't found anyone special. Not since you."

Matt wasn't sure how to respond, especially since he felt the same way—and he was desperately fighting that emotion. Experience told him he knew it was a one-way ticket to "Heartbreak Hotel."

But Honey pressed the issue. "How about you?"

"There's no one in my life right now. Several years back I was engaged to a nice Italian girl. My mom was happy as a clam." Matt groaned, thinking about his mother and her unabashed desire for more grandchildren. "My fiancée and I finally figured out we didn't love each other, so we decided to break up. Now she has four kids and lives next door to her mother.

"Like I told you before, with everything I have going on around here, I haven't had time for anything other than work and keeping track of the kids. I suppose I'm boring."

"No, you're not. You'd never be boring." Honey decided this was the perfect opportunity to ask the big question. "Do you think we'd still be married if my parents hadn't butted in?"

Matt shook his head. "I don't have any idea. What I do know is that I loved you. I would've done anything to make it work. Unfortunately, that wasn't to be. Your parents thought you were pregnant, didn't they?"

".Yes," Honey said with a grin. "They quickly found out I wasn't, and that really confused them. Their marriage is based on money and connections, so love is a fairly foreign concept to them. And it galled my mother no end that we got married by a justice of the peace. That, to say the least, isn't proper deportment for a debutante. She's really big on formal weddings. Although I suspect that even if we'd had a church wedding, complete with bridesmaids and a champagne reception, she still wouldn't have approved."

And that was the understatement of the century.

Chapter Six

The years seemed to melt away when she smiled at him. Had it really been a decade and a half since he'd pledged to love her forever? For Matt, that vow had never gone away—it had merely faded to a persistent ache.

Was he brave enough to put his heart on the line? A smart guy wouldn't go down that road again. And was this conversation really his idea? No wonder men shied away from the subject of relationships.

"I want to thank you for baking cookies with the kids. This is only their second Christmas without their mother," he said, abruptly changing the subject.

"It was my pleasure. They're great."

Matt's eyes lit up. "They are, aren't they?" He was surprised by Honey's reaction to being trapped in a house full of kids. She seemed to be enjoying herself.

How could that be? Honey was a high-powered businesswoman. She was used to dining in five-star restaurants, not chowing down on grilled cheese sandwiches or baking cookies with a bunch of rug rats.

Did he have a chance with her? That was up for debate, so he switched to a safe topic, the weather.

"The forecasters don't know when the snow's going to let up, but it won't be anytime soon. They say this storm will probably be a record-breaker." He was curious about her response to that news. It appeared they were destined to have an old-fashioned Christmas—truly old-fashioned—and Honey was going to be part of the celebration, whether she liked it or not.

"At least my friend knows I'm not out in the blizzard," she said with a frown.

That didn't sound like unbridled enthusiasm, but at least she was safe. Just the thought of what could have happened sent chills up his spine.

"Thank God someone found you. Where exactly did you leave your car?" The troubled look in her beautiful blue eyes made Matt want to kiss her silly—and *that* wasn't going to happen.

"I don't have a clue," she said. "I hope the snowplow doesn't destroy it when they finally get the okay to clear the roads."

"Me, too." Matt needed something to do with his hands. "Would you like a cup of tea?" he asked.

"That would be great."

"I'll put the kettle on." He hopped up to put some space between them.

HONEY HID HER SMILE. MATT WAS nervous. Now wasn't that interesting? "Christmas is in two days. Do you have everything ready for the kids?" She was sure he was on top of things, but if he needed help she was ready, willing and able.

He handed her a steaming cup of Earl Grey. Steeped just enough and with a hint of sugar, it was fixed to perfection.

"This is good," she said, taking a sip of the fragrant tea. "I can't believe you remembered how I like it."

"There isn't much I've forgotten about you."

She recalled a lot about him, too—his smell, the taste of his skin and the way his hands had memorized her body. Suddenly she had to fan herself. "Do you find it hot in here?"

His grin was pure devilment. Oops—he always had been able to read her mind.

"No. Actually, it's cold. And back to your question about Christmas—yes, I have it under control. Snow doesn't stop Santa. I thought you knew that." He waggled an eyebrow.

"That's right," Honey agreed with a giggle. Where had that come from? It'd been years since even a chuckle had slipped her lip.

"The only glitch is that I'm responsible for providing the church's Christmas tree. I don't know how I'm going to get it there, not with all this snow."

"Don't they have a tree they could use?"

"Their fallback plan is a pink retro monstrosity they have stored in the basement."

"Seriously?"

"Seriously. It's aluminum and even has its own spotlight."

Honey laughed at the image. "Will the choir be decked out in go-go boots and hot pants?"

Matt laughed, too. "Wouldn't that be a Christmas to remember? Too bad about the tree, though. I picked out a beautiful balsam last year, and I've been pampering it ever since. Not to brag, but I think it's the perfect tree. Unfortunately, until the roads are passable, it's going to stay right where it is."

"That's a shame."

"Yep. But I can't do anything about it." Matt leaned his chair back on two legs. "Right now I have to go out and feed the horses."

"Is that safe? You can't see your hand in front of your face. Won't you get lost?" Honey had heard stories about people venturing out in blizzards and not being found until spring.

"When I heard the storm was coming, I strung a rope from the barn to the back porch. I'll be fine."

"Okay." Just thinking about something happening to Matt made her queasy. "If you get hurt, I'll have to kill you."

HOT DAMN! SHE WAS WORRIED about him. "Yes, ma'am." When he touched her arm a spark of electric current almost fried his circuits.

"That's, uh…" The rest of Honey's sentence was interrupted by the sound of an argument.

"Uncle Matt, tell Patrick to stay out of my things!" Colleen was clomping down the stairs, accompanied by her brother, who was loudly proclaiming his innocence.

"You two deal with your own problems," Matt instructed them. "I'm heading out to the barn. If you guys wake up M&M, I won't be happy." Much to Honey's surprise, the combatants went to their separate corners.

"I'll be back in about an hour." He ran his finger down the side of her face. "If I'm not, don't come out to find me. Promise?"

"I PROMISE." AT BEST IT WAS A reluctant pledge, at worst a total lie. Who was she kidding? Of course she'd search high and low for him.

She was besotted, she realized—now and forever. So what should she do about it?

"Go on, we'll be fine. I'll make some hot chocolate. You can have yours when you get back," Honey said, knowing her perky smile lacked conviction.

MATT COULDN'T SEE A DAMNED thing. How could something as big as a barn go missing? Sheesh! Thank God he'd had the foresight to string the rope. If he hadn't, the horses would've gotten mighty hungry, and he'd be in real danger of getting lost.

Snow was supposed to be soft, wasn't it? This stuff felt as if it could scour the skin off his face. It was slow going, but by the grace of God he finally made it to his destination. Getting inside was another story. He'd exhausted every expletive in his repertoire before he managed to shut the barn door behind him.

The horses' body heat had made the barn warm and cozy. It was one of Matt's favorite places, so while he fed the grateful creatures and mucked out their stalls, he did some serious thinking.

When he and Honey were kids, they'd been knee-deep in teenage lust. The lust hadn't gone away, at least not for him. Neither had the love. But now it was tangled up with respect for the woman she'd become. But should he really trust her with his heart?

She'd only been back in his life a day, and already he had some big decisions to make. Could he convince her they had a future? What would the kids think about having Honey in their lives? And the biggest question of all—was she ready for a warp-speed courtship?

HONEY ANXIOUSLY WATCHED Matt disappear into the swirling snow. Concern for him sent her Protestant work ethic into overdrive. She cleaned the kitchen, made the kids a snack and straightened up the family room.

Not only was she worried about Matt's safety, she was scared stiff that she was falling in love with him all over again. Wait, amend that to she *had* fallen in love. In addition, the kids had quickly found their way into her heart. What was she going to do? She was smart. She was creative. She'd figure something out. So why was the *Green Acres* theme song playing in her head?

When Matt strolled in the back door her heart leaped with joy. Thank God, he was safe!

"Lucy, I'm home." His singsong parody of Ricky Ricardo on the *I Love Lucy* show sounded better than a choir of angels.

Chapter Seven

Should she or shouldn't she risk her heart? That was the question of a lifetime. One thing Honey knew for certain—if she let this opportunity for happiness slip through her fingers, she'd regret it forever. If he didn't reciprocate her feelings, it was his loss. In the big scheme of things, all she had to lose was a little dignity. And that was well worth taking a chance.

Matt was still shaking the snow out of his hair when Honey threw herself into his arms. How about that? He'd spent the past hour trying to decide what to do and then *she* took the initiative.

"That's the kind of greeting I like," he murmured, punctuating his delight with a nibble on her neck. He took her hand and pulled her toward the living room. "We can have a little privacy in here. Not much, but some," he said with a chuckle. "Hopefully the kids won't come looking for us. But I'm not all that optimistic. Until they discover we're missing, we can do some necking. That is, if you'd like to." He searched her eyes for any sign that he was on the wrong track.

"That sounds fantastic," Honey whispered, smiling softly.

They were lost in each other for almost thirty minutes—they'd kiss, cuddle, talk, and then they'd go back to kissing—before they were interrupted.

"Uncle Matt, M&M is up and she wants a snack. What should I give her?" Although Colleen was still in the family room, she was obviously heading in their direction.

"Busted," Matt muttered, running his fingers across Honey's lips. "But we're not through with this," told her with a wink.

"In the living room," he yelled.

"What are you guys doing in here?"

"Talking." Matt didn't even crack a grin.

"So what do you want me to give M&M?"

"I'll take care of it, but would you keep her busy for a few minutes?"

"Okay," she said, shooting them a suspicious look.

Matt waited until Colleen had left before giving Honey another heart-stopping kiss. "Why don't you come and help me?"

"Of course."

"I was going to tell you something interesting, but somehow I got…distracted," he said. "After I fed the horses I checked on the snowmobile. It's been moved." Matt frowned. "What do you suppose that's all about?"

Honey had a good idea, but she wasn't about to voice it. "I don't know. What do you think?"

"Beats me." He shrugged. "Oh well, after I make M&M a snack I need to take the dog out." He leaned over to pat Sweet Pea's head. "You're about to cross your legs, aren't you?"

The pup responded with a soft *woof*.

"Where do you take her? I never thought about doggy potty accommodations."

"I have a place outside the back door that's covered. As long as the snow doesn't swirl in and the roof doesn't collapse, we're fine."

"There's a chance the roof might fall in?" Honey asked with a squeak.

"Just on the shed. All the other buildings have roofs that are steep enough to keep the snow from accumulating."

Whew! Honey knew that snow was cold and wet, but other than that she was clueless. Her building supervisor dealt with things like snow removal.

"If it gets too deep, all bets are off. So in the morning I might have to climb up and shovel it," Matt said with a shrug.

"Is the blizzard supposed to stop?" If that happened, Honey would no longer have an excuse to stay. But whatever it took to make this part of her life come full circle, she was willing to try.

THE NEXT MORNING DAWNED CLEAR and very cold.

"Hey, sleepyhead. Up and at 'em." Honey peeked out from under the edge of the duvet. She didn't intend to leave her little nest—not unless someone provided some major motivation. And that inspiration came in the form of six feet of sexy male standing in the doorway. Yikes—she could see his breath in the air. She wouldn't have been surprised to discover icicles hanging from his ears.

"No," she muttered, pulling the pillow over her head.

"If you don't get up, I'll rip the covers off." His voice was getting closer.

"Go away!"

The mattress dipped as he sat down. Last night she would've given anything to have him in her bed. Although they were getting reacquainted, they hadn't become nearly as friendly as she would've liked.

Matt leaned over for an erotic exploration of her neck. "The kids are getting dressed to go outside and build a snowman. You've been invited to join them. And breakfast is ready."

Honey didn't know whether it was the children's request, his intimate cajoling or the lure of coffee—whatever it was, she couldn't resist. "Okay, hand me some warm clothes."

He took the terry-cloth robe off the chair and dropped it on the end of the bed. "I'm heating some sweet rolls I found in the freezer." He trailed kisses from her cheek to her collarbone. "It's time to face the morning," he said, emphasizing his assertion with a kiss.

HONEY HAD LEFT HER SKI OUTFIT—including her long underwear—back at the car, so she had to improvise. Matt's parka went down to her knees, Patrick's boots sort of fit, and Colleen had tossed in a hat and some mittens. Glancing in the hallway mirror, Honey thought she looked like a Pillsbury Doughboy that had run amuck at a Goodwill store.

The snow was knee deep, but due to the drifting, a small area of the yard was fairly clear. And that was where Colleen and Patrick decided to build a snowman.

"I'll help you guys when I get through shoveling," Matt said. "Honey, would you watch M&M? I don't want her to get too cold."

The child was flat on her back making snow angels. What three-year-old worried about the temperature?

"I doubt we could force her to go inside," Honey observed with a smile.

"You're right about that."

Matt gave Honey another kiss before ambling off to shovel a path to the front door. Now *that* was the way to start the morning.

Honey scrunched down in her borrowed parka. The temperature had dipped well below zero so she could see every breath she took. Wow! This was a scene straight out of a movie. It was beautiful. It was pristine. And if she really thought about it—it was terrifying. *Enough of that!* She was exactly where she wanted to be—thanks to her Willie Nelson Santa.

Matt had almost finished clearing a path to the front door. Who would've believed that so much snow could pile up in one place? The entire front porch was covered, and there were snowdrifts halfway around the house. Her poor BMW was probably nothing more than a bump on the landscape. In fact, they might not find it until the spring thaw. But did that really matter? If she didn't have a car, she couldn't leave. Now, that was an interesting thought.

After he finished his chores, Matt joined Honey and the kids as they made a life-size snow person—complete with a muffler and a carrot nose.

"Cute snowman, or is it a snowwoman?" Matt asked, leaning on his shovel and looking more attractive than any man she'd ever seen.

"What do you think, kids? Is this a boy or a girl?" Honey asked.

Her innocent question brought on a chorus of opinions.

"Enough, you guys," Matt ordered. "I want to show you our shop," he told Honey. "Kids, I'm going to take Honey out to the store. Why don't you come with us?"

Because of the huge drifts, Honey hadn't noticed the rustic structure that was only a hundred yards from the house, but based on the effort it took to get there, it seemed to be miles. Built of old barn boards and featuring a hand-carved sign, it was exactly what she would've expected. Matt was one of the most artistic people she'd ever known. When they were in high school, he'd won multiple awards for his oil paintings.

"I love the sign." It was more like a piece of art than the symbol of a business. "Did you do it?"

"Uh-huh. This was my first attempt at wood carving. It was fun." The sign depicted a gorgeous Christmas tree with lights, decorations and packages. The angel on the top was a miniature M&M.

"The Magic Tree Farm. That's so appropriate." Especially since

Santa had led her to Matt—even if her rescuer had looked like Willie Nelson. This was a place where magic happened.

"Who named the farm?"

"My uncle Pietro. He used to joke that he'd stick around just to make sure we ran it right. And frankly, if anyone could come back from the hereafter, he'd be the guy. He was a true believer in the magic of Christmas."

"I'm sure he'd be very proud of what you've done."

"I hope so." Matt pushed open the door. "It'll be cold in here. We have a furnace, but it's not connected to the generator. I do have a couple of the overhead lights hooked up, so at least we'll be able to see what we're doing. When the store's open we use the wood-stove for heat. People seem to think it feels more like Christmas." Matt made a sweeping gesture with his arm. "This is the center of our cut-your-own-tree operation. In November and December we have sleigh rides, decorated trees like you see here and homemade refreshments. Folks come all the way from Boston to get in the holiday mood."

"I'm not surprised. I love it." The interior was Christmas at its best. There were wreaths, stockings hung from the fireplace mantel, and several beautifully decorated trees—one had a Disney theme and another featured more traditional ornaments, while the third was a Victorian confection. Honey could imagine what a fairyland it was when the lights were on and twinkling.

"This is the fun side of our business; however, we make most of our money from our wholesale operation. We send trees and wreaths from Maine to Florida."

"I'm impressed."

"Thanks. We're doing well. I'm working hard to make this a legacy for my brother's children."

Honey nodded. That was exactly what she'd expect Matt to do. He always thought of others and he took his responsibilities seriously.

Then she noticed the wall of oil paintings. There was no doubt they were Matt's work. "This landscape is beautiful," she exclaimed as she examined one of the canvases. "Are you still painting?"

"Sometimes, but with everything else I have to deal with, it's hard to find the time."

"I know what you mean. I get so wrapped up in work that I forget to make time for the things I love." Perhaps she needed to start nurturing her artistic side again, Honey thought.

MATT WATCHED HONEY STUDY HIS paintings. He still loved her; damn, that felt good to admit. No more struggling against the Fates, no more second-guessing—Matt De Luca was a man on a mission. Honey Campbell had better watch out, because he planned to make her a part of his life. Nope, she didn't have a chance.

She was adorable in his parka with her bright eyes and pink cheeks. He could barely keep his hands off her. Soon, very soon, he'd have her in his bed, and then…

It was time to change the subject. Either that, or he was going to embarrass himself.

He turned to pull some snowshoes from the closet and held them out to her. "How about we snowshoe into the trees and cut down the balsam I selected for the church. That way if they plow the roads, we'll be ready."

While Colleen and Patrick were enthusiastic, Honey was unusually silent.

Matt was strapping on M&M's shoes when he started picking up on Honey's reluctance. "You do want to come with us, don't you?"

"I'd like to, but I'm not too sure about the snowshoes. People in Alaska use these things. I wear stilettos. I'm a city girl."

As Matt fastened M&M's, he raised his eyebrows. "Are you going to let a three-year-old show you up?"

"I guess not," she admitted. "But I don't know how to get them on. You'll have to help me."

"My lady, your wish is my command." Matt sketched a bow worthy of the finest courtier.

When everyone was fully equipped, they trooped out to the field where Matt's perfect tree was standing in all its snow-covered beauty.

"I've been giving this guy special attention ever since I found out it was my turn to provide the tree."

Honey had never really thought about the time and effort that went into growing Christmas trees. It obviously took an incredible amount of attention and a lot of hard work.

"I have an artificial one, but I usually don't bother to put it up."

"Artificial?" Colleen's expression said it all.

"You need a reeducation. We don't ever use the *A* word," Matt said with mock sternness.

"Yes, sir," she said with a mock salute.

Honey's answer gained her a hug and a lingering kiss. Now *that* was nice!

"Come on, guys," he called. "We have quite a hike back to the shop."

Colleen and Patrick were having a snowball fight, and M&M was asleep in Honey's arms. There was something comforting and warm about holding a tired child.

"I'm almost done," Matt said as he wrapped the tree in netting. Then he propped it against the side of the store. "If she's getting too heavy, you can take her back to the house," he told Honey. "I hope the church folks don't have to go retro. If they do, they'll be talking about it for the next ten years. In towns like Snow Hill, stories like that take on lives of their own."

M&M HAD SUCCUMBED TO SLEEP, and who could blame her? It was twilight before they returned to the house, and Matt saw that even the big kids seemed about to drop in their tracks.

He put his arm around Honey's shoulders. "I had fun."

"I did, too."

"It's Christmas Eve. That's a time for miracles. Do you think there's a miracle with our name on it?" he whispered.

"I certainly do. It's already happened. Otherwise I wouldn't be with you on the Magic Tree Farm." Honey wrapped her arms around his neck and demonstrated some magic of her own.

Chapter Eight

It wasn't a traditional Christmas Eve meal, but when it came to feeding kids you couldn't go wrong with hot dogs and hamburgers. For dessert they had Christmas cookies—baked by committee the previous afternoon.

"Uncle Matt, can we stay up late? Please," Colleen cajoled. "We never go to bed before midnight on Christmas Eve," she said. "Please, please, *please*."

"Yeah," Patrick agreed. "Christmas is like the Fourth of July, you get special dis…uh, dispersing on bedtimes."

"Dispensation, you dork," Colleen chided smugly.

"Whatever," he replied.

M&M was up from her nap but other than wanting to play with a strand of Honey's hair, she didn't seem to have an opinion.

"Tell you what, we'll play some games and see how it goes," Matt said. "You may get bored and not want to stay up."

"I suppose that'll be okay," Colleen agreed in her inimitable teenage way. "I'll get the Scrabble game."

Honey noticed Matt's grimace before he looked at her and mouthed, "She's a Scrabble shark."

Several hours later, Matt had gracefully bowed out and Honey was getting skunked again. What was it with these kids and games?

"Are you ready to…" Honey was about to suggest they quit when Colleen jumped up.

"What's that?" the girl exclaimed, peering out the window. "There's something with lights on out there."

Her comment got everyone's attention. Even M&M wanted to be part of the action.

"It's a snowplow! Uncle Matt, it's a snowplow and they're

driving up our lane!" Patrick was bouncing like a terrier on a biscuit binge.

Matt had given up on getting the tree to the church, but this *was* Christmas Eve.

"Sure looks like it." He glanced at Honey. He'd give anything to know what she was thinking. She'd donned her ice-princess face, which was almost impossible to decipher.

The road was clear, so Honey could leave as soon as they found her car. Would she really walk out of their lives? Matt didn't think so. During the past couple of days their spark had been rekindled. But he'd been blindsided before. Could he be mistaken this time?

"Look at all the people." Honey seemed transfixed by the spectacle going on outside.

And what a sight it was. Not only was there a snowplow, there were at least a dozen snowmobiles and an equal number of 4x4s.

Matt chuckled. "Those folks *really* don't want to use that seventies tree."

"Do you blame them?" Honey's icy demeanor had evaporated like water on a hot sunny day. And when she smiled, Matt was transported back fifteen years. He loved her, and this time, no matter what it took, he wasn't going to let her leave. He needed her. They *all* needed her.

"Listen, Honey—" He took her hand, ready to bare his heart. Whether her answer was good, bad or indifferent, he had to ask. "I—"

Matt didn't have a chance to complete his question before Colleen squealed, "We're outta here! Oh cool, we're outta here!" She pumped a fist in the air and danced around the room. "I can see my friends."

"You don't have any friends," Patrick retorted.

"Do, too, dipstick!"

"Kids, put on your coats and go greet our guests."

They dashed to the closet, each trying to beat the other out the door.

"Looks like we're going to have a party." Matt smiled sheepishly at Honey. He'd astonished himself by the use of *we,* but it was true—they were a *we.*

Before Honey could answer, the lights came back on. "Wow,

everything's happening at once." The road was passable again, they could deliver the tree and Honey had a sneaking suspicion Matt was about to say something important.

"Up," M&M demanded, raising her arms. Honey did as requested and then directed her attention to the citizens of Snow Hill who were arriving en masse at the front door.

"I think I should whip up some hot chocolate," Honey said, while Matt put on his coat to greet their visitors.

"That's a god idea," he agreed.

"Snookums, why don't you come help me."

M&M responded to the invitation with a giggle.

Honey couldn't imagine a better way to celebrate Christmas Eve than a party with people she loved, and a whole bunch of folks she planned to get to know. After she prepared a tray of refreshments, she carried M&M outside where Matt introduced Honey to what seemed like half the population of Snow Hill. The story of her rescue was met with a chorus of oohs and aahs. From their reaction, it was apparent they also believed in the magic of Christmas.

Some of the town's citizens were carefully hoisting the twelve-foot balsam into the mayor's four-wheel-drive truck, the snowplow driver was sipping on a hot chocolate with marshmallows, the party was in full swing and Sweet Pea was having a ball frolicking in the snow.

"I'm surprised we made it out here," the mayor commented, slapping Matt on the arm. "I'd hate to decorate the church with that ratty aluminum thing. I kept hinting that we should cut down a tree in someone's yard, but no one volunteered to sacrifice their landscaping. We've got a gorgeous tree now, though. Thanks for the donation, Matt."

Several of his constituents nodded in agreement.

"Mayor, look at the time." The preacher grabbed another cookie. "We have to head back to the church. We only have a couple of hours to get the sanctuary ready." He nudged Matt. "Thanks to you, we have the perfect tree. Wait till you see it all decorated." He turned to Honey. "And we're all thankful you're here. God works in mysterious ways."

Amen to that! "We'll be there," Matt said. "Won't we, Honey?"

He looked so hopeful she had to agree, but doubts kept creeping in. The problem? Her heart was vulnerable. She was in love—madly, irrevocably in love. She thought the feeling was reciprocated, but Matt had never actually said he loved her. Now that their isolation had ended and their special time was over, would he still feel the same way about her?

She wasn't sure if he loved her or simply liked her. Whichever it was, she refused to consider losing him again.

Chapter Nine

Everyone bundled up for the sleigh ride. Even fashion-conscious Colleen opted for comfort, donning Sorels and a down parka. M&M resembled a big pink marshmallow in her snowsuit.

"Are you absolutely positive you want to go into town in this rig?" Matt asked, affectionately patting the two draft horses he was hitching up. "We can use the truck. It's glacial out here," he said, hoping that would be his trump card.

"Nope. We want to celebrate Christmas properly. Colleen and I found a closet full of lap robes." Honey held up a scrap of plaid wool that had seen better days. "We'll be fine." She flapped the blanket. Whew—someone had had a moth ball fetish.

"Right, kids?" she asked. Honoria Campbell was a woman on a mission, and neither rain, nor sleet, nor the overpowering reek of mothballs could deter her. Her goal was to have the best Christmas ever—complete with the love of her life, three adorable children *and* a big, fluffy dog. How much better could it get?

Her decision to embrace Christmas and this family was the result of a long, sleepless night. When she was a kid, she'd let her parents plot her future. It wasn't that Honey didn't love her mom and dad, but they'd never had any idea what made her happy, and things hadn't changed much now that she was an adult.

It took her being dumped on Matt's front porch for Honey to realize she'd been wandering through life looking for a purpose. Three days with the De Luca family had put everything in perspective. Happiness wasn't about money or professional success; it was about love and family.

Although Colleen and Patrick had sibling sniping down to a fine art, it was obvious that they loved each other. They were working as a team at the moment, peppering their uncle with a chorus of "Please, please, please, we want to ride in the sleigh." Matt couldn't possibly resist that show of solidarity.

They were going on a sleigh ride.

M&M took a few steps before toppling over.

"Here you go, kiddo." Honey picked up the child, brushed her off and put her in the sled.

"I SUPPOSE WE'RE READY." MATT wasn't convinced this was a good idea. Although Dutch and Daisy were reliable horses, their road experience was limited.

"Everything will be fine, really it will," Honey assured him, wrapping her arm around his waist and giving him a squeeze.

Could she read his mind? He hoped not—especially considering the less-than-PG thoughts he'd been entertaining. When he was near her he felt like a testosterone-driven, hot and bothered teenager again.

That was why he couldn't resist tipping Honey's chin for a kiss. "Okay, let's go for it." He turned to the kids. "Hop in, guys. We have a Christmas tree to admire." So off they went in a flurry of snow-flakes and a chorus of "Jingle Bells."

When they arrived at the white, colonial-style church, Matt un-hitched the sleigh and tied the horses to a fence out front.

"Welcome to Snow Hill Community Church. What do you think?" he asked Honey.

"It's absolutely beautiful. For about half a second I was considering how perfect it would be for an advertising campaign," Honey admitted with an embarrassed laugh. Actually, she was thinking it was an ideal place for a wedding—hers.

Matt had seen the church a thousand times, but as with anything you see day after day it'd become part of the background scenery. He hadn't taken stock of his surroundings in quite a while. He glanced around at his adopted village and realized, not for the first time, that it *was* Christmas card material.

"This is like a Thomas Kinkade setting, isn't it?" He didn't wait for an answer. "But it's not as beautiful as you are." He emphasized his statement with a soft, inviting kiss. Matt heard more than one

"Good going" uttered as members of the congregation made their way into the church.

A resounding "Yuck!" from his nephew dragged Matt out of his trance. The comment was typical for a nine-year-old boy. Just wait until the kid was sixteen. Then he'd understand.

"Okay, well." He shook his head, noticing that Honey appeared a little dazed herself. "This church is probably the only place in New England that George Washington didn't visit." That was an inane comment, but considering his out-of-control hormones, it wasn't too bad.

"Come on, kids, let's go in," Matt said, noting that Patrick was engaged in a snowball fight with his best friend and Colleen was flirting with a lanky kid who wasn't faring well in the puberty wars.

"Hey, guys, get it rolling. Do I have to start my countdown?" Matt asked when Colleen and Patrick feigned deafness.

Honey gave him a wink before strolling up the steps with M&M in her arms. Matt followed with the two older kids reluctantly in tow.

As Honey opened one of the huge double doors adorned with matching evergreen wreaths, she spotted the Christmas tree nestled up next to a manger.

"Oh, my goodness!"

Adorned with twinkle lights, tiny red and green bows, strings of popcorn and homemade ornaments, the balsam was a festival of color in the otherwise pristine white interior. Even Honey's artistic mind couldn't have come up with a more ideal Christmas scene.

"Our usual spot is five pews up on the left." Matt's directions were a mere whisper, but they were enough to raise goose bumps on her arms. "Not that we have our name on it or anything."

Typical of a colonial church, the pews were partitioned into separate cubicles. That design had been created several centuries back so families could provide a source of warmth for their seating areas—not a bad idea when the church had been unheated and the temperature outside hovered at zero. Fortunately for everyone's tootsies, central heating had made its way to Snow Hill Community Church.

"COME ON, KIDS," MATT said. Colleen and Patrick were hanging back to see if they could find someone more interesting to sit with. Normally he wouldn't care, but the Christmas Eve service was a special family time. He glanced at the woman he realized he loved even more now than he had when they were young. She was playing patty-cake with M&M.

Could Honey—a big-city girl—be happy on a Christmas tree farm in New Hampshire? He couldn't leave the life he was making here and return to Boston. It wouldn't be fair to anyone.

He also couldn't ditch the work of several generations of the De Luca family; if he did that, Uncle Pietro would haunt him for the rest of his life. And the last thing he needed was a wine-swilling, grizzled old Italian invading his dreams.

Therein lay the conundrum. If he put himself on the line and Honey laughed—no, she was too much of a lady—or even worse he saw pity in those beautiful blue eyes, he'd die. Oh well, at least then he wouldn't have to deal with another broken heart. He wasn't sure he could live through that again.

HONEY TOOK A QUICK LOOK AT Matt. He'd been strangely quiet even though Colleen and Patrick were squirming as if they had a bad case of fleas.

He was a gorgeous man, not only physically, but deep down, where it really counted. How many guys would assume guardianship of three rambunctious kids? And not only that, he'd uprooted his life and given up his art to become a farmer. It wasn't often you found someone like that, and when you did, you kept him. That was exactly what Honey intended to do. So, considering their history, what was the best plan of action?

A jumble of thoughts whirled through her brain as the pipe organ heralded the beginning of the midnight service. What *should* she do? She pondered the question through "Deck the Halls" and "O Holy Night."

When Matt took her hand during "Silent Night," it felt so natural that any lingering doubts were dispelled. It was time to ditch the trappings and expectations of her upper-crust background and follow her dreams. She was in charge of her own destiny. It didn't matter what anyone thought—and that included her parents, her business partners and her friends.

Yeah! Honoria Westfield Campbell was ready to call the shots. It was liberating beyond belief. She crossed her fingers, hoping she wasn't being delusional.

Her dream was to be a wife, a mother and a full-time artist, and by gosh, she planned to make it happen! The only problem was how. Although Matt had been attentive and sweet, he'd never actually said he loved her.

MATT HAD BEEN MAKING A FEW decisions of his own. So what if she turned him down? So what if he got another broken heart? Like the old expression said, Nothing Ventured, Nothing Gained. And he planned to gain a wife, the girl of his dreams and a soul mate, all rolled up in one beautiful blond package.

Colleen was making eyes at a kid in the next pew, Patrick was secretly playing with his Game Boy and M&M was hopping on and off the pew. All was well in the De Luca world. Could Honey really become part of that madness?

As the ushers passed out candles for the final song, Matt picked up M&M. Excitement had gotten the best of the toddler, and she was sound asleep.

"She's a goner," he murmured.

"Uh-huh, she certainly is," Honey agreed, running her fingers through the child's soft black curls. "She really looks like an angel when she's asleep."

Mary Margaret wasn't the only one who could have posed for a master's painting, Matt thought, taking Honey's hand. Small candles provided a romantic glow, the choir was singing, it was almost Christmas—and it was now or never.

Matt took a deep breath and jumped in with both feet. "I love you, Honey Campbell. I have for years. I want you to live here with us." Not too bad for someone who was incredibly rusty in the romance department. She didn't do anything but stare at him, so he soldiered on.

"I want to marry you. Would you do me the honor of becoming Mrs. Matteo De Luca?" He ended his request with a gentle kiss. Considering that he had an audience and was holding a sleeping child, that was about the best he could do—no flowers or music, just a simple "Will you marry me?"

Honey continued to stare at him. That wasn't a good omen. Matt wanted to kick himself. Could he have been that dumb *twice?*

"You want to marry me?"

"Uh-huh," he responded, moving M&M to his other arm. He knew it was time to argue his case, but his ability to form a cogent sentence was suddenly missing in action.

"Are you serious? Really serious?"

"Yep."

By that time the people in the surrounding pews had discovered what was happening.

"Say yes, little gal, and put him out of his misery." That pearl of wisdom came from one of Snow Hill's crustiest citizens. Rumor had it he'd outlived at least three wives.

"Uncle Matt." Patrick was tugging on Matt's sleeve. "Are you getting married?"

"Married, who's getting married?" Patrick's question had gotten Colleen's attention. The two kids exchanged looks and focused their collective gaze on Honey, and then on Matt.

"If something's going on that will—" Colleen waved a hand in the air "—like, have something to do with us, we should be the first to know."

Although Matt didn't turn around, he could sense that their audience had grown. Timing had never been his strong suit, but this blunder had the earmarks of a debacle that would be rehashed for years to come. Why hadn't he waited until they'd returned home? At least that way he wouldn't have looked stupid in front of the entire town.

"Yes."

It was one syllable, but hearing Honey utter it almost knocked him over.

"Did you say yes?" Matt could barely believe his ears.

Honey traced the outline of his lips. "Of course I'll marry you, you silly man."

A stout lady with steel-grey hair leaned over the pew. "Why don't you hand me that child and give her a kiss."

"Yes, ma'am," Matt said, passing M&M to the grandmotherly woman. "Are you sure she won't be too heavy?"

"Nonsense. Now get busy."

"Right," Matt agreed, pulling Honey into his arms.

"Are you absolutely positive?" he asked, barely allowing her time to answer before he began kissing her into oblivion.

When they finally came up for air, half the congregation was applauding. The other half hadn't heard the news yet, but when they did, the entire church sent up a resounding Amen.

Chapter Ten

The excitement of the evening finally wiped out the De Luca progeny; even Colleen was down for the count. It was the perfect opportunity for Honey to call Bitsy and fill her in on everything that had happened.

After the kids went to bed, Honey and Matt had a long conversation about the future. "I can't believe everything that's happened. I'm so happy," Honey whispered, cuddling closer to the man she'd loved, lost and miraculously found again. A couple of days ago, she'd planned to spend the holidays skiing. Now she was about to up-end her entire existence.

Honey understood why Matt couldn't go back to the city. He'd made a wonderful life at the farm. That was the primary reason she was willing to ditch her advertising career. But the extra incentive was that art had always been her passion, and with the stress of a high-powered job, she'd had very little time to follow that dream. Now she could have it all—a family, a home, the ideal occupation and the love of a very special man. This was an answer to her prayers.

Her parents would *not* understand. They'd assume she'd totally flipped out. But what was new? They thought she'd gone to the Boston Arts Academy because she wanted to pursue a graphic arts career. In truth, she'd wanted to become the next Monet.

"What do you suppose your parents will think? I'm not exactly their favorite person." Matt raised her chin. He obviously wanted to see her reaction.

"To be honest, I don't know. But whatever they say, or think, is irrelevant. I love them, but they don't have any control over my life."

Matt grinned. "I'm glad your father doesn't own a gun."

Honey rolled her eyes.

"I hate to sound like a broken record, but are you *sure* you'll be happy on the farm? It's not very exciting."

"Are you kidding? How can life with three kids be boring?"

"You're right. There's never a dull moment around the De Luca house," he admitted with a chuckle.

"I have this idea." Honey sat up, demanding Matt's full attention. "I want to open an art gallery over in North Conway. Think about it—the resort town has a constant stream of skiers, leaf-lookers and vacationers. They have money and they're ready to spend it. I can make it work. I know I can. I'm not giving up a career. I'm making a huge lifestyle change. And best of all, it gives me a chance to paint. What do you think?" Honey couldn't keep the excitement out of her voice. "And since I can help you with the Christmas shop, you'll have more time to do things *you* enjoy."

"I can think of several things I enjoy doing with you," Matt said with a grin. "Want to practice a few of them?"

Honey playfully poked him in the ribs. "Hmm, sounds like a good idea to me," she said, scrambling onto his lap and kissing his neck.

"I could get used to this," he murmured.

"Me, too." Honey punctuated her admission with a giggle and another kiss. And that was the last of their conversation for quite a while.

WITH THREE KIDS IN THE household, they had to take their privacy where, and when, they could get it. And Matt intended to be with Honey every chance he had.

"Merry Christmas," he said, pulling her into his arms under the duvet. "In a few hours everyone will be up and raring to go." He chuckled, thinking about the chaos that was about to ensue. "You haven't lived until you've had Christmas with the entire De Luca clan."

Honey sat up, disturbing the warm nest he'd made. "What do you mean the entire clan? I thought it would be just the five of us. Who else will be here?"

"Uh-oh. In all the excitement I forgot to tell you my family's coming."

"Your family?"

"Yes." Matt counted the guests on his fingers. "My mom, my two brothers, my sister-in-law and last, but not least, my two nieces."

"Are you serious?" Honey asked with a squeak.

"Uh, yeah." This conversation wasn't going the way Matt had planned. Honey was scowling—not good. He loved his family, but as a group they could be intimidating. And there was a ton of history with Honey.

If he didn't immediately give Mama a heads-up about their plan to get married, there'd be hell to pay. So, as soon as the sun rose, he had a call to make.

"We always have Christmas dinner together. Honestly, it won't be a problem," he assured her. Together they could face anything— including their families.

Tugging the sheet over her breasts, she blew the bangs out of her eyes. "They all hate me. Hate me! The last time I saw your mother she was screaming at me and crossing herself. I felt like a Jezebel. I'm sure she has a voodoo doll with my face on it that she sticks pins in every night." Honey waved her hands dramatically, causing the sheet to slip. "And what's that curse called—the thing with the eye?"

"You mean *malocchio?*"

"That's the one. Your mother's going to give me that *look* the minute she gets here."

When Honey was right, she was right. But—and this was a huge *but*—Mom was a staunch Catholic. She believed in the concept of forgiveness. That went triple for John, the apple of his mother's eye and the only De Luca brother to become a priest. Good old John, he'd been the biggest hell-raiser in the North End until he went to the seminary. So things *would* be okay.

"As it happens, one of my brothers is a priest. He made a vow not to hold a grudge."

Honey gave him a look he couldn't decipher, so he pressed on.

"My nieces have more important things to worry about than me, ditto for my sister-in-law, and believe it or not, Mama's a big softie."

Honey responded with a snort.

"Okay, maybe *softie* is a bit of a stretch. But trust me, she'll come around."

Another snort.

"What about your other brother?"

That was a good question. Luke was the wild card. He'd been Matt's confidant throughout the entire Honey fiasco.

"Come here." He snuggled her close. "Let's discuss this in a civilized manner. We'll come up with a game plan, I promise."

"I hope you're right."

So did he! If he wasn't, this had the potential to develop into a Christmas fiasco that would become a family legend.

But whatever this day brought, Matt's primary consideration was Honey's happiness. And, somehow, he knew the De Lucas were going to adore her. He'd bet the farm on it.

Chapter Eleven

Honey was a whiz at advertising. She realized what happened on Christmas morning when kids were involved; convincing parents to buy their offspring the latest toy was her bread and butter. But understanding and seeing were two different things. From the moment the De Luca kids roared down the stairs until the last present was opened, it was sheer bedlam. Even poor Sweet Pea was buried in wrapping paper.

"Uncle Matt, this is so cool," Colleen squealed, holding up the latest in wireless telecommunication.

Patrick was trying out his new Xbox game and M&M was dressing her baby doll. Santa had outdone himself, and all was well in the De Luca household.

Honey was thoroughly enjoying her foray into the world of a child-oriented Christmas when M&M toddled over and climbed into her lap.

"Miss Honey." She'd finally mastered Honey's name.

"Yes, sweetie." Honey hugged the child.

"We have sumthin' for you."

"You do?"

"Um-huh. I made it, but Sissy helped." Colleen—aka Sissy— and Patrick plopped on the couch. It was a family moment that made her realize how much she'd missed.

"Here." Colleen held out a brightly wrapped package. The bow was off-center, and the Scotch tape was barely holding.

"For me?"

M&M gave her another hug. The other kids were more reserved. Their stand-back-and-watch approach was one Honey understood; it was a protective measure she, too, had learned as a youngster. Matt was the only person who'd ever broken through that barrier.

"Aren't you going to open it?" Patrick asked.

"Of course." She ripped into the wrapping and discovered a necklace fashioned from a bead kit.

It was long enough to wrap around her neck twice, and the beads were a wild array of different sizes and shades, but it was the best gift she'd ever received.

"I love it!"

"Do you really?" Colleen asked, her uncertainty apparent.

"I do." Honey hugged all three kids. In every possible way, it was a Christmas to remember.

Matt waded through the debris and sat down with the family. "I didn't have a chance to buy you anything, but I hope you like this." He plucked a small rectangular package from under the tree and handed it to Honey.

"Oh, Matt. I didn't get you anything."

"All I want for Christmas is you," he whispered, sending chills up her spine. "Open it."

"This is…this is wonderful." Honey pulled off the paper and discovered a small oil painting of the sun coming over a mountain. The orange, yellow and red splendor of sunrise melded with the deep purple of receding night. The scene's beauty brought tears to her eyes.

"At the right time of year you can see that from our back porch."

"It's gorgeous." Honey wrapped her arms around his neck. "I am so happy," she said with a sniff. "I want to put your paintings in my new gallery."

"My lady, your wish is my command."

SEVERAL HOURS LATER AS HONEY WAS showering, she had a terrible realization. She'd never cooked a turkey in her entire life. How long did you have to roast one of those birds?

She jumped into her sweats and was out of the bathroom in a flash. "Matt, we have a problem!" she yelled, skidding into the kitchen.

He was clearing off the table from their Christmas breakfast. "What's wrong?" he asked, folding Honey in his arms and proceeding to do a little PG-rated necking.

"Matt, stop that! What about the turkey?"

"What turkey?"

She looked up at him in disbelief. "The turkey we have to make for dinner. We can't serve your family peanut butter sandwiches."

"Oh that," he said, rubbing her back. "Trudy's bringing it."

"Who's Trudy?"

Matt lowered his lips to hers. "Trudy is my sister-in-law, Luke's wife," he informed her when he finally released her. "The De Luca ladies are bringing the entire dinner." Matt gave a self-deprecating laugh. "They don't think I can cook, and that's okay with me. We simply have to provide the dishes and the wine."

"Thank goodness." Now all she had to worry about was spending the day fending off *malocchio. Ye gads!* "Are they spending the night here?" *That* was a truly overwhelming thought.

"No."

Honey almost collapsed in relief.

THE KIDS AND DOG WERE presentable, the house was clean and Honey was about to chew her fingernails down to the quick. It was still an hour before Matt's relatives were scheduled to arrive, so there was time to kill.

"Is this your family photo album?" she asked, picking up a large padded book.

"Yep." Matt sat on the couch with her. "I'll show you pictures of the people you haven't met, like Trudy."

"Okay." Honey would take any kind of edge she could get.

Matt opened the cover, then almost immediately slammed it shut.

"What are you hiding?" She reached over to grab the book out of his lap.

"I guess you'll see it sooner or later." Matt reluctantly opened the front page, and Honey almost wished he hadn't. In the picture Matt was smiling and handsome. He was also wearing a cap and gown. Why hadn't she left well enough alone?

"It's my graduation picture. Dad was more excited when I graduated from high school than when I got my B.A." Matt traced his father's face with his finger.

"I suspect he was thanking the saints that I didn't have to spend the remainder of my senior year in jail."

"Dear God!" Honey had tried not to dwell on what her father had done, but this picture brought it all into perspective. He could have ruined the De Luca family.

"I am so sorry."

Matt stroked her cheek. "You didn't have any control over your father. He comes from a different time and he has his own perspective. I suppose he did what he thought was the right thing for you, although I obviously don't agree with him. All I know is that we didn't do anything wrong. We were captivated by our youth and our hormones, but underlying all that we loved each other. That was lost on your family, and that's their problem, not ours," he said. "Did I mention that I love you beyond reason?"

"I love you, too."

"I'm counting on it." Matt gave her a soft kiss. It was about the best they could do with a houseful of young chaperones.

"Let's look at the rest of the pictures."

Honey saw a parade of photos chronicling Matt's life. There were studio portraits of various family members, years of school photos and candid snapshots of the boys when they were young and then later as adults.

"Is this a picture of the kids' parents?" Honey pointed to a smiling couple in a wedding photo.

"Uh-huh, that's my brother Mark and his wife, Julie. I miss them like crazy. When we were growing up he was a pain in the butt," Matt said with a laugh. "One time when we were in high school he put a goat in my room. That animal did unspeakable things. Mark and my mother had quite a tussle over the incident. Guess who won?"

"I'll bet it was your mom."

"Absolutely. Mark was grounded for so long I thought he'd miss his graduation, and he was only a sophomore at the time. Plus, Mama made him clean all the carpets."

Honey had to laugh thinking about the antics of the De Luca brothers. "I always wanted a sister."

"Really?"

"Yeah. I didn't see any reason to discuss a pipe dream," she said with a shrug. "I'm not sure my parents even wanted *me*. And they certainly never expressed a desire to have another child. I think I interfered with their social life." Honey had finally acknowledged something she'd kept to herself for years. No one wanted to feel unwelcome—or to admit it. She quickly turned the page to avoid further discussion.

That was when she saw him. "Who's that?" She pointed at a picture of an old man with a beard—it was *her* Willie Nelson. She didn't have to have ESP to realize she wasn't going to like Matt's answer.

He was looking at her strangely, and why not? She was about to get hysterical.

"That's my uncle Pietro."

M&M wandered in and made herself at home on Matt's lap. "Would you like some milk?" he asked her.

She answered by sticking her thumb in her mouth. "Um-huh."

Honey wanted an answer, and she wanted it right that minute. "You mean the guy who's—" She finished her sentence by slashing her hand across her neck.

"One and the same," he answered.

M&M put her arms around Matt's neck. She was obviously picking up on their tension.

"Why are you asking?"

"Why am I asking?" Honey stabbed her finger at the picture. Her voice was getting louder by the second. "Why am I asking?" Okay, she'd officially lost it. This was bordering on *Twilight Zone* territory.

"Colleen! Colleen!" Matt yelled.

"Whatcha need, Uncle Matt?" the teen asked as she strolled into the living room.

"Would you take M&M to the kitchen and get her a cup of milk, please." He pried the child's arms from around his neck.

Colleen shrugged. "Come on, squirt. The grown-ups want to say something they don't want us to hear."

Matt sat down and pulled Honey close to him. "Sweetheart, what's the matter?"

She tapped the picture. "That's the guy who brought me here!"

Matt shook his head. "That's not possible."

"Why? Because he's dead?"

"Yep. That would make running around in a blizzard pretty hard."

Honey could feel the blood rush from her head. The guy on the snowmobile was a ghost!

Chapter Twelve

Honey took a deep breath. When that didn't do the trick, she took another. Nope, she still felt as if she was about to hyperventilate. Merciful heavens. She'd encountered a ghost! Not only had Honey seen him, she'd gotten on an Arctic Cat with him. How in heaven, or hell, had a ghost managed to drive a snowmobile?

"Hey, look at me," Matt demanded. "You're not going to faint, are you?"

Yes, no, maybe.

"Now look at the picture again. Please."

Matt's request deflated her impending hysteria. "Okay." Honey studied the photo. It had been dark that night, but there was no doubt about the identity of her rescuer.

"I'm positive. That's the guy. What—"

"What can we do about it?" Matt finished. "Nothing." He massaged the back of her neck. "He brought you here. I suspect it was his way of making sure we got back together. My mother's worried about me being alone, so I suspect she's been inundating heaven with prayers. She thinks the kids need a mother figure." Matt sighed. "I don't believe this is what she had in mind—us getting back together. But a Christmas miracle is the reason you're here, and you don't tinker with miracles, you simply accept them."

It *was* a miracle—a true-blue, full-blown miracle, and who was Honey to resist divine intervention?

She turned and threw her arms around Matt. "I plan to love you forever. Do you hear me? I will always love you!"

Matt lowered his head—anticipation at its very best. Unfortunately, they were interrupted by M&M. Such was the world of children. It would be a different way of life from what she'd experienced before, but Honey knew it would be an adventure.

"Uncle Matt, I still hungwy."

"Sweetie, come sit with us." Matt picked up his young niece, placing her on his lap. "Grandma and the rest of the family will be here in a couple of hours. And you love to play with Sarah and Jenny, don't you? It'll be fun."

"Um-huh," M&M agreed, popping a thumb in her mouth.

Fun was a matter of opinion. Honey was about to break out in hives just thinking about Christmas dinner. Matt had said it would be okay, and who could argue with his optimism?

"Can I have a samich?" When M&M was hungry, there was no distracting her.

"Sure. How about you guys? Do you want a snack?" Matt asked. The other kids had temporarily abandoned their Christmas presents and wandered into the living room.

"Whatever," Colleen responded with a wave of her hand.

Honey wasn't fooled by the cavalier attitude. At any rate, Patrick was more enthusiastic. Sweet Pea simply sat there with a big doggie grin on her face.

"Looks like we have some kids to feed, huh?" Matt linked his fingers with hers. She could see he was plotting something—she just didn't know what.

"Hey, guys. How do you feel about Honey and me getting married?" There'd been much excitement following the church service, but they hadn't had an opportunity for a family meeting. He prayed the kids would wholeheartedly approve—or, at the very least, not object too strenuously.

The littlest angel crawled into her lap. "You gonna stay?"

"I am," Honey said with a smile.

"Sweet." Patrick's endorsement was short and...*sweet*.

There was only one vote outstanding, and that would be the tough one.

Colleen waited a few seconds before she seconded her brother's observation. "I think it's cool. You can help me streak my hair."

Honey smiled at Matt. This Christmas was pure magic. As all three kids wrapped their arms around her in a hug, Honey could almost hear Uncle Pietro break into a huge belly laugh.

* * * * *

TANNER AND BAUM
Tanya Michaels

Dear Reader,

The holiday season is my very favorite time of year! Although I love the exuberant kaleidoscope of family outings and events, one of my treasured traditions is sipping hot chocolate or cider and rereading beloved holiday stories by the glow of twinkling Christmas-tree lights. Occasionally, the temperature here in Georgia even drops low enough that I can read by a crackling fire.

Given my fond recollections of carols playing softly while the kids slept and I lost myself in a book, I was delighted to have this opportunity to write a holiday story for others to enjoy. I hope you'll come to love Tanner Waide and Lilah Baum and the other citizens of their fictional hometown. In writing about Mistletoe, Georgia, I tried to create a place readers would want to visit again and again.

So take an hour or so away from the hustle and bustle of the season and indulge yourself. Grab some cookies and a mug of your favorite drink, get comfy, and welcome to Mistletoe.

Happy Holidays,

Tanya

P.S. Visit www.tanyamichaels.com for holiday giveaways and a list of some of those holiday stories I like to read each year.

Chapter One

As one might expect from a place called Mistletoe, everything about the town proclaimed holiday cheer. Twinkling decorations hung on streetlights, and pleasantly pungent smoke drifted from chimneys. Citizens were even being treated to the rare sight of snowflakes falling from the Georgia sky, dissolving into an ethereal mist before hitting the ground.

Yet despite the surroundings, Lilah Baum was not in a holly jolly mood. Nor was she motivated to profess joy to the world. Ditto donning gay apparel.

She'd managed to maintain her normal enthusiasm in front of her students, but, standing now on Aunt Shel's front porch, in the glow of tiny blue and green bulbs woven around the railing, melancholy soaked through Lilah like winter rain through mittens. When Shelby opened the door, Lilah's forced smile felt so much like a mask that she almost blurted, "Trick or treat." *Maybe I should.* A candy-induced sugar rush might improve her mood.

"Come in before you freeze!" Shelby Tierney was a silver-haired, five-foot-two bundle of energy and nurturing instincts. "Weather reports called for flurries, but I didn't believe it till I saw it."

Lilah followed her aunt through the foyer and past a cozy living room, where, in another hour, Uncle Ray would watch the evening news from his caramel-colored recliner. She breathed in the thyme-scented aroma of homemade lentil soup, which simmered quietly on the stove. *Nothing like the Tierney kitchen to warm the soul.* This olive-and-navy-decorated room, with its modest five-piece dinette set and abounding good smells, had been an unending source of solace and nourishment.

"My fourth-graders are hoping the snow will stick—" Lilah

shrugged out of her jacket "—and that school will be canceled tomorrow."

"Not a chance. Besides, they're lucky to spend the day with you. You're the best teacher at Whiteberry Elementary!"

"You're biased."

"Darn right I am." Shel beamed proudly. For a second, she looked so much like her late sister—Lilah's mother—that emotion clogged Lilah's throat.

Though Lilah had long since coped with her parents' deaths, healed by her aunt and uncle's love and her entire extended family of townspeople, there were moments when she missed her mother and father so much it hurt to breathe. Especially during the holidays. Her fingers went to the sparkling Christmas tree pendant around her neck. She and her dad had picked it out for her mom when Lilah was twelve—their last Christmas together before she had come to live with an aunt and uncle who'd married late in life and had given up on children of their own.

Aunt Shel's shrewd gaze didn't miss a thing. "Thinking of your mama?"

"Yeah." Lilah tucked the necklace into the draped collar of her sweater. "I'll be all right. If those kids are 'lucky' to spend their days with me, I've been downright blessed to have you and Uncle Ray."

Behind the bifocals perched on the woman's button nose, Shel's hazel eyes misted. "Don't you think of making me cry. Once I get into a state, my whole schedule will be off. Those cookies for the senior center aren't gonna bake themselves."

Shelby had been an assistant manager at the Mistletoe Inn when an out-of-town businessman named Ray Tierney had checked into the hotel and had quickly fallen in love with her. After Lilah moved in with them, Shelby had cut back to part-time hours. Still, all the volunteering she did around town was practically a second occupation.

"Cookies, right." Lilah blinked away the sting in her own eyes. She'd come over to help with some holiday baking.

Sounding more composed, Shelby glanced up from the recipe card she held. "Mindy at the center said you agreed to organize this year's Winter Wonderland dance."

Lilah hesitated. She hadn't mentioned it to her aunt yet because Shelby always praised her for carrying on the volunteer tradition…then followed up with a suggestion that it might be nice for her twenty-seven-year-old niece to have a man in her life *below* the age of fifty-five.

"I love helping over there," Lilah said. "And the dance seemed like a festive opportunity. I'm having trouble getting in touch with my Christmas spirit this year."

Shelby pursed her lips thoughtfully, a sure sign that advice would follow. Previous advisements had ranged from buying cheerful holiday sweaters to letting one of Lilah's many adoptive "aunts" set her up on dates with sons and grandsons. *Which is why I've been out to dinner with half the town's eligible bachelors, even though not one of them gives me that giddy rush I felt with—*

She crushed the thought. Five years was too long to pine over a man, even if she *had* expected to marry him. It was only her nostalgic mood that made her think of Tanner. The golden-haired hero of her high school and college years hadn't set foot in Mistletoe since the day he'd left, making it easy to banish him from her mind. Or, if not *easy,* then at least possible. Usually.

"I know!" Aunt Shel's declaration pushed Tanner back into the past where he belonged. "Kasey Kerrigan dropped off some wreaths and boughs at the inn. She mentioned they might advertise for extra help this season, since business has picked up the last few winters. You should call. They love you over there!"

Kasey Kerrigan was half of the husband-and-wife team currently running ninety-year-old Kerrigan Farms, which boasted blueberry picking and community cookouts in the summer; a pumpkin patch, complete with corn maze and hayrides, in October; followed by live tree sales and an amazing light display throughout December, with a live nativity scene the week of Christmas. Between seasonal busy times, the Kerrigans offered their farm as a site for events such as the school field trips that had strengthened Lilah's bond with them.

Lilah nodded slowly, envisioning the evergreen rows of Leyland cypress and Virginia pine, the charming little shop full of handmade gifts. "Good idea, Shel." Kerrigan Farms should provide lots of old-fashioned Christmas spirit.

That is, as long as Lilah didn't think too hard about the families coming to shop—apple-cheeked kids anxious to help select and cut down a tree, husbands buying cups of cocoa for their wives—and wonder if she would ever find that for herself.

IN THE SCHEME OF THINGS, five years wasn't such a long time. An early milestone for a long-term business plan, the run of a moderately popular television show. Yet, as Tanner Waide parked in one of the dozen paved spaces outside Waide Supply, it hit him hard how much a man's perspective could change in five years. He'd peeled out of this very parking lot in a beat-up Mustang he and his brother had partially restored, determined to go find where he *really* belonged. Atlanta.

And now he was back.

He'd seen his family in the interim, when his mom or sister ventured out of Mistletoe for more extravagant shopping options, and at his brother's wedding in South Carolina, where the bride's parents lived. But he'd delayed coming home until…

Until what? He didn't even know anymore. Maybe he'd been waiting until he'd achieved success, although he wasn't sure exactly what measuring stick he'd planned to use. Not that it mattered. A little over three weeks ago, he'd lost his footing on the ladder of success. Rather, he'd been shoved off. Despite the luxury car he drove and the cashmere sweater he wore, Tanner felt like the poster child for Colossal Failure.

At least the holiday season gave him an excuse to return. It would have been much harder to stroll into the family store in, say, mid-March, and announce—

"Hey!" A small, feminine fist rapped against the car window. His younger sister smirked through the glass, her voice raised. "We don't feature curbside service, big shot, so if you want something, you'll actually have to get your butt out of that sweet ride and come in."

His mouth quirking into a grin, Tanner waited for Arianne to move before he opened his door. Her blond hair swished halfway to her jeans, considerably longer than when he'd last seen her.

"I see you inherited Dad's customer service approach," he teased.

She scowled. "Don't start. You haven't even been here ten seconds."

He supposed he'd deserved that.

"Gone by the house to see Mom yet?" she asked.

"No, once I got off the Interstate, coming into town this way was faster." He stretched, his spine and shoulders cracking audibly. Should a man who wouldn't hit thirty for another year and a half be creaking? "Good to be out of the car. Traffic was insane."

Arianne appeared to be looking down her nose at him…even though he had six inches of height on her. "Move to the city, get city traffic. Would've expected a smart guy like yourself to figure that out." She pivoted and flounced toward the store. In spirit, at least.

Technically, she'd probably stopped "flouncing" about the same time she'd had her braces removed. The girl who'd been a teen when he left had grown into something perilously close to a woman. *Scary thought.* Tanner and his older brother, David, were two years apart, but there was triple that gap between Tanner and twenty-two-year-old Arianne.

Neither Ari nor David had ever voiced any aversion to working at the family store. It was only Tanner who'd chafed at the implied restrictions on "What I Want to Be When I Grow Up." Thinking of the sleek, contemporary office in Atlanta—and the pitying and even suspicious glances people in that office had sent his way—he grimaced. He'd grown up to be a fall guy, easily duped by the mentor he'd admired. Comparatively speaking, that made part-owner of Waide Supply seem like a dream job.

Arianne paused in front of the door, glancing over her shoulder. Genuine concern had replaced the irritation in her expression. "You coming?"

"Yeah." But what kind of reception awaited? His mother, when he'd called to ask about staying for a few weeks in December, had been ecstatic. Zachariah Waide might be less so. Then again, facing the old man wouldn't be half as difficult as facing his own past mistakes.

A copper bell chimed above his head, marking the moment he set foot inside. Concrete floor stretched straight ahead, and to his left, the aisles sectioned off in categories, such as Gardening Accessories, Fireplace Maintenance, Poultry Supplies, Camping Gear and Tools. Near the front counter that ran along the wall to his right, someone—Ari, or their mother—had stacked red boxes of grease guns and electric sanders into an approximate Christmas tree shape, topping it with a glittery gold bow.

Zachariah Waide himself stood behind the counter, ringing up poly tarp for a balding man in flannel. The customer turned, smiled at Arianne, then did a double-take. "For a minute, I thought that was David. With longer hair and fancier duds."

"No, that's my other son." Zachariah smiled tightly. "Tanner."

My "other" son. Good thing he hadn't expected a hearty welcome.

So, he'd been right about something. But he'd been wrong about so much more. Like his misplaced faith in the embezzler who was probably living large in the Bahamas. Like the way Tanner had blithely assumed he would never miss his hometown. In college, he'd been delighted by the four years of escape, although now he realized that his many visits back to Mistletoe had served as a touchstone. Bittersweet wistfulness for this place had snuck up behind him and kicked him in the ass too many times.

But missing the town was nothing compared to the perpetual ache of missing the woman he'd left behind. He'd dated plenty in Atlanta, but no one had looked at him with the trusting adoration of Lilah's doe-brown eyes. She had loved him absolutely.

The balding man trying to place Tanner slapped his palm on the counter. "I remember! You were engaged to that nice Baum girl."

Tanner flinched. Technically, they'd never been engaged, although they'd talked more than once about being married someday. About the bright future they'd imagined and hoped to share. "A long time ago."

Ari inserted herself into the conversation. "You have a good day, Mr. Jebson. Next time you come in, I'll help you pick out a miniature decorative windmill for your wife. Dad, I'm gonna take Tanner back so he can say hi to David." Without waiting for any male to respond, she grabbed her brother's hand and tugged him none too gently through the double doors marked Employees Only.

On the other side was a long, narrow hallway. There was a restroom, a closet, a small break room—more of an alcove with a coffeepot and microwave, really—and, at the end of the corridor, an office with a closed door.

Tanner took a deep breath. "So, that guy…Jebson? He mentioned Lilah."

"Uh-huh."

"You rarely talk about her." Ari had come to stay with him once that first year at his apartment in Atlanta. They spoke on the phone, they exchanged e-mails, but she'd never mentioned the young woman who'd practically been a member of the family. Tanner had resisted asking, hoping that not hearing about Lilah would help him get over her—a plan that was perhaps his most spectacular failure to date.

"No, I don't talk about her. Not with *you*." Ari's tone held a surprising jolt of anger. "Do you know how long it took her to speak to me again?"

"She was mad at you?" That sounded nothing like the generous-spirited woman he'd known.

Ari shook her head, muttering about moron brothers. "She was hurt. How could she be around us without thinking about you? Until you left, she was like a sister to me."

Lilah had always said the same thing, that being with the Waide siblings made her feel less like an only child. Had he ruined that? "Arianne, I'm sorry. Truly sorry."

She gave him a level look. "Okay." It was an acknowledgement of his apology, but it was not forgiveness. Certainly not information.

Now was probably not the right time to ask if Lilah had fulfilled her certification to teach…if she lived near her aunt and uncle…if she was dating anyone.

Ari opened the office door and their brother, David, having just hung up the phone, straightened in his black leather chair. The two-sided desk was obviously shared by him and their father.

"The prodigal moron has returned," Arianne proclaimed.

Tanner shot a look over his sister's head. "I don't remember her being so much of a brat."

"Oh, she was." Grinning, David stood. "You just get in? Rachel can't wait to say hi. We'll be over for dinner tonight."

"Looking forward to seeing her, too," Tanner said, returning his brother's one-arm hug. He'd always thought David and his wife, Rachel, made a great team.

They'd make great parents, too. Tanner was surprised there'd been no announcement that they were making him an uncle. An e-mail from his brother last spring had implied they were ready to start a family. A pang of regret wrenched in his chest. Lilah had wanted kids. *His* kids.

"You okay?" David asked.

"No, I'm a moron."

"Told you so," Arianne said cheerfully.

"I've…missed Lilah. I don't expect her to miss me—I know I gave up that right. But I should apologize for the way I left. She's still here, right? Teaching at Whiteberry?"

David rubbed a hand over his jaw. "Do you want to apologize for her sake or yours?"

"Both." Tanner wished he could argue that his motivations were unselfish, but that wasn't completely true.

"Maybe she's better off not hearing from you." David's blue-green eyes were full of apology. And resolve.

Clearly, his siblings weren't going to help. But this was Mistletoe, an old-fashioned small town lying between Atlanta and the North Georgia mountains. If Lilah was here, it wouldn't take him more than a day to find her.

After all the time he'd already lost, even a day felt too long.

Chapter Two

"Should you be grading papers instead of helping me?" Vonda Kerrigan asked. The seventy-three-year-old woman was Kasey Kerrigan's mother-in-law and the reigning cribbage champion at the Mistletoe Senior Center.

Lilah laughed, carrying a white vinyl tablecloth toward where Vonda stood in the center of the rustic room. "Kasey and Jim are *paying* me to help you. I'll grade book reports this weekend." School was in session until next Wednesday, then students and teachers had two-and-a-half weeks off for winter break.

The Kerrigans had been happy to give Lilah some evening and weekend hours at the farm. There wasn't much business early on a Thursday evening, but a few people would trickle in after six and the place should be packed on Saturday. Lilah and Vonda were setting up a tabletop display of green jalapeño jelly and sweet red pepper jelly. When more customers arrived, they'd set out crackers and cream cheese so that patrons could taste a sample.

"I have some new recipes I've been itching to try," Vonda said, "but Kasey doesn't think the general public is ready for my liberal use of habañero."

"Probably not," Lilah agreed. Her tongue burned just thinking about it.

"Sissies." Vonda snorted. "That's okay, more habañero for me. Besides, who am I to look down on the visitors who keep this place going? Bart and I got married here, and eventually I came to love this farm nearly as much as I loved him, God rest his soul."

"I know what you mean." Lilah looked around the wooden interior of what had once been a barn, breathing in the scent of cinnamon and cedar, gingerbread ornaments and vanilla candles. "When Mom and Dad used to bring me to visit Mistletoe, I sensed it was special. But when I came to live here, it became an almost magical refuge. Everyone was so welcoming, I never felt like an outsider." She'd felt safe, loved.

Of course, Tanner Waide walking away after their being together for six years had been a reminder that pain still existed, even in Mistletoe, but she could hardly blame the town for that. Unlike his valedictorian older brother or adolescent sister, Tanner had always had a rougher edge, just enough of a hint of rebel to attract a good girl such as Lilah without scaring her away. She should have anticipated that he would one day rebel in earnest, deciding that small-town life and a small-town girlfriend weren't for him.

She pushed thoughts of Tanner away—the point of helping out at the farm was to find her holiday spirit. "Vonda, do we have a radio around here? Some Christmas carols would be lovely."

"They would indeed. Let me jet on over to the main house," the woman volunteered. "The radio here in the storeroom is busted. Jim keeps forgetting to fix it."

"Oh, that's—"

"It'll be my pleasure." The woman's bright red lips broke into a smile. "I love zooming around in that golf cart they got me. Be back in a flash!"

"Okay." *When I'm seventy-three, I want to have that kind of energy and zest for life.* Heck, she'd be happy to have that kind of enthusiasm *now*.

While they'd counted inventory earlier, Vonda had confessed that she was dating a "younger man" and that she was trying to decide the right time to tell her son and daughter-in-law that she'd invited the sixty-five-year-old "hunk" to Christmas dinner. Then Vonda had asked if Lilah had had any hot dates lately. *Ha.* At this point, lukewarm was a stretch. Some of the other teachers at Whiteberry had set her up with neighbors and in-laws, but only a handful of first dates had led to second dates. There had been no third dates. When you've known the person sitting across the table since junior high, there isn't a lot of discovery left.

One of the ladies at the senior center had persuaded Lilah to have dinner with her great-nephew, who lived about half an hour away. From what she could tell, the shy bank manager was convinced that making jokes was the best way to break the ice.

While complimenting her dress, he'd told her she was "da Baum," and the puns had come fast and furious after that, accompanied by his titters of nervous laughter. The only words she'd gotten in edgewise had been to the waitress, who'd sent Lilah more than one look of sympathy. He was probably a nice guy, really. He just wasn't…

The front door opened, gusting cool air through the room. The draft helped clear Lilah's head, and she glanced up with a smile. "May I— *You*."

Her first thought was that her eyes must be deceiving her. All the Waide men had similar features and eyes of varying shades of blue. So this was probably David or some cousin, and her nostalgia had led to momentary hallucination. But even after she blinked, Tanner Waide still stood in the doorway.

Tanner's back. He couldn't have been in town long. Today, maybe yesterday. Any sooner than that, someone would have told her. Warned her. Why the devil hadn't Ari called?

Unable to look away, Lilah indulged in a visual tour that left her tingly. He still wore his thick, dark gold hair a bit longer than his father would approve of, and his jaw was just as chiseled as ever. He hadn't acquired the softness some of his fellow high school athletes had developed. Although the jeans and long-sleeved Henley he wore were casual, the hunter-green waffle-knit shirt accentuated the green in his eyes and his jeans fit *really* well. He looked like Santa's gift to womankind.

She wondered what Old St. Nick's return policy was, because Tanner Waide was the absolute last thing she needed this Christmas season.

LILAH WAS SO BEAUTIFUL TANNER felt winded just looking at her. She'd been a lovely girl in college, with hair that glinted red in the sunlight, porcelain skin and a ready smile. The color of her auburn hair, worn wavy and loose, had deepened. Her face had filled out from the wide-eyed, hollow-cheeked orphan who'd first arrived in Mistletoe. All of her had filled out. She'd been on the thin side when he'd last seen her, but her curves had ripened into fulfillment of their soft promise. The long skirt she wore over boots and the coppery sweater that clung to her in a knit embrace were like the polished setting for a glowing gemstone. She was mesmerizing.

One of them should say something.

Probably preparing to do just that, she licked her lips, but the action drew his focus to her mouth. He stared, and she watched him stare, and the frozen silence stretched on between them. The air crackled with awareness and memories and the desire to touch. How had he ever walked away from this woman?

One tenant in his condo building had been big into crystals and feng shui. While that stuff had never resonated with him, if anyone had an "aura" it would be Lilah. An almost visible purity of heart that both contrasted with and complemented her earthy sensuality, the full lips and rich hair. Faces flashed in his mind of women he'd known in Atlanta. Georgette, whose beauty had been obvious but somehow brittle, the assistant who'd hinted he should feel comfortable calling her after hours if *any* need should arise. Leslie, the successful businesswoman he'd dated for over a month until he'd been uncovered as a close colleague of an embezzler. Suddenly, Leslie hadn't returned his calls.

Lilah would have. She would have stood by someone she loved. Shame flooded him.

"Wh-what are you doing here?" she asked.

Hating myself, mostly. "I wanted to see you. To talk to you."

Her russet eyebrows drew upward in a stern expression he didn't remember. He suspected it was effective in the classroom. "I don't have a lot to say to you."

He shoved his hands in his pockets, took a step forward. Was it his imagination or did she take an almost imperceptible one back? "Well, I never gave you a chance to tell me what a jerk I was. You could start with that." His goodbye had been a note because he'd known he couldn't face the tears that might have convinced him to stay. He'd worried that there would come a time he'd resent both himself and Lilah for that decision. Conversely, it had seemed selfish to ask her to leave.

For a moment, her eyes widened at his candid words, his regretful tone. Then she regained her composure, squaring her shoulders. "Don't be silly. That's ancient history, and I was raised better than to hold a grudge."

She would have been more convincing if her voice weren't tight with restrained emotion. *Thank God.* Even displeasure to see him was better than indifference. Or worse, a perky, philosophical announcement that he'd been right to go because she'd then met the man *truly* right for her. If Tanner were a better person, wouldn't he want that for her, to know things had worked out for the best and she was happier with someone else?

Experimentally, he tried to envision her kissing some faceless guy good-night and feel happy for her. He clenched his jaw so tightly his teeth ground together. *Hell, no.*

Behind him, the door he hadn't completely shut opened again. He turned automatically to find a white-haired woman wearing a quilted jacket over a bright purple sweatshirt. She had astute gray eyes, a beak of a nose and a mouth painted in a glossy red more vivid than her shirt.

"Evening, ma'am," Tanner told her.

Squinting, she sized him up, reminding him in the strangest way possible of Clint Eastwood. "You're one of Zachariah Waide's kids."

"Yes, ma'am. Tanner Waide."

She darted a glance to Lilah, then back to him, so quickly he almost missed it. "Heard you'd moved to the big city."

"I'm home for…" He'd started to say "the holidays," but he didn't want Lilah to think this had been an impulsive hello because he was in town for a week and had looked her up on a whim. "Well, for the near future. I took a leave of absence from my job." *A permanent* leave.

It had been hinted by the partners at the development company, where he'd been second-in-command to the chief financial officer, that if he quit, it would save them the trouble of getting rid of him. Though he hadn't technically been guilty of any wrongdoing, he hadn't caught all of the financial discrepancies and had been gullible enough to trust that the CFO was looking into the ones he had caught. Investors had wanted a scapegoat. Since the real criminal was probably drinking mai tais in Montego…

The woman snapped bony fingers in front of his face. "You always space out like that? I don't remember Zachariah having any slow-witted kids. I had a slow-witted nephew once, sweet boy with about the best gift with horses I've ever seen. You any good with animals?"

"Er, no." He'd veered off track. Lilah was supposed to be listening to his apology; instead, he was being interrogated about livestock.

"Huh, no job and no skills." The woman shook her head, and there was a muffled sound behind him that sounded suspiciously like Lilah trying not to laugh.

Tanner felt compelled to defend himself. "I never said I didn't have a job."

"Leave of absence? Sounded like a euphemism for *unemployment,* the way you said it." She tapped the side of her head. "I've been around seventy-three years, son. Tough to pull one over on me."

He nearly smiled. If she weren't making him look bad in front of Lilah—something he was capable of doing all on his own—he would have really liked the old firecracker. He held out his hand. "And you are?"

"Vonda Simms Kerrigan." She shook his hand crisply.

"Nice to meet you, Mrs. Kerrigan." He leaned toward her, adopting a conspiratorial tone. "But I was hoping for a few minutes alone with Lilah."

The woman beetled her eyebrows. "We won't have any hanky-panky going on in this store!"

This time, the sound effect from Lilah's direction was more choked than amused.

"Nothing like that," Tanner said. *Unfortunately.* "It's just that I…screwed up. And I owe her an apology. While I don't mind admitting that in front of other people, I have a few things I'd like to add privately."

They both turned toward Lilah, who was looking down, so Tanner couldn't read her expression.

"Well?" Vonda prompted. "You want to be left alone with this young buck or not?"

"I really don't." Lilah raised her head, her gaze containing not a single trace of the warm, worshipful affection he'd stupidly taken for granted. Now, her eyes resembled frozen chocolate chips. "Tanner, I appreciate the sentiment, but Vonda and I have work to do."

Her after-school job, so to speak. His mother had cracked after breakfast this morning, while the two of them did dishes, saying that someone in town *might* have mentioned "that nice Baum girl helping out the Kerrigans with the Christmas season rush."

"I see," Tanner said softly. His innate stubborn streak warred with the knowledge that he'd already hurt her once and should probably respect her wishes. Where was the line between persistence and stalking? Was he being an irritating old flame who didn't know when to admit the spark had died? Or been murdered, in this case. He'd snuffed it out himself.

Without another word, Lilah made her way behind the counter to the small storeroom in the back.

"So." Vonda regarded him. "Looks like you flopped."

"Looks like."

"You gonna give up on her and stay away like she asked?"

A better man would. "No, ma'am."

That maraschino-cherry mouth split into a wide grin. "Might be some hope for you after all... But I wouldn't bet on it just yet."

Chapter Three

The phone was ringing when Lilah unlocked the door to the one-bedroom home that was her half of a brick duplex; second-grade teacher Quinn Keller lived in the adjoining half. They each had their own entrance and driveway but shared a common front and backyard. They'd hung decorations outside together over the weekend, but that had only temporarily lifted Lilah's spirits.... She hadn't been able to shake the dread plaguing her like a Dickensian Christmas ghost. And now she knew why— Tanner Waide was back.

Then again, if she'd been feeling uneasy because she'd sensed his impending return on some heretofore undiscovered psychic level, would she have really felt so stunned seeing him earlier? It had been like the paralyzing, breath-stealing, icy shock of falling into a frigid pond. She froze in the act of picking up the cordless phone that hung in her shoebox-size kitchen. He couldn't possibly be calling her, could he?

"H-hello?"

"Lilah?" The hesitant female voice on the other end belonged to a Waide all right, but not the one she'd feared. "It's Ari."

For a second, Lilah said nothing. When she spoke her tone held more resignation than rancor. "If you're calling to let me know he's here, you're a little late." Though Lilah had assured people after Tanner's defection that she would be fine and that their parting ways sooner rather than later was for the best, her aunt Shelby and Arianne Waide would know how much it had shaken Lilah to see him today.

"I'm sorry. I didn't know what to do! My policy is to try to steer clear of anything between the two of you and stay neutral, like the Swedes."

"That would be the Swiss."

"Them, too."

Lilah sighed. "I know he's your brother, and you don't have to feel awkward. There *isn't* anything between me and Tanner, hasn't been in a long time."

Ari sighed, too, but Lilah couldn't tell whether it was an exhalation of relief or regret. The two women used to giggle about how great it would be to become sisters-in-law. Ari had grumbled about her brothers outnumbering her and needing another female around. *Well, now she has Rachel.*

"David and I tried to tell him to leave you alone," Ari said. "For whatever it's worth, I didn't give him your phone number or anything to help find you."

Lilah laughed in spite of herself. "This is Mistletoe. You hardly need a private detective in order to track someone down."

"He said he wanted to apologize for the way he left."

"Yeah, that's what he told me, too." Of course, the sentiment might have been a touch more meaningful 1,840 days ago…give or take. "Ari, if it comes up again, you can tell him it's all water under the bridge and to let it go."

"I'll tell him," Ari said, sounding skeptical that the relayed message would keep Tanner from determining his own course. "But you know my brother."

I thought I did, once. They said their goodbyes and hung up.

Despite the years that had passed, Lilah recalled vividly the day she'd found his note. She'd known Tanner was unhappy, restless— he and his father had been butting heads since Tanner's adolescence, and it had only worsened when Tanner returned from college with innovative ideas for growing the family business. But she'd never dreamed, even in her nightmares, that he was capable of abandoning her without a backward glance.

When her parents had been taken away from her in a small plane crash, it had been the worst day of her life. But she'd known in her heart they never would have voluntarily abandoned her. Reading Tanner's words had produced a different but equally unbearable pain. He'd had a *choice!* And he'd made it for both of them, without consulting her. Though she'd never admit it to anyone, even Shel, she remembered, verbatim, the handful of words that had ripped her world apart for the second time.

Lilah, I know this note is the coward's way out, but I also know that if I tried to tell you in person, I wouldn't be able to walk away. As much as I love you, I can't stay in Mistletoe. I'll always be Zachariah Waide's son, David Waide's little brother. I'll never figure out who I am. But this town means so much to you. I can't ask you to leave, to give up your plans for the future and what little family you have left. This way is best for both of us. I hope one day you'll forgive me, but mostly, I hope you have the wonderful life you deserve. Tanner

Just his name. No Love, Tanner or Yours, Tanner. Not even a hollow promise that he'd always remember her and what they shared.

A light knock sounded at the front door, jarring Lilah back to the present. It was soft, but carried effectively in the silence.

When she opened the door, she found Quinn, a woman who'd been named in honor of her mother's family and blessed with the angelic features that ran on her father's side.

"You're not headed to bed anytime soon, are you?" Quinn asked. It wasn't uncommon for the two friends to have late-night snacks together or to join each other to watch rented DVDs. "*A Christmas Story* is coming on in five minutes, and it's funnier with someone else."

"Come on in. A movie and some caramel-covered popcorn sound great." One of her students had brought her a large tin of the sweet, salty snack. Presents trickled in during the weeks between Thanksgiving and Christmas break, mostly of the edible variety, and she'd be lucky not to gain fifteen pounds by the new year.

Quinn laughed. "Would that be caramel-covered corn from Aisha Lewis? I have her little brother in my class and got a tin today, too."

"I keep hoping I'll get one of the Oster kids some year. I hear their mother's homemade fudge is to die for."

Ten minutes later, they'd found the right television station, popped off the top of the decorative popcorn tin and poured apple cider. But Lilah's genuine enjoyment of Quinn's company and the quirky movie couldn't keep her mind from wandering back to Tanner's unexpected visit at the farm. Thank God Vonda had been there to run interference. Lilah had faked composure for a few moments, but she didn't know what would happen if she were alone with him for long.

And she had no intention of finding out.

TANNER OPENED HIS CAR DOOR, and a voice immediately called out in the dark, "Hey, little brother."

As he walked up his parents' driveway, Tanner squinted, the white icicle lights hanging from the roof providing just enough illumination for him to see David on the top porch step. "What are you doing sitting out in the cold?"

"Came by earlier to see if you wanted to shoot some pool at On Tap, and Mom said you weren't here. Then she and Dad left for this couples' book club she made him join."

Made him? Susan Waide had always been more of a stand-by-your-man kind of wife, who rarely voiced a dissenting opinion and looked pained whenever Tanner did. "You could have waited inside, where there's heat and a television." Despite his own words of wisdom, Tanner sat on the cold stairs next to his brother. He glanced upward, marveling at the thousands of stars in the clear sky. When he was younger, he'd taken this kind of night sky for granted, but five years in the city had cured him of that. *I took way too much for granted.*

He turned toward his older brother. "I saw Lilah."

"Figured as much."

"God, she looks…"

"Yeah."

She was more beautiful now than she had been before…. She was also more guarded. "I've really screwed up." It was the kind of thing he wouldn't have been able to admit before, but he was realizing now that there were things in life more important than pride.

"No argument here."

With a shove at David's arm, Tanner demanded, "Are you just going to sit there agreeing with everything I say, or do you have some brotherly advice?"

There was more surprise than sarcasm in David's expression. "As I recall, you never took advice well."

True. Their father hadn't tolerated anyone's viewpoint but his own, and David had come across as the know-it-all sibling, quick to correct baby brother. Tanner had been so eager to prove himself. He'd been benched during a major football game in high school because he'd changed a play his coach had called. Even though his family was well-liked and he personally had been fairly popular, there had been days when he'd felt as if the only person who believed in him *unconditionally,* who saw his true potential, was Lilah Baum.

"I thought I knew everything. Turns out, I'm an idiot."

David regarded him with wry affection. "That could be said about most guys in their teens and early twenties."

"As I recall," Tanner mimicked, "you had your act together even then. A fact that Dad never refrained from pointing out. 'If you worked harder, you could make varsity *and* honor roll, like Dave.'"

"Dad wanted what was best for you and pushed because he cared. But he should have left me out of it. He was wrong to compare us."

Tanner huffed out a breath. He'd let angry resentment shape his actions for too long. He'd barely even recognized his own sister because she'd grown up so much in between the times they'd seen each other! If David and Rachel had a baby, did he want to be the bitter absentee uncle who never came to Thanksgiving dinners? Feeling smothered and unappreciated in his early twenties, he'd tried to run from his problems. Yet he'd only created different ones.

"We should go inside," David said. "My butt's numb."

"Or we could head into town and wager on that pool game you mentioned. If I win, you have to spill your secrets on a successful love life." David had snagged a gorgeous woman with a formerly high-powered career and somehow convinced her that she wanted to spend her life with him in Mistletoe.

David's laugh was abrupt. "I don't think I'm the one to give you advice on romance."

"Why? What's wrong? You and Rachel didn't have a fight, did you?" At dinner the other night, the two of them had seemed as happy as newlyweds, all smiles and stealing secretive glances at each other as though they couldn't wait to be alone.

"It's complicated." For a minute, it was easy to picture him as the eleven-year-old who'd once condescended to his younger brother—*You wouldn't understand.* "Speaking of complications, you want to tell me what's really going on with your job situation? We're all thrilled to have you home for the holidays, but…"

Tanner stood. "I'll give you the candid rundown, but we definitely have to go to the bar." There was only one in town—On Tap. Everyone over legal drinking age went there. You were just as likely to find yourself sitting next to the school district superintendent's wife chatting with one of her matronly friends as you were scandal-plagued loner Gabe Sloan.

David nodded. "Fine by me. I'll drive."

Good. For Tanner to admit how he'd found a substitute father figure who believed in him wholeheartedly, who encouraged his individualism and helped him climb the ladder of success, only to push him into a free fall from one of the top rungs…well, that conversation was going to require significant quantities of beer.

"CUTE BLONDE CHECKING YOU OUT, three o'clock," David muttered.

Tanner took a swallow from the bottle he held and glanced down the length of the teak bar. There was indeed an attractive blonde sitting with an equally pretty brunette.

"She can't be much older than Ari," Tanner protested. He'd also noticed that the brunette was sending appreciative vibes in David's direction—she was too far away to notice the slim gold wedding band.

"Do you really think she's too young for you to talk to, or is it just that you prefer redheads?"

Redhead. Singular. He preferred the woman who had paradoxically seemed an old soul, probably the result of losing her parents so young, yet had worn her heart on her sleeve and looked forward to events with a wide-eyed, almost childlike enthusiasm.

Tanner fidgeted on his bar stool. "Looks like one of the pool tables just opened up." There were three in a recessed pit to the left of the bar.

"You're changing the subject." Nonetheless, David slid off his stool.

"Hey, I already shared the embarrassing tale of how I came to be unemployed. Let's save some wounds to poke for another night."

David paused. "Believing in people is an admirable quality, Tanner. That man's betraying you was his flaw, not yours. You have no cause for embarrassment."

Tanner ducked his head, his big brother's absolution carrying more weight than he would have expected.

But then David followed up with, "Now, the way you handled things with that nice Baum girl…*that* you can be ashamed of. It was shabby."

"Dammit, don't you think I know that?" He'd known it when he wrote her that note, but he'd pushed his conscience aside, telling himself he and Lilah had separate destinies. She'd always praised Mistletoe as the home of her heart, her sanctuary; to him, however, the town had become a cloying pen of limited opportunities.

Ironically, the more he'd succeeded over the years, the more she'd haunted him. He'd impress one of his supervisors and want to tell her about it. He'd get a great bonus and think of the cute necklace he could surprise her with—Lilah had loved surprises. Dating had become a process of elimination for him, each girl who wasn't quite right bringing him closer to a truth he'd resisted.

He followed his brother down the two steps that led to the pool area. Four men were playing a team game at the first table, and a guy who barely looked old enough to be in a bar was teaching his date to shoot pool at the far end. Tanner and David took the middle table.

Tanner pulled one of the cues off the wall, going through the motions of evaluating it even though he could have been holding a tree limb for all he noticed. "Do you think five years is too late to try to win her back?"

"Yes." David racked up the balls.

"That's it? Just yes? What about second chances and perseverance?"

"Are you going to break, or not?" Once it was his turn, David called a side pocket and said as he leaned over, "Real perseverance is following your heart whether other people tell you it's impossible or not. 'Course, if Lilah's over you, perseverance could seem a lot like stalking."

Was she over him? "Does she have a boyfriend? Any serious relationships in the last five years?"

"Ask Ari." David knocked in his yellow, but miscalculated a bank shot and didn't sink the blue. "She'd know more than me."

"Ari is stonewalling me."

David grinned. "Female solidarity."

"You wouldn't find it so amusing if the women were united against *you*."

"I go out of my way not to tick them off. Do I look stupid to you?"

"Thanks," Tanner said as he not only missed the ball he was aiming for but sent the cue ball sailing into a corner pocket.

"Scratch," his brother said cheerfully.

Tanner stepped aside, scowling. Tomorrow, he needed to casually question some of the town's citizens and find out more about Lilah's life. If she'd truly moved on and was happy without him, he wouldn't press the issue. He wasn't such a bastard that he would mess with her happiness twice in one lifetime. But the vulnerability she'd so carefully tried to disguise when he saw her spoke of unfinished emotional business. Even if she never trusted him with her heart again, he had to at least try to apologize and make sure she understood that his leaving was no reflection on her.

Although it was a skewed comparison, discovering that Royce MacKenzie, the man he'd affectionately called Mac, had used Tanner as a patsy had given Tanner clearer insight into the way Lilah might have felt. Not merely angry—which was well within her right—but perhaps self-doubting, wondering if she should have seen signs of Tanner's leaving, wondering if she could have done anything to stop it.

On his next turn, Tanner managed to avoid pocketing the white ball. Instead, he landed the eight ball.

"Game over." David shook his head. "Man, you don't even *need* an opponent. You're your own worst enemy."

Tell me about it.

Chapter Four

Since Tanner hadn't actually imbibed much in the way of beer the night before, he was spared the hangover that would have made his head pulse with pain when his mother rapped at the bedroom door. "Tanner? There's someone to see you."

Opening one eye, he peered at the ancient radio alarm clock. Barely seven in the morning, an unusual time for visitors.

He pulled on jeans and, on the slim hope Lilah had changed her mind about never wanting to speak to him again, tucked in a dark blue T-shirt. She'd always loved him in blue. Unfortunately, short of a shower, there was little he could do about sleeping on his hair. Maybe the advantage of a shorter, more "respectable" cut (as his father put it) was that there was less to stand straight up on one side. Still, he refused to waste time on grooming. If it *was* Lilah waiting, an extra minute could be all she needed to change her mind about seeing him.

He skidded in sock feet down the hardwood floors of the hallway and around the corner to the kitchen. His mother, sipping coffee at the kitchen table, pointed wordlessly toward the living room, giving him no hints as to who sat on the other side of the wall. Shelby Tierney, as it turned out.

At the sight of Lilah's aunt perched on the ivory sofa, he drew up short. A barrage of memories assailed him. Shelby making him a batch of snickerdoodles for luck before a homecoming game; Shelby waiting on the front porch the first and last time he'd brought Lilah home past curfew; Shelby studying him over Thanksgiving dinner when he'd come home his freshman year of college, as if she had somehow *known* he'd taken her niece's virginity the night before; Shelby looking sympathetic the day she'd come into Waide Supply for some gardening tools and had found Zachariah lecturing Tanner on the money he was investing ("wasting") to refurbish a dilapidated Mustang.

"Hello, Tanner."

"M-Mrs. Tierney."

The twist of her lips was a parody of the smile he remembered. "I believe at one time you called me Aunt Shel." A habit he'd picked up from Lilah when he'd discovered for himself how welcoming the Tierneys could be.

"Well, that was before I broke your niece's heart," he said.

"Quite right." She stood then, bringing them marginally closer to eye level. "I hear you've already been to chat with her."

"Lilah told you?"

"No." Shelby's tone was bemused, reflecting surprise that Lilah *hadn't* been the one to mention it. The two of them were close. "But I'm sure you know news travels fast. It's hard to keep secrets in a small town, or to have private pain without every third person asking how you are."

He and Lilah had been together for six years. And he'd left her to deal with well-meaning condolences and less well-intentioned gossipmongers when he had slunk out of town. "I made bad mistakes. I'd like to try to atone for them."

Shelby pursed her lips. At last, she said noncommittally, "Well, that's not up to me. Now, if you'll excuse me, I have to get to work."

He opened the front door for her. "Do I have your unspoken approval, or are you going to recommend to Lilah that she'd be better off never talking to me again?"

"Neither. But I'll tell you this much." Shelby's eyes narrowed in a gaze so piercing he was tempted to check his chest for small, bloody wounds. "You ever hurt her like that again, you'd better go a lot farther away than Atlanta. This time, I won't bother talking Ray out of running you down."

"Yes, ma'am." He swallowed. Though she might be a five-foot-two bit of nothing who often smelled like cookies, she was a Southern lady from the same hearty stock as Vonda Kerrigan and as women who centuries ago had held plantations while their men were off fighting.

Tanner would just as soon take his chances with a cranky mountain lion as a Southern woman protecting her family.

BY EARLY AFTERNOON, TANNER WAS thinking that the shower he'd taken before lunch had been a waste of soap and water. Lugging boxes down from the attic at his mother's request had left him grimy. She, however, looked fresh as a daisy, digging through tissue paper and bubble wrap in the family room. How had she unpacked a half-dozen heirlooms without getting even a speck of dust on her white sweater set? It was unnatural.

"It's so nice to have you here to help with this!" Susan chirped. "I've been wanting to tackle this project for months, but your brother and father are always so busy with the store. I know you had ideas to expand the business, but they already have more than enough work to stay occupied."

"So he always said." Tanner, exasperated by his dad's "dinosaurlike" resistance to the Internet age, had insisted the store could benefit from a Web site, shipping some of their smaller items as unique, homey gifts to people who lived in less rural areas. Zachariah had thought that sounded like a lot of extra labor for a negligible profit and that they should continue to focus on the local townspeople who had supported Waide Supply for two generations.

Susan's cornflower-blue eyes dimmed. "Though I suppose if your dad had been willing to entertain any of those ideas, you would have stuck around to help."

He hadn't intended his leaving to be a temper tantrum, the adult version of "*if you won't play the game my way, I'll take my ball and go.*" "I just needed space, Mama."

"I know." Her smile was both understanding and sorrowful. "You were always the child most like him, which wasn't easy. For either of you."

Like his father? Tanner had considered them opposites in nearly every way.

He turned his thoughts over as he made another trek up the folding stairs and carried down a heavy cardboard box labeled "Turkey" in unfamiliar handwriting. His great aunt's, he surmised. When his mother's parents had gone to a sunny retirement community in Florida, they'd not only given a number of their possessions to Zachariah and Susan but had passed along boxes of things that had belonged to Susan's aunt Midge. Susan, hoping to unclutter the attic, wanted to see if there were any hidden treasures that would either be useful in Ari's new apartment over the Malcolms' garage or that could be donated as antiques to the town's annual charity bazaar.

He took the box to his mother for inspection. "Any idea what *turkey* means? The farther I go into the back of the attic, the less painstakingly the boxes are marked." He'd known exactly which boxes his mother had packed—Susan had often helped with store inventory, and her descriptions tended to be thorough. His grandmother's had been less specific but still understandable, with labels such as Kitchen Stuff. But Great-Aunt Midge had favored oblique, one-word references.

Although, as it turned out, *Turkey* was a dead-on description of the first thing his mother removed from the box. He sat at the hearth drinking ice water and watching.

"Holiday decorations," Susan said, staring at what had to be the world's ugliest turkey centerpiece. It looked fragile and home-made—maybe papier-mâché. Then she pulled out much cuter, albeit chipped, pilgrim salt-and-pepper shakers that he vaguely remembered from childhood, and smiled at something else down in the tissue. "Ooh, these are pretty. I bet they brought them back after Uncle Henry was stationed in Germany."

He admired the colorful glass ornaments, then went to retrieve more boxes. By the time he returned, his mother had begun sorting Christmas stuff into four piles—the pieces she wanted to keep, those she planned to offer Ari, the few damaged items she was throwing out and some that she wanted to give to the senior center.

"They might want them either for the lobby or to use at the Winter Wonderland dance." The dance, which worked as a fund-raiser for the senior center, was as much a part of Mistletoe tradition as the tree lighting in the town square. "Would you be willing to run this stuff over to the center for me?"

"Sure." Looking at the ornaments she'd set aside, Tanner thought of another errand. "You and Dad don't have a tree yet."

"No. We all went over to decorate David and Rachel's on Thanksgiving weekend, and Ari has some funny little fiber-optic tree that she plugs in, but your father and I just haven't... It's different now that it's just us left in the house."

"How about I take care of the tree?" he volunteered. "I'll find one and be responsible for putting everything away after Christmas."

She beamed, looking thrilled to share this holiday ritual with him after several years of his not even coming home. "That sounds lovely." It apparently didn't bother her that he had blatant, ulterior motives.

He knew exactly where to look for the perfect tree.

WHOEVER COINED THE PHRASE "Thank God, it's Friday" had probably been a teacher. Even the most studious among Lilah's class had been hyperactive by the time the bell had rung at the end of the day. With only three days of the semester left after this weekend, the kids had holiday fever and were atwitter with talk of plans for Christmas shopping, baking and ski trips to North Carolina. She suspected she'd see more than one student at Kerrigan Farms, enjoying the light display that would start this weekend or the visits with Santa Claus that would begin soon.

Speaking of the farm… She glanced at the clock in her car's dashboard to make sure she had enough time to get to the senior center, then home for a change of clothes and early dinner before she was due at the farm. She had some receipts she wanted to take to Mindy, as well as edible goodies from her growing stash that she planned to drop off for residents.

Once she'd reached the center, Lilah parked in a visitor space. She grabbed her purse and a manila folder full of information on the Winter Wonderland dance. At the moment, Lilah and Mindy were a committee of two. Gina Van Hoff, who had helped organize the dance and sell tickets for the past two years, was recovering from a double knee replacement, and noted town philanthropist and perpetual volunteer Stanley Dean was overseas with a church group doing mission work in the Czech Republic.

The lobby of the senior center—which doubled as a recreation area with a big-screen television, vending machines, Ping-Pong table and several donated dinette sets, where people could play cards and board games—was surprisingly empty. Lilah nodded to Judith Clusker, who worked the front desk.

"Where is everyone, Mrs. C?"

"Up on the third floor. There's a bingo tournament going on in the cafeteria." Judith smiled. "But you'll probably run into Dana Mae. She claims she's taking her exercise by going up and down the hallway with her walker, but I think she's just trying to get a better look at the hunk with Mindy."

Hunk? Mindy was the widowed mother of two high schoolers and possibly the only single woman in town who dated less than Lilah. Good for her, if she'd met someone to help break up the loneliness of the holiday season! There were some gaps in life that couldn't be filled by the adopted family of senior citizen residents.

Filled with friendly curiosity, Lilah peered around the corner and into the doorway of Mindy's office. Her mouth dropped open. *What is* he *doing here?* It was like one of those diabolical looping nightmares, where you think you've woken up but you're actually just dreaming that you're awake in bed and the nightmare keeps rolling on. Except that Tanner's broad shoulders and well-muscled legs—*Lilah Anne Baum, don't you dare look at his butt*—were more like something from an erotic fantasy than a bad dream. She jerked her gaze up to the back of his head, safer territory, and noticed that the burnished copper hair curling against his collar looked damp. Had he just showered?

She thought of the tiny apartment he'd had his senior year of college. Theoretically, there'd been a roommate, but said roomie had spent all *his* time at his girlfriend's, so Lilah and Tanner had enjoyed a lot of privacy. She remembered Tanner in the shower with her, helping her wash out temporary hair dye after a Halloween party. Bathing with someone was an intimacy she'd never shared with another man.

"Oh, Lilah. Perfect timing!" Since Mindy had spotted her, it was probably too late to flee. "I was just telling this nice young man that you're the person to talk to about the dance." Because of the age difference between the two women and the fact that Mindy had been coping with her own husband's death right around the time the town was buzzing with news of Tanner's departure, it was clear she didn't know Lilah and Tanner's history.

"Hi, Lilah." Tanner's dark velvet voice rasped against her overwrought nerves like sandpaper. Darn it, he'd relinquished his claim on Mistletoe—this was *her* town, and it wasn't fair that he was every place she turned around.

Something like a snarl sounded in her throat, and she tried to disguise it as a cough.

"Lilah?" Mindy looked worried. The Winter Wonderland coordinator needed to be a people person; feral noises were not going to help raise money for the center—unless Lilah scared people into donating. That was an approach they hadn't tried.

"I'm fine, just a…tickle at the back of my throat. Nice to see you again, Tanner." *Wow*. She was probably one lie short of lightning striking the center.

"Nice to be seen." The surprise that had been in his gaze when he first swung his head around had mellowed into something more flirtatious, something that magically erased the years between them and once again made him a self-confident high school senior offering to carry her lunch tray.

"Tanner came in with some decorations he thought we could use for the dance," Mindy interjected. "I was explaining that your committee's short-handed—"

"We're not short-handed!" *Oh, crap*. There she went with the lies again. How had she never realized in the six years they'd been together that Tanner brought out latent dishonesty in her?

Tanner blinked at her denial, then his mouth curved into a lazy, knowing grin. "Is that so? And here I was about to volunteer."

"Fantastic!" Mindy was pushing forms toward him before Lilah had a chance to groan.

He didn't take his eyes off Lilah. "This won't be a problem, will it?" His tone was more sincere than challenging, as though he was giving her an honest chance to object and would honor her choice if she wanted him to walk away.

But she hesitated a moment too long, and Mindy asked, "Is there something I should be aware of?"

"No," Lilah said brightly, unable to admit how much sway this man still had over her emotions. "We appreciate your helping out, Tanner. I was merely thinking of your family. You've come home so seldom that I didn't want to cut into your time with them before you leave. Again."

"No need to worry about that. I'm here for the indefinite

future. Things didn't work out in Atlanta." His words were carefully chosen, purposely vague. Had something happened to cause him pain?

The old Lilah, the one who used to fall asleep at night mentally reciting *Mrs. Lilah Waide,* the one who'd had her first orgasm at Tanner's hands, the one who'd cheered him on at every football game and winced every time his father wounded his feelings, wanted to comfort him. She actually caught herself with one hand raising toward him, then checked the motion. While she didn't actively wish him harm, whatever had injured his heart or ego was none of her business.

"That's a shame," she said neutrally. Then she switched her attention to Mindy. "I have to go because I'm helping the Kerrigans tonight, but I wanted to drop off some stuff for you." Blindly, she thrust the folder onto Mindy's desk. Then she told both Tanner and Mindy that she'd be in touch when she had more time and spun around to leave.

He caught up to her just as she was reaching for the lobby door. Why couldn't he have changed his cologne after five years? The familiar scent was bringing back far too many memories and sensations. "You probably think I'm following you around town, but I didn't come here looking for you, Li."

"It's Li*lah*. And it doesn't matter why you're here."

He continued, infuriatingly, as though she hadn't spoken. "My mom asked me to do her a favor. I was trying to help."

"Yes, I saw how very *helpful* you are when you volunteered to be on the dance committee." She was giving too much of herself away by letting him see her anger, but she couldn't help it. A girl could only repress her emotions for so long.

He rocked back on his heels, having the gall to smile at her. "Okay, that part might have had something to do with spending time with you. But how can I show you I've changed if I'm nowhere near you?"

"I don't care whether or not you've changed!" Realizing she sounded bitterly unhinged, she tried to lower her voice. "You made it clear that I should get on with my life and let you go your separate way. Join the committee, don't join the committee. It no longer matters to me."

"Oh God, Li." His normally smooth voice was harsh with apology and self-recrimination, and he lifted his hand almost to her cheek, then stopped in unconscious parody of her own actions back in Mindy's office. "I was a selfish bastard, but I never meant to hurt you so badly. I was trying to spare you making a decision you'd regret. I couldn't bear to think that you'd leave with me, only to be mis—"

"Yeah. I got the note." She wanted to hate him for that, but the naked pain in his eyes made it difficult. Looking away was difficult but crucial to preserving her sanity. "Forget about it. That was five years ago, Tanner. Everyone does things they regret."

"What about you?" he asked. "I can't imagine you doing anything stupid or petty that would haunt you. Do you have regrets?"

Falling in love with you. Those six years with him, of reveling in his strength and wicked smiles and the way he made her feel cherished, had been some of the high points of her life. Would she have sacrificed them if she'd known how it would turn out? Honestly, Lilah didn't know. "I have to go."

He nodded. "It's a small town, though. We're probably going to bump into each other."

He was right about that. Mistletoe had pretty much one of everything—one main grocery store, one library, one movie theater, one nice hotel. A disproportionate number of restaurants, though, now that she thought about it. People in Mistletoe really liked to eat.

She shrugged. "Then I'll see you soon."

"Soon," he repeated, his gaze making it a declaration of intent.

Chapter Five

"You have *got* to be kidding me!" Lilah's words were quite audible over a jazzy carol being crooned in the background by Harry Connick, Jr.

Tanner faltered in the doorway, stepping aside to make room for a departing customer, but he paused only a second before conjuring a purposeful smile. Despite the temper his once-gentle former lover had acquired, earlier today he'd seen the old Lilah, the one who wore her emotions for all to see. And he'd been forced to confront the damage he'd done. Now, he was a man on a mission. He had to make this right, as much as that was possible five years after the fact.

Still, the way she was glaring at him from behind the counter made it clear his would not be an easy quest. Slaying a dragon with his bare hands might have been simpler.

Petite Kasey Kerrigan, whose Sunday-school class he'd once attended, had jerked her head up at Lilah's dubious greeting, but when she turned from the box of fragile figurines she'd been unpacking and saw Tanner, her expression hardened. Hmm. Not many allies in the gift-shop-cum-diner tonight. Vonda was seated at one of the three small tables, her eyes laughing as she blew on a spoonful of warm soup. He'd asked Ari to come with him as backup, but her response—"Oh, hell, no!"—hadn't been encouraging.

Deeming it a tactical error to appear weak, he sauntered toward Lilah. "I'm sure what you meant to say was, 'How may I help you?'"

"You don't need my help," she retorted. "You need a good therapist. And what I *really* meant to say is a word I respect Vonda too much to use in her presence."

"Don't mind me," Vonda called, cheerfully eavesdropping. "My Bart was a Navy man and taught me to swear in four languages!"

"Mother Kerrigan, please." Kasey didn't sound appalled so much as resigned.

Personally, he found the woman's multilingual cussing abilities endearing and would have winked at her if his instincts weren't warning him that it would be bad to turn his back on Lilah. "I'm here strictly as a paying customer," he said, his eyes all innocence.

"That look didn't work on me when Tommy Blaine tried to convince me his gerbil ate his spelling homework, and it's *certainly* not going to work on me now." Lilah propped her elbows on the counter and leaned forward, letting her gaze run over him in an obviously unimpressed perusal. "You're nowhere near as cute as Tommy Blaine."

He almost laughed, enjoying her spirit. "I told my parents that I'd find them a Christmas tree this year. Not just any tree, the perfect tree. If I don't find one tonight, I may have to come back." He lowered his voice so that Vonda and Kasey couldn't hear. "It's always been my philosophy to keep trying until I get the job done right, remember?"

Lilah blushed straight past pink and cranberry and right into scarlet, then jerked back from the counter. "You may have noticed that we keep the Christmas trees *outside,* Einstein. So just haul yourself back out the door, and I'm sure Jim will be happy to assist you."

Behind them, Vonda hissed at her daughter-in-law. "What did he say? Did you catch what he said? That girl looks the way I used to when I was having a hot flash." Kasey shushed her, and Vonda harrumphed.

Tanner turned and faced the septuagenarian. "I was just explaining to Lilah how important it is that I do this right. This is my first Christmas home in a long time. I stayed away even after I wanted to come back, because it was… When you walk out on people you love the way I did, you're not even sure they'll want you home. I know now it hurt my mother that I missed so many holidays, and now I want to find her the perfect Christmas tree. It won't undo anything or change the pain I caused her, but I have to start somewhere."

Vonda studied him with those crinkled eyes that missed nothing and then nodded sharply.

Behind him, Lilah was less moved. "You're not exactly subtle, Waide," she accused in a whisper.

He risked a grin over his shoulder. "I have many charms. Subtlety isn't one of them."

BY THE CONCLUSION OF THE weekend, big-hearted Lilah Baum, town good girl and fourth-grade teacher, was considering murder. Whenever she wasn't working the register, she was casting her gaze about the gift shop for *Sopranos*-style inspiration. She was a bright, creative woman. There had to be a way to make Tanner's demise look like an accident.

It was Sunday, the third consecutive day he'd been at Kerrigan Farms, ostensibly looking for his "perfect" tree.

"I've known people who were less picky about who they married," she'd snapped yesterday evening when he hadn't settled on one.

He'd sent her a look so intense that the tiny resin snowman statuettes on the shelf behind her had started melting. "Yes, but I'm on a quest. I don't take it lightly."

Yesterday had been so crowded with customers that she should have barely noticed him—he did spend a fair amount of time out on the grounds—but it was as if she could only breathe his understated but extremely masculine cologne whenever he was in the renovated barn. Somehow Tanner drowned out the scents of pine, hot chocolate and vanilla candles. Just as his laugh at some observation Vonda made had drowned out all the other voices. Each of Lilah's five senses were perfectly attuned to him: sight, sound, hearing. She wished she could tell herself that she remembered nothing about taste or touch, but that wasn't true. And the more he was around, even on the periphery, the more she found herself thinking about exactly those things.

Maybe her feelings of barely contained violence stemmed from sexual frustration.

After all, she hadn't made love in two years. Months after Tanner had left, a girlfriend had invited Lilah on a roadtrip to Biloxi, where they'd planned to have a wild weekend at the casinos. Motivated by three strawberry daiquiris and a misguided need to replace the memory of Tanner's loving her, she'd engaged in her only one-night stand. She'd thrown up afterward, hated herself for weeks and hadn't touched a strawberry daiquiri since. Later, she'd been friends with a man she regularly joined for dinner or a movie. They made sense as a couple—they laughed at the same jokes, his family liked her—and she'd tried to convince herself that she could fall for him. After months of nothing more than kisses, she'd invited him to stay the night. In the morning, it had been clear they were intended to be platonic friends and nothing more. Which they'd remained up until the time he'd moved to West Virginia.

Annoyingly, Tanner's repeated visits seemed to be good for business. On Friday, he'd bought a chili-making kit and one of Kasey's homemade angel chimes and given shy Chloe Malcolm, who'd graduated in the top ten of Lilah's high school class, heart palpitations by winking at her. On Saturday, as he'd been purchasing stocking stuffers for people in his family, Lilah had sniped at him more loudly than she'd intended and several people nearby had looked on with interest. One woman had laughed outright and reached immediately for her cell phone. Come Sunday, at least a dozen people seemed to be loitering aimlessly and waiting for Tanner to make an appearance. Vonda sold them cups of spiced cider in the meantime. The worst part was that Lilah caught *herself* waiting for him, glancing up expectantly, her breath hitching every time a swirl of cold air came in, signaling that the door had been opened.

He'd arrived earlier that afternoon, but after making a point to greet Lilah and tell her how nice she looked today, he'd gone out to find his tree. With any luck, a fellow customer chopping down a pine would forget to yell "timber" and one would fall on Tanner's head.

Behind the counter with her, Vonda handed a customer change, then glanced at Lilah. "I think you've earned a break. You look…flushed."

"Well, we've been busy. Especially with repeat customers, I've noticed." She couldn't keep the sardonic note out of her voice.

Vonda merely laughed.

Lilah turned a wry eye on her much older friend. "You've been encouraging him."

"Well, he is helping us turn a profit. I haven't seen this many people coming and going since the year the Rubik's Cube came out and we were selling them as novelty items. Who knew those little suckers would catch on so fast?" She smiled fondly. "My Bart never could get his to work out right. He'd get two or three sides the same color, but then…"

Despite the fact that Vonda had a more active social calendar than Lilah herself, it was also clear that Vonda still missed the love of her life. He'd passed away decades ago, but Lilah supposed that some things you never got over entirely.

Impulsively, she kissed the woman's pale cheek. "I think I will take that break and get off my feet for a few minutes. But if you get slammed, I'll—"

The door opened, and several people in the crowd called out greetings, including, "Hey, Tanner, how's that tree hunt going?" The man who asked had such a smirk in his tone it was clear no one believed a *tree* was what Tanner hunted. Amid hellos, Tanner headed toward the counter, people obligingly making way for him and falling noticeably quieter as they listened to what he said.

He nodded to Lilah and Vonda. "Ladies."

"You become any more of a fixture around here," Vonda said, "we might have to charge you rent."

"It's possible you'll be seeing less of me." He leaned casually on the counter. "I think I've found the tree. She's slender and just the right height, but has a personality that keeps her from blending into all the other rows of trees. I can easily envision her at home, part of the family."

"Great. We're very happy you found the tree of your dreams." Lilah didn't even bother trying to cover her relief.

He turned toward her. "I might just take tonight to think it over."

"Don't strain yourself," she muttered. Then she squared her shoulders, deciding to meet his blatant metaphor head-on. "Aren't you worried that someone else will buy this tree? You can't just walk away and expect it to be waiting there for you when you decide to come back."

"Very true," he said softly. "I guess I'll go get the purchasing slip from Jim. And I need a few other holiday items." He didn't elaborate, but he was staring so hard to Lilah's left that she couldn't help but turn.

Sprigs of the town's namesake were for sale, wrapped in lush red ribbon.

She grabbed one of them and shoved it gracelessly in his direction. "Here."

A private smile played around the corners of his lips, as though they were the only two people in the room. "Maybe I should test it out first? Make sure it works." Another pointed glance, this one to the framed cross-stitch behind the counter that proclaimed The Customer Is Always Right.

Ha. The Customer, in this case, was the devil. She untied the silver-smeared apron she'd put on earlier that day when helping some of the farm's younger visitors spray-paint wooden snowflakes. "As it happens," she said sweetly, " I'm on break. But I'm sure Vonda would be happy to help you."

There were a few muffled guffaws from behind Tanner, but he ignored them. Instead, he gamely held the sprig over his head and leaned over the counter.

Vonda raised up on her tiptoes, then paused, her voice carrying through the crowd as sharply as the whipcrack sound effect in "Sleigh Ride." "Son, I'm afraid I might be too much for you and inadvertently ruin you for all other women."

He laughed, and choruses of "Oo-ooh" "Re-*ject*-ed!" came from the crowd. Both Tanner and Vonda glanced toward Lilah, who'd been trying to make a cowardly getaway. *Oh, for crying out loud.* This was ludicrous, and she intended to put an end to it once and for all.

She flounced around the side of the counter, stopping mere inches from Tanner. Her voice was low. "If I kiss you under this freaking mistletoe, do you swear you'll get that purchasing slip from Jim and drop all this nonsense about looking for a tree?"

"Yes." He locked gazes with her, waiting for her to make the next move.

God, his eyes were blue. The deep, deep, green-blue of Caribbean waters she'd seen photographed in travel brochures. They'd planned to honeymoon in the Caribbean. It had sounded so exotic to her; Tanner had joked that any place where she spent half the time in a bathing suit was okay by him. Of course, they'd both known they'd spend most of their time naked. He'd been an amazing lover, bold and determinedly thorough, and she'd been eager to please.

Vestigial traces of anger and lust she'd had no real outlet for in the past five years worked their way to the surface. She was so… How *dare* this man! Did he really think some stupid kiss was going to change anything, melt her into the little puddle she'd once been at his feet? They had witnesses, for heaven's sake. This was a perfunctory holiday tradition, nothing more. It wouldn't be like the kisses they'd once stolen behind the football bleachers at the high school or in the stacks of obscure reference books at the back of the university library. *She'd chosen her college based on where he'd attended!* He'd been like a god in her world, a sun that she'd mindlessly orbited, blinded by his light.

But no more.

Not closing her eyes—it wasn't that kind of kiss—she let him see her full disdain as she lifted up to meet him halfway. He sucked in his breath, then his lips brushed hers. Shock radiated through her like an earthquake, starting as a small tremble where their mouths met and growing into something cataclysmic. *Good Lord.* He must have had some of the spiced cider outside; he tasted like cinnamon and nutmeg and five years of pent-up longing, dredging up the same yearning in her. Though she'd told herself that, after all this time, in front of all these people, it couldn't possibly be the kind of kiss he used to claim her with, so hot that it felt like an invisible brand, it was *exactly* that kind of kiss. And some uncontrollable part of her was kissing him back, branding him just as indelibly, marking him as hers.

But he's not. Suddenly, their kiss tasted salty, and Tanner released her, his expression stricken.

"Are you all right?" he asked in a gruff whisper, catching a tear with his index finger.

She opened her mouth to assure him she was just fine, but only a sob came out. Mortified, Lilah turned and rushed toward the door. Once again, Tanner Waide had made a total fool of her in front of the people she considered family—worse, this time she'd helped him do it.

Chapter Six

Tanner was rooted to the spot, poleaxed by the rapid succession of extreme emotions he and Lilah had just shared. Though their kiss had been brief, its impact on him was shattering. Kissing Lilah was a more intense and meaningful experience than having sex with a woman who *wasn't* Lilah. He'd been startled to find himself so quickly aroused.

Of course, he'd been turned on to some degree during their verbal sparring all weekend. He'd never realized before what a sharp tongue she could have…or how much fun it could be to match wits with her. But she hadn't been having fun. Her expression when she'd pulled away, the tears shimmering in her eyes, punching holes in his soul… What had he done?

He gave a brief shake of his head, feeling as though he were returning to his own skin after an out-of-body experience. Without sparing a glance toward any of the onlookers, he raced after Lilah.

She was fumbling with her keys at the driver's side of her car and ignoring his presence, though he'd seen her tense as he approached. Thank goodness she'd locked her car, though many didn't in such a friendly environment. Otherwise, she probably would have taken off already, and she shouldn't drive when she was this upset.

He closed his hand over hers and helped her turn the lock. "I'm sorry."

She drew a shuddery breath, still not looking at him. "I've been hearing that a lot from you lately. You know when it would have been helpful, Tanner? *Five years ago!* When I was rehashing everything I'd ever said or done and wondering what I could have done differently, when I was crying at night because I felt like part of me had been ripped away and wondering if I'd ever love again."

"Have you? Loved anyone else?" The question escaped without conscious thought—he knew he had no right to a response. Instead, he gave his own answer. "I haven't. I've met some wonderful women, but none of them were right for me. None of them were you. I should have stayed, Lilah. I ran from this town, full of people who'd known me since I was in diapers, and from my father, from my mother's disappointment that I was always disrupting the family peace, and I ran from the expectation I saw in your eyes. I should have found ways to compromise, should have appreciated how lucky I was."

"But you didn't." She swallowed. Her tone was calmer now, but infinitely sad. "I don't know who you are these days, but I'm not the same worshipful girl I was five years ago. Whoever we were, whatever we had, is gone. I'm sorry if your conscience bothers you, Tanner, but you're just going to have to deal with it."

Then she climbed into her car and left him in the dust.

As LILAH STEERED INTO HER driveway, Aunt Shelby was pulling in behind her. Either Shel had ESP—which Lilah could believe—or someone had phoned her. Lilah opened her car door, feeling slow and old beyond her years.

In moments, Shel was at her side. "Kasey Kerrigan called."

Lilah tried to grin. "Try saying that three times fast." Neither of them laughed at the feeble joke.

"Oh, honey." Shelby squeezed her niece's arm in a quick gesture of encouragement.

"Come on." Lilah quickened her pace. "I have to get inside before I fall apart in the front yard and have poor Quinn worried that her next-door neighbor has gone mental."

"Quinn would understand. She loves you. We all love you," Shelby said.

It was meant to be a reassurance, but it came out as irony. So many people in these parts had loved her, had protected her and nurtured her and cheered her on. Yet the person who had once meant the most to her… *Why couldn't he just stay gone?*

But it was a half-hearted thought because even before Tanner had returned, she hadn't been entirely happy. Maybe he'd been equally unhappy and had come back because he needed closure. They couldn't possibly get much more *closed* than they had today.

Inside, Lilah's aunt followed her to the kitchen. It was smaller than Shelby's and never smelled quite as good, but their best talks had always taken place there. Shelby rummaged around, pouring tea and discovering leftover cream cheese marble bars while Lilah sat at the table and sank her head into her hands.

Finally, she looked up. "Did Kasey call you before or after the kiss?"

"During, I believe. She said Tanner looked playful, you looked furious and half the town was looking on."

An exaggeration, but half the town would probably know about the kiss by tomorrow.

"Kasey worried that it might end badly, which she verified, then asked me to pass along her apologies. She feels that she or Jim should have asked him to stop coming to the farm."

"No. If I'd wanted him to stay away, I should have spelled it out. I know Tanner. If I'd told him with any real force that I didn't want to see him, he'd have honored the request." *I know Tanner.* Had more contradictory words ever been spoken?

In some ways, she did know him—the familiar feel of his lips and the way her own had responded were proof of that. She knew that despite the uneasy relationship he'd had with his father, the two men loved each other. She knew that despite having a fundamentally good heart, Tanner had always possessed a certain arrogance. As an adult, she could see it as a flaw; as a girl, she'd simply been awed by his confidence. She knew that, however convoluted his attempts at reconciliation had become, he was legitimately sorry for the way he'd left.

But was it simply for the way he'd left—the note with no warning—or did he regret leaving at all? His voice, racked with emotion, echoed in her head. *I should have stayed, Lilah.*

She'd coached herself to not torture herself with what-ifs. In order to rebuild her friendship with Ari, Lilah had had to stop looking at the younger woman and thinking of Tanner, wondering what would happen if he'd stayed or what would happen if Ari mentioned Lilah the next time she talked to him. What-ifs were a short road to crazy. Yet now, she couldn't help herself.

He said he should have stayed...would he have been happy? Or would he have become just as miserable, constrained by the small town and his place in the family business, as he'd predicted she'd be if she moved away from Mistletoe? While she could theoretically teach anywhere, this was her home. Because Lilah had lost the two most important people in her life at such a young age, she loved fiercely, not wanting to let go. She loved this town with everything in her. And had loved Tanner that way, too.

She met her aunt's compassionate gaze. "You know, for the first time, I think I really get why he left. I always knew why, on some intellectual level, but I couldn't put myself in his shoes. I couldn't process it emotionally. Maybe it was best that he went to Atlanta."

"He obviously doesn't feel that way," Shelby mused.

"Something went wrong." She recalled his expression at the senior center, the hurt in his eyes. Was his pain caused by a woman? That didn't fit. He'd seemed sincere today when he'd claimed never to have loved anyone except her. She ignored the way her heart leaped at that admission. "I don't know what happened, but he came home to lick his wounds."

"One of the benefits of having a home and people who love you. Zachariah Waide is a good man but demanding and difficult to please. I hope Tanner and his father use this opportunity to work out some issues, man to man."

"I hope so, too." Lilah's tears seemed to have cleansed most of her anger. "It's important to fix what you can while there's still time."

"Does that extend to you and Tanner, as well?" Shelby asked quietly.

For an instant, Lilah let herself bask in the warmth of what-if, then shook her head. "No, some things you have to let go." Maybe now, she finally could.

Shelby hesitated.

"Aunt Shel?" Lilah had never known the woman to be shy about sharing advice.

"You've both changed, grown. Maybe you owe it to each other to get to know the people you've become. You're a wonderful woman with a lot of love to give someone, but..."

But she'd rejected all candidates. Was it because she was too picky, because she just hadn't found the right man yet? Or because the right man had been in Atlanta, and now life was giving them a second chance?

TANNER WAS RUSTY WITH HOLIDAY traditions, but surely not all family gatherings to trim the tree felt this stilted. Though Susan Waide was in a festive mood, whistling as she hung keepsake ornaments and periodically beaming at her middle child, Zachariah kept sending inscrutable glances toward Tanner and saying nothing. Had the old man heard about Tanner's very public display of affection at Kerrigan Farms? While Zachariah and Susan had been happily married for decades, they weren't the type to kiss in public. Tanner had once noted, after a ballet recital when their father waited until they were in the car to tell Ari what a wonderful job she'd done, that it was bizarre how a man could be more comfortable criticizing than hugging. Was it because of how Zachariah himself had been raised?

Well, when I have kids I'll— Tanner drew up short, unable to complete the thought since having kids meant first finding a mother for them. Right now, there was only one woman he could imagine in the role, the one so anxious to get away from him that she'd fled her part-time job in midshift. He wanted to ask Ari if she'd talked to her friend, if Lilah was all right, but he didn't dare. His sister had *definitely* heard about the kiss and disapproved. She glowered at him even as she dutifully handed Susan silver icicles to be placed on the fir branches. Tanner might have looked to his brother for moral support, except that David seemed preoccupied. He'd explained that Rachel was home with a migraine headache, but otherwise, he was uncharacteristically silent this evening.

Susan planted her hands on her hips. "I want Christmas cheer, people! Look alive."

"Sorry." David gave their mother a rueful smile. "Guess I'm just worried about Rachel. I could sing carols, if you like."

Having heard David sing before, the entire family groaned at his offer. Tanner caught Ari's gaze, and she flashed a tiny smile of sibling commiseration. It faded as quickly as it had appeared but still helped ease the pressure around his heart. He may have screwed up with Lilah this afternoon, but perhaps he still had a chance of making things right with his family. He'd missed them over the past few years and regretted the pride that had kept him from coming home. Awash with guilt, he'd noticed the tears in his mother's eyes when she'd stepped outside to study the Christmas tree strapped to the top of his car. They'd been happy tears, but Tanner had been hit by the thoughtlessness of his staying away so long.

She turned to smile fondly at him now. "Tanner, you brought us this beautiful tree. Why don't you put the star on top and we'll plug in the lights to see how everything looks?"

He thought again about pride. "Actually, I think Dad should do it. He's the head of the household. I can take my turn next year."

Susan's eyes went wide with surprised pleasure at Tanner's implied promise to come back; Zachariah nodded briefly to his son, then climbed on the small step-stool to place the star. David plugged in the strand of lights, and a rainbow of twinkling colors spilled into the room.

"Perfect," Susan declared. "It's absolutely perfect."

"Does that mean we can eat now?" David demanded boyishly.

As the rest of his family filed into the kitchen, Tanner took a moment longer to stare at the tree. Perfect? Not quite. Just as he wished his sister-in-law could have been with them tonight, he wished Lilah were here. Laughing along with Ari as they untangled lights, snuggling up against Tanner's side as they studied the picturesque holiday scene. She'd always fit in so well with the Waides; it was *Tanner* who'd sometimes felt like an outsider under his own roof. Ari and Susan shared a special mother-daughter bond, and David had been less of a disappointment to their father. Tanner had so often felt like the odd man out, his unspoken insecurities had become a self-fulfilling prophecy.

"Tanner?" His sister's voice was soft in the doorway behind him. "You joining us for dinner?"

"Absolutely." When he turned, he saw the warning in Ari's expression. He wouldn't have been surprised is she'd told him to leave Lilah alone, but instead, she cautioned him about Susan's feelings.

"You made Mom's entire holiday by coming home, getting the tree, suggesting that you'll be back. I hope you meant it. She'll be crushed if they were just empty words."

"I meant it." The specifics of his future were hazy, but his past was becoming clearer and clearer. With maturity and perspective, it was easier to acknowledge the mistakes he'd made. Why had he arrogantly believed running off to Atlanta would solve his problems? There was nothing in the city he truly missed. Certainly there were conveniences there that Mistletoe didn't have, but when he weighed the occasional Falcons or Thrashers game against a closer relationship with his family…

And, as he was reminded when he sat down at the table, despite Atlanta's many wonderful dining options, no restaurant could quite duplicate Susan Waide's home cooking. He was resisting the urge to groan in ecstasy when his mother called for everyone's attention.

"Ari and I were chatting earlier and we have a suggestion to make. I know it can be hard to find time to do holiday shopping, especially since store options here are limited. If the three of you would like to drive to some of the nearby outlet centers one day this week, we're fully capable of running the store."

Three pairs of blue Waide eyes stared at her, uncomprehending.

"Shopping?" Tanner echoed, not sure he'd heard right. "Actually, I've picked up a couple of small gifts this week."

"Well, good for you, not putting it off till the last minute," Susan commended him. "Your father is a notorious procrastinator when it comes to things like that. In his defense, I'm sure it would be easier for him if Mistletoe were big enough for a mall." The Waide women, along with many other female citizens, satisfied shopping urges with a string of brand-name factory outlet centers that were half an hour away.

"Even without a mall, gifts can easily be ordered off the Internet for delivery," Tanner pointed out. As soon as he said it, he waited for his father to grunt about people's dependence on computers.

Instead, Zachariah was nodding enthusiastically, "Yeah, what he said. I could do that."

David laughed. "See, Mom, men don't really bond over shopping the way women do. A day at the outlet centers sounds more like a chick excursion."

Susan glared so effectively that Tanner almost choked on his pot roast. David shrank two inches in his chair and Zachariah announced that Tuesday was good for him. Ari smirked.

Later, as the Waide siblings cleaned and put away the dinner dishes, Tanner asked, "Is it me, or has Mom become…feistier?" It was both a valid question and a preemptive strike to keep anyone from mentioning Lilah.

His sister nodded cheerfully. "Rachel said some women get more empowered as they hit their forties and fifties. Whatever caused it, I know Dad wouldn't have let me go to Florida with friends freshman year if Mom hadn't intervened." Ari had commuted three days a week to a small college but had lived at home.

Reaching for a dark green towel to dry dishes, David added, "I think it's because of you, bro. After you left was the first time I'd ever heard Mom and Dad argue."

"You're kidding?" Tanner had assumed that peace in the Waide kingdom would be restored once he was gone.

"I think she felt bad about not sticking up for us more. Not that we were always right or that Dad should have taken all your just-graduated-into-the-real-world advice, but he could have considered it more carefully. That's what Mom told him. She's been more kick-butt and take charge in the last couple of years, but the surprising thing is, he doesn't seem to mind. He just needed someone to call him on it."

"Hey, I tried to call him on it," Tanner reminded them.

David laughed. "Yeah, but you were obnoxious. Mom's more diplomatic and way better-looking, which probably helped win Dad over."

His brother had a point. After today, Tanner couldn't argue that diplomacy was his strong point. He scrubbed a plate with more force than was probably necessary, searching his mind for a new plan of action.

What would it take to win over Lilah?

Chapter Seven

"All right, all right, give her some space, you vultures!" Shooing faculty with one hand and cradling a mug of hot coffee in the other, Quinn placed herself on the seat next to Lilah's in the teacher's lounge.

"Thanks," Lilah said drily. Though she'd expected plenty of people to be curious about her public lip-lock with a former flame, she wasn't equipped to deal with so many questions before the school day had even started. She'd never been a morning person; it was something she and Tanner had in common. One time, after they'd spent the night together at his college apartment—

"Earth to Lilah?"

Lilah blinked. Good grief. The man had crept into her thoughts in a hundred little ways since she got out of bed. Probably because of the unbidden dream she'd had while still in bed. Her face flamed. *Stupid kiss*.

Quinn peered at her, worry in her green eyes. "You don't look well. We could find a sub to cover for you today."

"No, I'm fine." How pathetic would it look if everyone heard that she'd fled Kerrigan Farms in tears yesterday, then hadn't even been able to show her face at school? She had a responsibility to her kids. "I just didn't…sleep well last night."

"Had Tanner on your mind, I guess."

If you only knew. "You heard about the kiss?"

"Girl, everyone heard." Quinn lowered her voice. "And most of us are jealous. It sounds exciting to have the love of your life come crawling back to declare he can't make it without you. I understand he's every bit as good-looking as he always was."

More so, in some respects, but best not to dwell on that. "His being here has been taken out of context. He did not come back because he couldn't live without me," she said dismissively. "He's home to spend Christmas with his family."

"Uh-huh." Quinn sipped her coffee, regarding Lilah from over the rim of the mug. "Yet he spent all weekend trying to get whatever time he could with *you*. Just tell me this and I swear I won't ask for any other details. That kiss, on a hotness scale of one to ten?"

Eleven, easily.

"WELL, HELLO, HANDSOME." Vonda Kerrigan looked up from a card table where she was playing cribbage with a white-haired man in a reindeer sweater.

Tanner gave her a grin of sincere affection, although seeing her there at the senior center was a reminder of what an ass he'd been yesterday. "Good morning, Vonda."

She gestured toward her opponent. "This is Peter Joel, a dear friend of mine and decent cribbage player, even if he is a youngster."

Tanner managed not to smile; the "youngster" in question had to be at least sixty-five. "Nice to meet you, sir."

"Peter's also donned the red suit and requisite padding to be Kerrigan's Santa for the past few years," Vonda continued as the two men shook hands. She turned to Peter, a mischievous note creeping into her tone. "And, of course, you've heard of Tanner's recent exploits."

Shifting his weight, Tanner stammered, "I hadn't meant for that to get all over town."

He wished he could claim that, living in Atlanta, one forgot how quickly word spread in smaller communities, except that wasn't true. While the average person on the street might not know that he'd left his job in disgrace by association, fellow professionals in his social circle had found out immediately. Their reactions, ranging from open curiosity to an aversion to hanging out with him, hadn't been pleasant. He should have been more sensitive to making Lilah the topic of gossip. Dammit, he had to learn to put her feelings over his needs!

That's why he was here.

As though she could sense his thoughts, Vonda asked, "What brings you to the senior center?"

"I signed up recently with Mindy to help on the dance committee—"

"The one headed up by our very own Lilah?"

"I was coming by to explain that it's probably best if I back out."

Vonda's brightly painted lips thinned. "So that's your answer? To run away, again? Frankly, I'd come to expect a little more from you."

"It's not like that." Tanner shoved a hand through his hair. "I'm trying to do what's right for her."

"Men." Vonda snorted. "No offense, Peter. Why did you leave town with only a note? Wasn't that because you deemed it best for Lilah?"

"You know about the note?"

"I know *everything*."

Yes, he had partially left the note because he'd suspected he could convince her to leave and that she'd regret it later. But it had also been the easy way for him because looking her in the eye and breaking up with her would have crippled him. *Selfish.* If he had it to do over again...

"I stalked Lilah at the farm, and I don't think she appreciated it," he said ruefully. "She's over me, and I should stay out of her life."

"Over you?" Vonda echoed. "Ask anyone who witnessed that kiss, and I bet they'd tell you different. You can't make up her mind for her, but you could at least be around to give her the information she needs to make a decision. Let her see who you've become, let her see that you're going to stick around. And under no circumstances drop off that committee! In fact, if your calendar's not too full next week, Peter here was just complaining about his knee. Old football injury. Might not be a good idea for kids to climb in his lap this year."

Peter blinked. "I never played football."

Vonda shot him a quelling look that suggested his injury could either be of the "old football" variety or she'd arrange for something less fictional.

The man cleared his throat, then looked at Tanner. "You'd be doing me a real favor if you could play St. Nick this year."

"Well," Tanner said drily, "since it *is* to help a fellow ex-football player..."

LILAH WAS TENSE WHEN SHE walked into the Dixieland Diner to meet Mindy and Tanner. Would Tanner be angry after their parting yesterday? Would he continue to flirt?

To her relief—and darn it, she *was* relieved, not disappointed— he was the very picture of polite but platonic gentleman, greeting her with the same cordial nod he gave to Mindy, who arrived moments after Lilah. The two women sat on one side of the booth with Tanner opposite. A yellow-aproned waitress took their drink orders; then, as they were perusing their menus for dinner choices, Mindy's cell phone chirped.

"Hello? You're kidding!" She listened, frowning, then responded, "Okay, I'll be right there." Folding the phone, she explained, "My oldest had a minor fender bender. Nobody's hurt, but he's shaken, so if you two don't mind doing this without me…"

"Of course not," Lilah assured her, thinking that Mindy was a model mom. If Lilah had a child who'd been in even a minor car accident, she doubted she would be quite so calm.

"Great!" Mindy stood, grinning once before she bounced away. Her sly, self-satisfied smile brought to mind an inept con man who'd just pulled off his first successful sting.

As Lilah mulled that over, the waitress returned with a diet cola and Tanner's sweet tea.

"No lemonade for Mindy?" Lilah asked sardonically.

The waitress flushed. "I, uh… Didn't I just see her leaving?"

"Yeah." But not with enough time to return an extraneous drink to the kitchen, even if the waitress had intuited that Mindy was leaving for good and not just getting something from her car. The problem with having a town full of extended family meant that there were plenty of meddling "relatives" to drive you crazy.

Once they'd ordered and were alone again, Tanner commented, "So, this is awkward."

"You didn't have anything to do with Mindy's sudden and patently unconvincing emergency, did you?"

"No." He grinned boyishly. "But it would make my day if you told me *you* did."

Though she shouldn't encourage him, she laughed. "No,

they came up with this all on their own." Mindy and Vonda, she was guessing.

"They think they're helping you find happiness. We did have a lot of good times...." The comment came out hesitantly, as though he expected contradiction.

The uncertainty was charming. This wasn't the swaggering young man she'd known. "We had wonderful times." They'd almost never argued...although part of that was because she couldn't have imagined disagreeing with anything he said. She scowled at the memory of what a mouse she'd once been. "I couldn't have been a very interesting girlfriend."

He raised an eyebrow. "Why would you say that?"

"Looking back on it, I think I was overly agreeable."

"Not 'overly.' Besides, even if you were, you've definitely grown out of it."

Recalling some of the comebacks she'd tossed at him over the weekend, she returned his smile. For a moment, sitting across a dinner table and teasing each other, it was as if they'd never been apart. Luckily, the waitress delivering their food broke the spell. As they ate, they discussed the plans for the dance at the inn. They read over the notes Mindy had made confirming catering arrangements, talked about Tanner playing deejay with borrowed stereo equipment so that they didn't lose money paying someone, and finalized decorations, including who would pick up what and when they would have it to the hotel ballroom. Lilah was feeling pretty pleased with the work they'd accomplished when the waitress brought their bill.

Automatically, Tanner reached for it and Lilah blushed. Maybe because his action reminded her of dozens of dates with this man and the steamy way those dates had ended.

"I'll get this." She grabbed for the check, freezing when her hand met his. He had strong fingers but she knew they were capable of featherlight caresses.

"You sure?" His tone was neutral, but his eyes were a smoldering blue, as if his thoughts were running in the same direction as hers.

"Y-yeah. After all, I'm the committee chair, and you're here as a volunteer. I insist." She wiggled the paper out of his hands, trying to bring their fingers into as little contact as possible.

He smirked at her efforts but said nothing. As she pulled cash out of her wallet, he drawled, "It's probably just as well, since I'm more or less between jobs."

"Really?" There'd been speculation around town about his employment situation, but no one seemed to know for sure what had happened.

"I worked my way close to the top of the accounting department of a fast-growing Atlanta corporation. But then my supervisor and friend—well, I thought he was a friend—skipped the country with embezzled funds."

"That's awful!" Particularly the way his mouth had pinched at the corners when he'd mentioned his "friend's" betrayal. Whatever the theft had done to him professionally, it had also hurt him personally. "Surely your employers don't blame you?"

"Yes and no. They investigated me closely, which was uncomfortable, but didn't make any charges against me. Still, they needed a scapegoat. It's hard to make an example out of the guy buying drinks for the locals in some bar in Aruba."

"Tanner, I'm so sorry." Much as she'd never wanted him to go to Atlanta in the first place, she'd loved him too much for too long to hope he failed.

He shrugged philosophically. "Maybe it was for the best. I was caught in inertia. I hadn't been truly happy in months. If I ever had been. I liked the challenge of my job and the pace of the city, and felt I was learning a lot about business and schmoozing from Mac. It was interesting and fast-paced, but just because you're not bored doesn't mean you're satisfied with your life. Eventually, things even stopped being all that interesting, but you know how an object in motion tends to stay in motion?"

"I might have covered something like that in one of my science lesson plans," she kidded gently.

"This will come as a shock," he said with a self-deprecating smile, "but I'm a stubborn man. It's hard to admit I'm wrong. So, even though there was this niggling voice in my head saying I'd made a mistake, it wasn't enough of an impetus to actually backtrack and change my life. But then when Mac left… Maybe it was fate's way of kicking me in the butt."

Sounded more like Mac's criminal tendencies than fate, she

thought uncharitably, wishing the man tropical sunburn and jelly-fish stings. "Good for you on turning this into a positive! So you're going to look for a new job once you get back to Atlanta, give yourself a fresh start?"

"A fresh start...." He stared at her so steadily that she shivered. He'd had that look right before he'd kissed her for the first time, before his best football games and the night he'd told her he loved her. "I've been thinking about it, even since before I left the city, and I don't plan to go back. What do you say, Lilah—is Mistletoe big enough for the two of us?"

"I'LL BET MOM WOULD LIKE THOSE," David said, peering over Tanner's shoulder.

Maybe. Tanner glanced back at the pretty topaz earrings, keeping to himself that it hadn't been their mother who'd come to mind when he'd spotted them. "You having any luck? There's got to be something in here Rachel would want."

"What she wants, we aren't going to find in a store." He sounded weary.

"Everything okay?"

"Yes and no." David hesitated, then shook his head. "You have your own problems. Rachel and I love each other, and I'm sure everything will be fine."

At least one of the Waide men was having luck. Zachariah walked back toward them, holding two small bags. "This place is great," he enthused. "Terrific savings! I got a bracelet for your sister, a necklace for your mom and the matching earrings to give her for Valentine's Day. I can stuff 'em in the back of my sock drawer and not have to worry about more shopping between now and then."

"Gee, Dad," Tanner drawled. "You're such a romantic."

The sarcasm was lost on his father. "Well, I have to try. Once you kids all left the house, she decided I'd been taking her for granted. I don't...I don't want to lose anyone else in my family."

Tanner started. *Does he mean me?*

At lunch, Tanner and his dad sat together while David went back to the counter for extra ketchup. Just as he had the other night,

Tanner caught Zachariah watching him. On Sunday, Tanner had assumed the glances signified disapproval; now, he wasn't so sure.

"Dad, is there something you want to talk about?"

Zachariah looked pained but determined—like a kid about to get a shot. "I'm glad you're home for Christmas, son."

"For more than just Christmas," Tanner said slowly. "I didn't expect to miss the town, yet I—"

"Missed the people in it?" his father suggested. "Heard you've been wooing that nice Baum girl. We all like her."

"Thanks, but I screwed that up years ago."

"You were young and stupid," Zachariah said gruffly. He ran a hand through his hair. "I don't even have that excuse. I was just old and proud. When you came back from college, so sure of yourself and lecturing me on modern business practices...I felt obsolete. But it wasn't my intention to run you out of town, or even out of the family business."

Tanner knew an admission like this had to be difficult for the man whose stubbornness he'd inherited. "Dad, my heart wasn't in the family business. No disrespect, but I want to build something that's mine. Maybe hang out my own shingle and offer up book-keeping and accounting services to businesses in Mistletoe."

"Really?"

"I do have a favor to ask, though. Maybe I could use you as a reference?"

Zachariah laughed, suddenly looking like a younger man. "I think we can manage that."

Clutching a handful of packets, David dropped into the third chair. "Did I miss anything?"

Only Tanner and his father making a concerted effort to put the past behind them and embrace the future...not that he would ever admit to his mom or Ari that the menfolk had bonded during a day of shopping.

Chapter Eight

Lilah opened her door, fully expecting to find Quinn. Instead, Tanner grinned down at her, and her breath caught.

"Hi," he said. "Is this a bad time?"

"No, come on in." She glanced at her grubby jeans and snowman-appliquéd sweatshirt; she hadn't worked at the farm tonight and had changed into comfy clothes after school. "I was just watching old Christmas cartoons and wrapping presents."

He glanced over at the television, grinning at the animated classic. "I love this one."

"I remember." They stood smiling in mutual recollection of holidays past—presents exchanged, carols sung off-key and the tickle-fights that ensued when she couldn't help giggling at his giftwrap attempts. "So…were you stopping by because of the dance?"

"The farm, actually. Vonda convinced me to do a favor, but I wanted to make sure you're all right with it before I show up."

"The Santa gig?" Kasey had called to ensure Lilah wouldn't mind.

"You already know? News really does travel fast in this town. Look, Li, I don't want—"

"The kids will love you. There's no reason to turn it down because of me. We're just…old friends."

He eyed the television set once more, then sniffed the air as if scenting the brownies that sat on a plate in the kitchen. "Are old friends allowed to stay for Christmas movies and help wrap?"

"I assume that by 'help wrap,' you mean scarf down baked goods?"

"Hey, I can stick my finger on the ribbon while you tie. I'm useful."

So he helped her tape up boxes and relieved her of some of the caloric-temptation in the house. He was interested in seeing her place, small though it was, and listened as she talked about teaching. She got so caught up in their evening that it wasn't until the next day at school that she realized Quinn had never shown.

Lilah leaned in the doorway of her friend's classroom. "You stood me up."

"I noticed the visitor's car in your driveway…that was still there when I went to bed."

"You could've joined us."

Quinn smiled. "Are you sorry I didn't?"

Lilah couldn't help smiling, too. "No, not really."

"HO, HO, HO!"

Lilah glanced up from the register with a grin. Hard to tell that a male model's physique was buried beneath the red velour robe and generous padding. "Hey there, Santa. Kasey's got a corner all set up for you." The green and gold throne they'd been using for a decade sat along the far wall, next to a table of cookies and an illustrated copy of *The Night Before Christmas* and the more modern children's book *Santa's Stuck*. There were several designated "Stories with Santa" times, and Tanner already had a waiting audience of two little boys.

Tanner winked at Lilah. "Have you been a good girl this year?"

No, not if one counted the thoughts she'd been having since their kiss, thoughts that had only grown more frequent and heated after their cozy evening at her house and during their companionable lunch the other day to finalize some details for the dance. Tanner had changed. He was still clever and flirtatious and strong-willed, but he'd also mellowed and matured. He'd told her over pizza how he and his father were finally talking—the man was actually going to hire Chloe Malcolm to create a Web site for the store, but Tanner was no longer hell-bent on his father taking his advice. Paradoxically, the corporate "failure" in Atlanta had helped Tanner overcome his need to prove himself, as if bottoming out had taught him he could still go on, even enjoy reinventing himself.

Though Lilah smiled at every customer who brought purchases to the counter, she kept half an ear on the story circle, enjoying

Tanner's rich voice and thinking that the kids in her class would love it if he dropped by next semester to read for them. Who was she kidding? *She'd* love the excuse for his company.

Late Saturday afternoon, Tanner was finishing up a break and ambling back toward his corner when skeptical fourth-grader Kyle Nugent put himself in Santa's path, eyeing Tanner up and down and casting a glance toward Lilah, who was straightening a collection of ornaments.

"Ms. Baum, do you actually think this is Santa Claus?"

Tanner smiled at Kyle. "I know you asked for a Wii game system."

The kid shrugged, unimpressed. "So did half the other boys in town."

"All right," Tanner said. "What if I told you that I knew what Ms. Baum asked for when she was your age? A Princess Galaxia doll."

Kyle frowned. "Never heard of Princess Galaxia."

"Well," Tanner said, merriment evident in his deepened Old St. Nick voice, "that *was* a long time ago. Ms. Baum's not as young as she once was."

"Watch it, Kringle," Lilah threatened with mock indignation.

"But her very favorite Christmas present ever," Tanner continued, "was a snow globe with carousel horses inside."

It had been a gift from her mother, a musical globe that Lilah used to wind up when she was missing her parents. "I can't believe you remember that," Lilah said softly.

His gaze met hers—incongruously somber beneath the fake bushy white eyebrows and wire-rim costume glasses. "I never forgot a thing about you. Even when I tried."

"Dude!" Kyle Nugent was appalled. "You're not making googly eyes at Ms. Baum, are you? What would Mrs. Claus say?"

LILAH WOBBLED INTO THE Winter Wonderland dance feeling absurd. It had been ages since she'd worn high heels, but Quinn agreed they made Lilah's calves look shapely. As she watched her neighbor drift off to greet friends, Lilah thought sardonically that she couldn't recall worrying about her calves when she attended the dance *last* year.

She'd been here earlier, working with volunteers and hotel staff to get everything set up, but she and Quinn had arrived later than she'd planned. (Apparently, primping was time-consuming.) There was already a crowd. Lilah couldn't see past everyone mingling and enjoying appetizers to glimpse the dance floor or the table where they'd put stereo equipment.

"Whoa!" Ari, looking quite attractive in a slinky green dress, turned away from the cash bar with a glass of white wine. "You're wearing makeup."

"I always wear makeup," Lilah protested. *Lip gloss counts.* "This is just more dramatic because it's for evening."

"And you curled your hair." Ari inspected the complicated arrangement, a partial topknot secured with a jeweled barrette that left the rest falling in loose ringlets. "You're *gorgeous.*"

Let's hope your brother thinks so. The words "Have you seen Tanner yet?" spilled out of her mouth before she could check them. Though he would have cleaned up by now, she'd thought he looked dangerously attractive this afternoon, carrying tables in his black T-shirt and jeans, his discarded sweatshirt hanging on the back of a chair. He might not play football anymore, but Lord, his biceps and shoulders…

"Nope, haven't seen him." Ari grinned impishly. "I'm avoiding my brothers in case they have the same reaction to this neckline as my dad. But Tanner's here. I walked in while he was admonishing the crowd that *someone* had to be the first on the dance floor. Then he thanked Vonda for tugging her date out there."

"I should go make sure Tanner doesn't need anything. See if all his…cables are working correctly," she finished lamely.

"Well, if that's what you kids are calling it these days." Ari smirked. "Here. You probably need this more than me. Tell my big brother I said hi."

Lilah's eyes narrowed, although she accepted the glass of wine. "Keep teasing me, I'll tell him what you're wearing."

"Won't matter. Once he sees you, he'll forget who I am."

TANNER DUG THROUGH THE CD collection but couldn't find the hip-hop band Vonda had requested; most of the music the library had supplied was mellow—holiday tunes and a few ballads interspersed with older favorites like "The Twist." He was surprised and touched at how many people had stopped by the table tonight to say hello and express their pleasure that he was coming back to Mistletoe. A number of his friends and classmates had moved away, but a good percent had put down roots here in town. One former buddy had already approached him about playing softball in the spring.

"Pat Donavan's gonna try to recruit you," Nick had predicted. "So I wanted to beat him to it!"

Thinking about spring in Mistletoe, Tanner glanced up. His gaze collided with Lilah's. It was the sappy kind of moment he would have mocked if he'd seen it in a movie, but right now, he was too paralyzed by the way she looked to be amused. He doubted she knew she was the most beautiful woman in the room.

For a moment, she stood equally paralyzed. But then she resumed her path toward him. "H-hey."

"You're stunning."

"You look pretty nice yourself." She took in the black suit he'd borrowed from David and wore without a tie. "I mean, it's no fuzzy beard and red suit, but…"

"I had a lot of fun playing Santa for the past few days. I see why you enjoy working with kids."

On Sunday, he'd left his corner to grab something to drink and had encountered Lilah talking to an adorable curly-haired toddler. Lilah had bent down to hear the girl better, and with their two dark heads so close together, they could have easily been mistaken for mother and daughter. It had been like a punch to his solar plexus.

"Dance with me," he said.

She wet her lips as though the prospect of his holding her made her nervous. "Now?"

"Yeah, I can program the next couple of songs. Besides," he cajoled with a grin, "they can't fire me—I'm a volunteer."

He grabbed the James Blunt CD he'd glimpsed earlier and crossed around the table to take Lilah's hand as the first notes of "You're Beautiful" played. He pulled Lilah into his arms, not even waiting until they were on the dance floor.

"You take my breath away," he murmured.

"Same here." Her voice was husky. "Can I lead?"

He laughed. "Am I boring you with the swaying back and forth?"

The look she shot him made it clear she was anything *but* bored. She proceeded to maneuver them backward, toward a corner volunteers had enlivened with festive decorations. Finally, she had him where she wanted him and pointed upward.

Mistletoe.

With the groan of a drowning man reaching for a life preserver, he lowered his mouth to hers, burying his hand in her hair and belatedly realizing he was probably destroying a style she'd spent a lot of time on. But he couldn't bring himself to loosen his fingers. If the way Lilah thrust her tongue against his was any indication, she didn't mind. He kissed her for an aching eternity, the noise of the surrounding crowd drowned out by the blood pounding in his ears like the roar of the surf. Either he'd pulled her even tighter to him or she'd stepped closer—their bodies were pressed together in a sweet friction that only made him want more.

Lilah pulled back with a sigh, blinking dewy eyes up at him.

Was it wrong, surrounded as they were by half the town, including the aunt and uncle who'd raised her, to want to make love to her this badly? He almost smiled. If it was a crime, he'd been guilty of it plenty of times over the years.

"You look pretty pleased with yourself," she observed.

"I was remembering a Fourth of July picnic where we snuck off and made our own fireworks."

She leaned into him, her words muffled but discernible. "I wish we could sneak off now." Tilting her head back, she said, "I rode here with Quinn. Could you…give me a lift home later?"

The question she was really asking was clear in her eyes, and he could barely get enough blood to his brain to tell her yes.

LILAH FLIPPED ON THE LIVING room light, glad to give her hands something to do. Was it foolish to be this nervous with someone who'd already seen her naked countless times? *Get a grip, it's Tanner.*

Hence the nervousness: it was Tanner. The only man she'd ever truly loved, the one man who'd broken her heart. And though he'd seen her naked plenty, she hadn't exactly gotten any younger since then.

"Lilah? You okay?" He'd removed his blazer, and the buttons on his white shirt were like small beacons. With just a few flicks of her fingers, she could truly touch him again.

"I was…thinking about brownies," she said absently.

His eyebrows raised. "Really? You're hungry?"

She laughed, not volunteering the information that she'd gained a few pounds since they'd last made love and that she'd been wishing her students would start bringing in fruit trays and carrot sticks to celebrate major national holidays. "No. I'm not that kind of hungry."

His eyes gleaming, he moved toward her. This kiss was even hotter than the three they'd stolen throughout the evening. During their last kiss, he'd jokingly whispered something about renting them a room there at the inn, and Lilah had blushed like a sixteen-year-old girl. No *way* was she going upstairs with Tanner Waide at the hotel where her aunt worked.

"You make me feel young," she whispered between kisses.

"Twenty-seven is hardly old." He found the sensitive spot on the back of her ear, just above the lobe, and she shivered.

She hadn't been talking about age, really. More a state of mind, when they'd seemed to have their entire futures ahead of them. She began working on those buttons, enjoying the sensation of his hands on the nape of her neck and the curve of her butt. She no longer knew what the future held in store—but for tonight, he belonged to her.

Chapter Nine

Lilah had awakened this way hundreds of times, although not in this house. Morning sun slanting through the blinds, Tanner's body warm against hers, a muscular arm tugged snugly around her as if he'd never let her go.

Which had turned out to not be true.

Gently edging away, she blinked back sudden tears. Last night had been incredible. Making love had been even more amazing now because they knew what it was to be without each other. They'd tried to make up for the lost years with thorough, bold exploration and whispered endearments. It had been almost dawn when he'd murmured *"I love you."* Had it been real or a dream? Which did she want it to be?

Because as fondly as she recalled those mornings where she'd awakened like this, feeling deliciously languid, she remembered with equal clarity those mornings after he'd left, when she'd waken hoping it had all been a bad dream, her heart shattering anew as she forced herself to face reality. Well, now it was reality time.

"Lilah?" His voice behind her was a sensual invitation to curl back up with him.

"You should go." The words tumbled out involuntarily.

"You have somewhere you need to be?"

"No. But your family probably noticed you didn't come home. Quinn has probably noticed your car. You should just go!"

He sat, kissing her shoulder. "Are you okay?" Although she was facing away from him, the hysteria in her voice was unmistakable.

"No, I'm not okay! I'm...I'm a pushover. I have no self-discipline when it comes to you." She stood, taking the sheet with her as she searched for clothes.

Tanner, unbothered by his own nude state, watched. "You're

sorry about last night? It was your idea." He said it with no trace of accusation, merely confusion.

"Last night was phenomenal. I'm worried about the nights to come, the day when I wake up and find you gone again." Dammit, she was crying. She hated that she was crying in front of him!

"That's not going to happen," he said patiently. "Once I get my stuff from Atlanta, I'm settling here."

"For the right reasons? Tanner, I don't want to be your consolation prize. I'm sorry a colleague screwed you over, and I'm glad you're considering coming back—your family missed you while you were gone."

"Just my family?" he challenged. His eyes were beginning to reflect annoyance.

"You haven't even been here a month! And I'm supposed to just accept that you'll be here, what, forever?" She glared through her tears. "I'm less likely to believe in forever than I once was. You could give me your word…but I'm less likely to believe that now, either."

TANNER SAT IN HIS LUXURY CAR—honestly, he should trade it in for something more practical; he felt like an idiot driving it around the small Georgia town—and wondered where to go. His sense of direction was all mixed up right now, thanks to Lilah's sudden one-eighty. It seemed as if the car started driving of its own volition, and he found himself en route to his brother's house.

Rachel opened the door, looking adorably rumpled in a peach robe and crooked ponytail. "Mornin'. I was just pouring myself a cup of coffee. You want one?"

"Sure." He had a pounding headache. Maybe the caffeine would help. "Is David awake?"

"In the shower. Was he expecting you?"

"No. I just showed up like a mannerless bore."

His sister-in-law chuckled. "Don't sweat it, some of my best friends are mannerless bores. I'll go tell Dave you're here."

Not five minutes later, his brother stood shirtless in the kitchen, a towel slung around his shoulders. "Rachel's right. You look rough."

From the other room, Rachel chided, "David! Be tactful."

David pursed his lips. "You want to tell me what's up? I'm not sure I can drag it out of you and be tactful at the same time."

"Lilah." Tanner sipped his coffee, trying to figure out how to say the rest of it. Admitting that *she'd* asked *him* over for the night seemed ungentlemanly. Yet the very fact that she'd suggested it had left him completely unprepared for her change of heart this morning. If she'd had doubts about their getting back together, she could have voiced them before they'd made love multiple times.

David poured himself a mug of coffee. "Ari said you left with Lilah. I would have expected you to be in a better mood this morning."

"I woke up in an excellent mood that quickly went downhill when she kicked me out of her house. I don't even know why! I thought we were…"

Dave arched an eyebrow. "I'm sure five years ago *she* thought you 'were…' before you took off one day with virtually no explanation."

"Hasn't anyone noticed I've been trying to make up for that?" Frustration swelled inside him—frustration with his past mistakes, frustration that Lilah wouldn't believe him and that David wouldn't take his side. Mostly, he was frustrated because he didn't know how to make the people who mattered most to him listen.

Something Mac used to say came to him: *"You want people to listen, kid, talk with action, not sentences."* Although Mac had turned out to be an amoral SOB, the old cliché about actions speaking loudly was still true. Maybe it was just as well that Tanner hadn't stayed at Lilah's and talked until he was blue in the face.

Maybe once he started to put some plans into *action,* he'd begin to earn back Lilah's trust. And, if he were truly fortunate, her heart.

LILAH STUDIED HER REFLECTION in the mirror and tried to conjure a smile festive enough for the New Year's Eve party at the principal's house. Though she wanted to stay at home in her pajamas, Quinn had threatened to drag her out by force if necessary. *That's only because she doesn't realize what lousy company I'll be—if she knew, she'd let me stay home for the other guests' sake.* It was bad enough that Lilah had turned Christmas with Shel and Ray into the dreariest holiday she'd had in years.

Shelby had patted her arm. "I'm sure he'll call to wish you a Merry Christmas."

But he hadn't. Lilah hadn't spoken to Tanner since the morning after the Winter Wonderland dance…no surprise there, the practical part of her reasoned. After all, she'd pushed him away! Did his not trying to fight for her prove that she was right about his lack of emotional staying power, or was his disappearing out of her life a second time around *her* fault? There was probably only so much fighting for a woman any self-respecting man could do before he gave up gracefully; maybe he'd reached his limit.

Her doorbell sounded. "Coming!" Thank God. For as much as she hadn't been looking forward to this party, perhaps it was healthier that she be among people than at home brooding.

She opened the door and stared at Tanner. He had the kind of stubble that movie stars always managed to make sexy, although she couldn't say that the circles under his eyes upped his hotness factor.

"You're not Quinn," she said blankly.

"Not last time I checked. Can I come in?"

The smart answer was probably no. "I only have a few minutes. Then I have a party."

"And *Quinn's* your date? There must be something very wrong with the men in this town." He followed her to the living room.

Lilah felt too nervous to sit, but she figured that if she didn't, neither would he. Standing in close quarters with him hovering over her seemed unsettling. He joined her on the couch, though, making her wonder if standing hadn't been the best option after all. Was it too late to shoot to her feet inconspicuously?

"I wanted to come sooner," he blurted, "but I was in Atlanta."

"Ari mentioned." After some prodding. Dragging Ari into the middle of this hadn't been Lilah's proudest moment.

He didn't seem to have heard her. "Plus, banks and government agencies are closed for the holidays, which makes getting stuff done at Christmas tough."

"What kind of 'stuff'?" She held her breath waiting for an answer.

His gaze was a caress. "Planning-for-my-future-and-praying-you'll-be-in-it stuff. I signed a short-term lease at the Rivermill apartments. Hardly luxury condos, but my unit will work until I have a house built. I found a beautiful piece of land, and I was hoping that sometime…you might go with me to see it. And I've been checking into the licensing I'd need to start taking on clients. Dad and David agree that in the meantime they could use some help getting last year's taxes in order."

Lilah felt as if she were having a strange dream. The very sexy man sitting with her was talking about taxes, his voice strangely calm considering her own racing pulse. "You're staying," she heard herself say. "You're really staying?"

"I am. I'm sorry it took me so much longer than it took you to realize where I belong, but I'm really enjoying being back. Well, except for Christmas. I was miserable."

"Me, too."

He scooted closer, taking both of her hands in his. "You know how I told you that I wanted to find the perfect tree?"

Her laugh was half sob. "I think most of the town remembers your so-called quest."

"I failed this year. It can't be the perfect tree unless you're sitting underneath it with me on Christmas morning. I hate myself for the Christmases we missed together, the birthdays I—"

She pressed her hand to his mouth. "Tanner, I forgive you."

He looked at her with eyes nearly as damp as her own. "I love you so much."

Lilah barely got out her own "I love you, too" before his mouth claimed hers in savage joy. *Welcome, home.*

OUTSIDE, TINY FLAKES OF SNOW fell gently as Quinn Keller grinned at the couple silhouetted in the living room and turned to walk away. It looked as if Lilah had found her own way to celebrate the New Year…and a new beginning.